KILLER'S GIFT

KILLER'S GIFT

Hugo W. Matson

03/26/03

To order additional copies of this book, contact:
Xlibris Corporation
1-888-7-XLIBRIS
www.Xlibris.com
Orders@Xlibris.com

Contents

To all who served in Vietnam. We will not forget your sacrifices.

ACKNOWLEDGEMENT

Very little has been written about the tunnel rats in Vietnam but the best source of information about these brave but unheralded heroes is The Tunnels of Cu Chi by Tom Mangold and John Penycate. Leonard Grissom and all of the other characters in this novel are the product of my imagination. A special thanks to the various work shops who were exposed to this story and who probably learned more than they ever wanted to about life in the tunnels.

PROLOGUE

Leonard heard the rustling, a whisper of sound, moving toward him, like someone crawling, clothes dragging along the dirt floor. Slowly. He didn't use his flashlight. They'd be waiting for that. Waiting for the light. Waiting to squeeze the trigger, not having to aim. They couldn't miss because he filled the crawl space. Even though he was no bigger than the VC, he filled the cavity like a loose tooth in an infected gum. Even if he lay prone or flattened himself against the dirt wall, the AK 47 would catch him in its cone of fire.

The sound grew closer, all around him, a frictionless whisper that crawled up his arms, into his hair, his ears, wading through the salty rivulets of sweat coursing down his face, tracking across his shoulders, his chest and along his legs, burrowing into his pants under his belt, under the ties that bound his pantlegs so they wouldn't scrape along the ground, tug at a root or catch on a stone. He slapped at the bloated bodies; beat at the web that collapsed in sticky threads around his fist but continued to advance, its veined membrane torn, its movement caught in the beam of his flashlight he had flicked on just before he shut his eyes. He squeezed his eyelids together to keep them from digging under his eyelashes even as they stung his face.

He held each side of his nostril and tried to blow out the ones that had gained entry. He used both hands, swiping at his face to stop the flow of traffic, but others replaced them. He clamped his mouth shut in mid-scream as the spiders marched across his teeth and onto his tongue. He tried to sputter them out without opening his mouth, but they burrowed into the crevice between his stretched lips through which he was trying to breathe, and he swallowed the ones that reached the back of his tongue. He tried not to think of them crawling around inside his stomach.

The rope tugged at his waist. He must have signaled to be pulled up. He realized that he had been firing at the massive, black web, the rounds spanging against the ceiling and ricocheting off the walls and floor of the tunnel sending bits and pieces of earth against his face and arms and tearing ragged holes in the fabric of the moving web. The sound filled the blackness and the cone of light but was muffled by the spiders clogging his ears.

He pushed himself backwards, his feet tangling in the rope behind him; his hands covered with spiders clinging like fur to his fingers, his wrists and arms. He found a space where the tunnel widened enough to turn around and blindly scrambled back to the entrance.

They pulled him out, his eyes swollen shut, his body wearing a hair shirt of spiders. Someone yelled for the medic. Hands swept his face and mined his ears, and he heard their curses and their pity. A rag beat at his body. Fingers unlaced his boots. They stood him up and pulled off his pants. He didn't feel the air. The medic spread ointment on his face and body and he felt a needle in his arm, which, in moments, relieved the stinging.

He stayed in base camp several days until he could open his eyes, and the burning from the bites ceased, and his nausea disappeared. A week later, out of the tunnel, on a search and destroy operation, Private E-2 Leonard Grissom stepped on a mine.

I

Leonard Grissom stretched out on his recliner, letting his thoughts drift from the images on the 26" TV, housed in the Spazio wall system with its multi-tape deck, VCR, and array of speakers. He was in a reflective mood. Leonard, he thought, you've never had it so good. His eyes glanced off the open-beam ceiling to the shining, customized parquet floor of the living room. He had drawn the drapes, shutting out what was left of the day's sunlight. The gas flame in the fireplace danced across the faux logs behind the glass fire screen adding to Leonard's sense of well-being. A shiver of pleasure ran through him.

They had bought the house during a depressed market. It had been a steal. Pure luxury, Leonard reasoned. Not bad for a guy who bounced from one foster home to another back in Detroit. He wondered what they—the foster parents, the teachers, the social workers—would say if they could see him sitting in his high grade Italian leather-upholstered recliner, a thick Karastan rug spread on the floor around him like an Indian potentate's. He would show them the limited edition prints, paintings and watercolors covering the walls. None of those bowls of fruit, or vases of flowers or dead ducks for him. No sir! So the rug wasn't a Bokhara, and maybe the paintings weren't Picassos or Wyeths, but they were all signed by the artists. He had found the paintings through an art dealer who said they were done by local 'emerging artists' which didn't fool Leonard a bit. He bought them as much for the sales pitch as for the paintings themselves. Besides, both he and Mickey liked them. He wasn't into watercolors, but as she pointed out, the artist had captured the subtle shades that only these paintings could replicate. Like when they traveled north on I-87, the

Northway, up to Montreal, and on a clear day, north of Albany, could see the foothills flowing into ever fading nuances of color to the bluish-gray mountains on the eastern horizon. Only watercolors could do that. They had time to enjoy their home, that was the best part. Leonard didn't have to punch anyone's time clock, not that he ever had. Well, except in the Army and those first couple of years in the Bronx. He'd had no choice then.

No, Leonard thought, no one would have predicted that he, Leonard Grissom, would be living in a $250,000 dollar house in the suburbs of Newburgh, New York with no mortgage hanging over his head, a BMW and Range Rover sitting in the two-car garage. He couldn't remember the number of times he'd heard he wouldn't amount to anything. He had to admit to himself, later, he'd given them good reason to think that. As a kid he'd been a delinquent, running away from one foster home after another. Skipped school every chance he got. School had been boring, too confining. They had him tested because they'd thought he was a retard. When they saw his IQ, they bugged him about making something of himself. He didn't need an IQ test to tell him he was smart. How did they think he kept money in his pocket and never got caught? But that was years ago.

Life had been good to him. It had given him opportunities and a chance to use his God-given talents. The thing was, he recognized opportunity, looked for it, could spot it even when there was only a crack in the door. He didn't have to be battered around the head to respond to it. He knew instinctually what he had to do to take advantage of the chance that had been laid at his feet. That's what was so great about this country. Opportunity was everywhere.

It hadn't always been that way. Hunger had been his first memory. Hunger and darkness and sitting in his own shit, pants wet. As a child he couldn't remember when he didn't feel the hollow inside, the vast cavern that seemed bigger than himself, like he was inside it looking out. That it had swallowed him. He remembered crying from hunger, and she'd shake him and that would make him cry harder until she locked him in a closet where the crying didn't do him any good and only brought darkness. Leonard learned not to cry. So she wouldn't have an excuse to lock him in the closet. Sometimes he ended up in there for no reason other than it seemed to be the best place to put him. To get him out of the way.

> *"Get the kid outta here," man's voice.*
> *"What d'ya want me to do with 'im?"*
> *"Ya din't tell me ya had a fuckin' kid."*
> *"What difference is it gonna make?"*
> *"I don' like havin' him hangin' aroun' watchin' me."*
> *"Aw shit. What am I gonna do with 'im?"*
> *"Jus' get 'im outta here."*
> *"C'mon, ya little shit. I'll put'im in the closet."*
> *"Do it."*
> *"Ahh, your fuckin' pants are wet again. Mummy'll change ya later. Stop your fucking cryin', ya hear? Stop it!"*

No reason at all. So he learned that he could be punished for not doing anything, for just being alive. He'd hear voices and laughter and moans and glass breaking, and he knew it was glass breaking because he could see the shiny bits and pieces under the door or when she let him out of the closet if she remembered, and once out, he waited to see what he was supposed to do or allowed to do. He avoided the glass because he had cut himself once and the only way he could stop the bleeding was to suck it until it stopped. The finger bled for a long time. She had been upset that he had cut himself. She had called him, 'stupid.' After that she called him stupid all the time. He wondered if it was because he didn't cry anymore or speak? Keeping silent reduced the possibilities of punishment or eliminated it altogether.

Sometimes she put him in the closet with something he could eat and a bottle of water. He knew she'd be away a long time. He knew this because it had happened many times—with enough food to last through several meals: half or three-quarters of a box of cornflakes, or a partial loaf of dried bread, or day-old or two-day old doughnuts, but he ate everything at once and it filled the hollow inside him, for a time. When he no longer cried or even moaned in the closet, because it didn't do any good and sometimes brought a hammering on the door which scared him, he learned to listen and came to understand the sounds from outside the door, her voice sounds: laughter—she was happy; crying—she was not happy; moans and groans—she was hurt or … she was happy.

He could identify the smells inside the closet. The smell of her few clothes, a dress, a cloth jacket, hanging above him and dirty clothes she threw in a corner of the closet—ragged jeans, T-shirts, a tank top with the scent of her drug- or booze-dried sweat. A smell he came to recognize later. Perfume on a dress. A party dress. And there was the smell of shoes: sandals and a pair of sneakers, pungent. There was his own smell. The smell of urine. And dried shit. He remembered sleeping for long periods of time on a pile of dirty clothes, hers, and if he awoke during the night, he wasn't sure if he'd ever see again. Sometimes it was the clothes that blocked the crack of light that stopped outside the door. Sometimes it was the darkness itself through which no light penetrated. He knew it wouldn't do any good to cry. He'd resolved that long ago and so his hands became his eyes in the dark closet, tactile, exploring the limited space with fingers sensitive to the different fibers of the clothes and the worn, cracked leather or canvas shoes, the grain of the wood in the floor, the rough surface of the plaster, the ragged edge of wallpaper still adhering to the wall which he picked at until he loosened a piece and was able to peel it off or his fingers found a seam in the wallpaper which formed an overlapping thickness and another problem for his fingernails already bitten to the quick. He could only see when light slanted under the door because someone turned on a light bulb or raised a window shade on the other side of the door. He would sit and watch the churning dust motes twist and turn as they rode the sun under the door. Sometimes he lay on his side, his face pressed against the floor and tried to see what was beyond the door. Usually, all he saw were feet, bare feet, men's feet—black and white, and her feet with toenails painted red and chipped, the polish shrinking on the toenails; sometimes she wore sandals, but usually she was barefoot, and he came to know her feet better than anything else about her.

Sometimes he was so hungry he ate the bugs that made their home in the closet. No bug was safe. His fingers explored the cracks in the floor and the molding around the edge of the wall, and he became very familiar with all the crevices, fissures, chinks, and crannies in the closet and traced them as they meandered up the wall in the darkness. He ate the plaster and chewed the wallpaper, licking the glue that had long dried on the back of the scraps that he pulled from the wall. He also ate his own shit but there wasn't much of that. It wasn't only the hunger and the darkness, there was also the thirst because she sometimes forgot the water. He was always thirsty. When she let him out, he asked for water. He didn't cry if she ignored him. He held up a glass or cup and followed her around until she filled it. Once he found a glass on an end table after a party the night before and thought it was water and he drank it down, and it made him very sick. After that, he always smelled what was in a glass, even when he heard the glass being filled from a faucet.

He came to terms with the closet and the darkness. Except for the terrible hollow inside him and the thirst that burned his throat when he tried to swallow, the darkness became a refuge. He would go to the closet when he was afraid.

One night, much later, the last sound he heard from her, a chilling shriek, left him huddled in the corner of the closet under a pile of her clothes, afraid the shriek or what caused the shriek would follow him through the door. The police came and opened the door and took him out. Someone had reported a bad smell coming from the flat where they lived. He hadn't noticed it at first because it hadn't yet seeped through the space under the door into the closet. No one had opened the door for three days. She had not left any food or water.

"Jeezuz," a voice said—the voice of the policeman who picked him up and wrapped him in a blanket.

"Fuckin' bitch," another voice said.

He knew they weren't talking about him although someone had called him a 'poor little fucker,' and put a hand on his forehead. He couldn't say why he remembered those words but it was probably when they put him with his rail-thin arms and legs and swollen stomach and his already little, old man's face and large, unblinking eyes into the warm water in a bathtub and gentle but firm hands scrubbed the caked dirt, which had almost become an outer layer of skin, from his body and removed the myx that had dried yellow around his nostrils where his tongue couldn't reach and his hand wiping it, only spread it laterally in silver streaks on his cheeks. Then came clean white sheets with railings along the sides of the bed and tubes in his arm which filled his belly and he slept, no longer hungry or thirsty. He was surrounded by light and when night came—and he could now distinguish between day and night—there was always some light near him. It took him a long time to be able to sleep with so much light. He would close his eyes tight to shut it out and would walk around in the darkness in his head.

Later, when he asked for 'mummy', he learned that the bad smell had come from her and she had been dead three days. He also learned that she was his mother, offcially. He wasn't sure what that meant. Leonard didn't have any frame of reference for understanding the meaning of this word because he couldn't remember when the warmth of her arms stopped—he did have vague memories of that—and the darkness began. Or why? Someone had found, after rooting and sifting through the papers stuffed in kitchen drawers, that his name was Leonard Grissom. Maybe it was a birth certificate or maybe just a name on a scrap of paper. Or maybe on a doctor's bill. No middle name, as if she had wanted to limit his identity, or didn't want to take the trouble to come up with one since there was no one important enough to her to be remembered. They never were able to find any living relatives. Or if they tried, no one owned up to it.

They guessed his age. Wrote it down on the official papers that followed him around from the time they discovered him. He was seven years old, although he didn't look it because he was undersized; other times, he appeared older with his pinched features and the lines that furrowed his face as if the seven years he'd already lived had been multiplied ten times. He realized, later, that if they had given him his name from a birth certificate they would have known his age. That lack of information never troubled Leonard. When they found a foster home for him it seemed nice to have people call him by his name, although most people ended up calling him Lenny. He was registered in the first grade because he was behind in his education, never having been to school. And he was comfortable because his classmates were all his size but a couple of years younger. For a while he enjoyed learning and being around other children, but he didn't talk much, nor laugh, nor shout nor share in their games. And when he moved from grade to grade his classmates grew taller and he lagged behind. That didn't bother him. They left him alone. Until later.

When he met the first bully in his life, Benny Fowler, Leonard didn't know what to do. He couldn't run. There was no place to run. He had to be in school. Benny stole Leonard's lunch, took it out of the bag, stepped on it and ground it into the pavement. When the other kids began to do it, Leonard ate his lunch before he arrived at school. He stuffed the food in his mouth, gulped it down and hiccuped the rest of the way to school where he headed straight to a drinking fountain, peered from left to right to make sure no one would push his face into the fountain before he drank, and held his breath until the hiccups stopped.

His tormentor, a large, foul-mouthed kid, taunted him by making fun of his size and his little, old man's face when he was serious which was most of the time.

"Hey runt," Benny would holler in his face, "When you gonna grow up?" The other kids would laugh.

"Your daddy a midget? Is that why you're such a runt?" Someone else would say.

Benny began bumping him in the hallway or during recess, which escalated into pushing and punching him and when he went down, the last time in the schoolyard, began to kick him. As Leonard rocked from side to side to avoid Benny's feet, he rolled over the neck of a broken bottle. He gripped it and as the bully stood over him, Leonard thrust the shard of glass up into Benny's inner thigh. He screamed in triumph when the broken glass tore through the thin pantleg and into his tormentor's leg. He rolled away as Benny fell. Leonard scrambled to his feet. As he was ready to thrust the sharp edges of the bottle into the bigger boy's face, a hand grabbed his arm. It was the principal.

"Easy son. What's going on here?" The man looked around. He didn't release Leonard's arm.

"He stabbed Benny," someone piped up.

"Yeah, he stabbed 'im'."

The principal ordered one of the kids to find the school nurse. They moved Leonard to another foster home. And another school. There was a succession of foster homes for one reason or another and a succession of schools. He'd stayed at the last foster home the longest.

As a kid, in the summer, Leonard slipped out of his room at one or two in the morning when everyone was asleep. He'd sneak down the stairs and through the kitchen into the darkness outside where he'd stand listening for a moment; absorbing the pulse of life that beat under the cover of night; his senses alert to the sounds around him. Satisfied that everything was as it should be, he wandered through the alleys. He listened to the snores coming from open windows, the hum of air conditioners, a car door slamming, the wail of a distant police siren, until the scrape of approaching feet along the pavement forced him to crouch, barely breathing, heart pounding, among garbage cans as the footsteps receded past him; moving again, past whispering voices on back porches and cigarettes which glowed red like feverish fireflies and past the moans of kids making out like bandits in the bushes. He glided past all this, a wraith, comfortable with the darkness, pulling it around him like a cape while he prowled, unseen, through the shadows. When he came to one of the neighborhood bars, he squatted in an alleyway until a drunk came staggering out, followed by the music of Teresa Brewer or the Ames Brothers or Julius La Rosa on the juke box. Then came 'good nights', hyena-like shrieks or deep rumbles of laughter. A triangle of light carried tattered ribbons of smoke and the smell of beer—spilled on tables and the bar, in empty bottles, belched from bloated guts, or dried on the floor and in corners where the mop never reached—until the door closed leaving the drunk wavering on his feet, orienting himself with bleary, light-blinded eyes until he remembered where he was or who he was and where he roosted.

Sometimes, the mark staggered as far as an alleyway and fell sprawling on the sidewalk or in the gutter where Leonard pounced, bending low over the man's body, hugging his back to avoid a flailing arm, the smell of the beer, by now, sour and mixed with the odor of vomit and the muttering of a guy who was powerless to avoid what was happening. Quick hands sliced open the back pocket with a razor blade and snatched out the wallet; nimble fingers sure and steady from months of on-the-job training, self taught, practiced, unhesitating, prepared to flee at the first sign of danger, pulling out the bills and pushing the wallet through the thick hair under the back of the mark's collar but repulsed by the touch of the hair on his fingers. And then it was away from there! He made his way home through the alleys, quickly but patiently, slipping across the back porch and through the unlatched door of his home like a gust of wind leaving the hot sounds of the city panting behind him. If he didn't score with the wallet, he didn't linger. At fifteen years of age, he knew his limitations.

Leonard was careful with the money he picked up this way,

and he didn't flash it. He kept it hidden at home. He knew that 'Ma' checked out his room every day, usually looking for girlie magazines. Once she'd found a copy of PLAYBOY under his mattress, and she'd boxed his ears, wanted to know where he got it and chewed his ass. It wasn't in the trash later so she must have given it to 'Pa'. Leonard learned to discipline himself about the money because at school, anyone who had money could be expected to be shaken down. The gangs took care of that. Carfare, lunch money, walking around money, pocket jingling money, security money, 'big deal' money. Until the predators raped your pockets leaving you a low life again. Bitter and ashamed and powerless. Being a loner and small for his age, he was fair game for the teenage packs although he had incredibly strong hands, and he was not only agile but very quick on his feet.

He generally avoided the street gangs. When push came to shove he gave as good as he got which gained him a measure of respect. That was before kids started coming to school armed with a piece or a shiv and the schools had to hire security guards and later, install metal detectors. Yeah, he gave as good as he got. Except when they piled on. Even then, they had to be hard pressed to jump him because when he couldn't run away, he attacked. The thing was, they never found any money on him. You didn't need a genius IQ to figure out that there wasn't much point intimidating a kid who didn't have any dough and could cause you a world of hurt even when you were kicking the shit out of him.

Leonard had always been a player in life, even back then. He just avoided center stage. He looked across the room at Mickey, sitting on the matching leather sofa, her back supported by a chenille cushion, knitting, concentrating on her latest project, her long red nails flashing in the soft light from the lamp beside her. Probably a hat, or ... booties for a new baby in the neighborhood. They didn't know their neighbors very well. Mickey was shy, and Leonard thought their attitude was very patronizing. Their self-assurance turned him off.

They both knew that when they moved into this affluent neigh-borhood of stockbrokers, lawyers, businessmen, school adminis-trators and accountants, with their houses set back from the wide, tree-lined street overlooking manicured lawns and barbered bushes, and garage doors that didn't front the street, that they might have trouble fitting in.

Mickey looked up, catching his intent gaze. She sent him a fleeting smile, concentrating on binding off the ends of the yarn. Finished, she smiled again, setting the knitting aside.

"Why do you keep doing that, the knitting? You think they care?"

"I do it for me," she replied.

"I wonder what they really think. They ever use the things you make?"

"Does it matter? I do it because these babies might never have something that was made just for them. Mothers don't have time to make things for their babies. That's why I do it."

"That's the only reason? C'mon," he smiled. "Our neighbors see us differently. If they see us at all. These things aren't going to make any difference to them."

"No, love, I don't think that's true. Don't forget we're the new kids on the block, and we don't have children. Our life has been different. That's what sets us apart. They try. I told you we've been invited out several times, but you've been away, and you know I don't like going out alone. I don't think it's proper."

Leonard conceded that she was probably right. They wouldn't have gotten to where they were now if it hadn't been for Mickey's persistence. Mickey had been the one who insisted that they had to change if they wanted to get out of that two-room apartment in the Bronx. And she had the farthest to go to make the adjustment. It hadn't been easy. They had worked very hard for their veneer of the cultured, well-spoken, well-dressed, well-read, educated people the world saw.

Mickey had adapted easier than he had. She was more driven, more ambitious, saw the advantage of changing appearances, understood the difference in perception when people didn't see or hear what they expected to see or hear. She said appearances were everything. She was right. First, she started on the way she talked. And then the way he talked. She was an excellent mimic, and he was surprised when she began speaking in the broad English accent that she had developed from watching and listening to tapes of Alister Cook and the programs on *Masterpiece Theater.* She just whipped it on him one day. Out of the blue. He'd had no idea how long she had been working on it. The shock of hearing her was the same as when he heard a British heavyweight boxer speaking English during a TV interview. In the meantime, they worked on their education, after their shift in a fast-food joint. They went to classes with the smell of hamburgers and onions clinging to them like a rumor. Leonard already had his GED from the Army. One of the few things he'd done right. Mickey earned hers after many months of hard study. From learning to speak respectably and starting their education, they began learning to dress properly.

It cracked him up when Mickey devastated uppity sales girls in Macy's or Bloomingdales if they ignored her or delivered a put-down when she demanded service. She became very English and in quiet measured tones gave them a brief lecture on the limits of democracy in the workplace and the imperatives of good service to the paying customer. Mickey even coerced him into reading *The New York Times,* and on Sunday; after reading the news, they pored over the Book Review and Arts sections and discussed the fashions and planned the furniture they would someday own when they were able to buy a house in the suburbs. Those years had been tough years while he learned and honed his skills. But they'd arrived.

II

Mickey was as beautiful as the day he first met her in that crummy bar off Tu Do Street in Saigon. So many years later and she still looked like that young girl. Except for the long, thin, pale, barely visible scar that ran from out of her hairline down the side of her face. She no longer tried to hide the violation they had inflicted on her. Hadn't for years. Wore it like a badge of honor now but never talked about it nor about the scars left inside her head. Her bright blue eyes still remained unfathomable to him despite their clarity.

Mickey was a 'hostess' in the small bar. Leonard was eighteen and had been in Vietnam four months. He was out to get a piece of ass, and he wasn't sure how to go about it. Not in a foreign country. He had drifted away from his buddies and found himself in this hole-in-the-wall with three tables with chairs and three bar stools spaced along a narrow bar—crowded under a ceiling fan that barely moved the sluggish air. Several girls sat together at one of the tables and giggled and nudged each other when he walked in. He took a stool at the bar and ordered a Coke. The sweat rolled down his back and from his armpits, and formed a beaded mustache over his upper lip. He flapped his fatigue jacket several times to cool his body. He wiped the top of the can and popped the lid and took a long swallow. There weren't any other GIs in the place. He checked his watch, a Post Exchange (PX) Seiko. It was too early for the rear echelon desk warriors. He'd read everything that there was to read on the Coke can and sent a sideways glance at the three girls. One of the girls stood, ran her hands down the front of her dress and strolled past him. She wore a mini-skirt, high heels, and left a trail of perfume in her wake.

Leonard was drawn to the small Eurasian girl who sat with them, but didn't seem to belong there. She had long, dark brown hair that fell straight to her waist, unlike the other two with their teased, sprayed hair that sat like stiff wire hats on their heads. She appeared to be the youngest of the three. Leonard swung around on his stool and stared at the young Eurasian. She dropped her eyes to avoid his eye-fucking gaze. Leonard couldn't bring himself to think that she could be a whore. She seemed ... fragile. Just didn't seem right to think it. Seemed dirty. But she was the one he wanted.

Hell, was she any different than Rita, loud with big tits, back in foster home number three? Who'd suck your cock for a couple of bucks and spread her legs for a sawbuck. Or Angela, now there was a name for you, who liked to be gang-banged more than eat although she did that too. Overweight with plucked eyebrows and greasy hair and smeared lipstick and smelled like bad fish when she took off her pants. Leonard always had to pay even to feel 'em up. They didn't give freebies to a ... runt like him. When he paid it was slam, bam, thank you, ma'am. But when he was done they gave him a speculative look and later when no one was around, Rita or Angela would grab his crotch, "You got any money, Lenny, pussy wants her big Tom." But that was if no one was around. It was never free.

Leonard realized that in his clean but baggy combat fatigues and soft jungle hat pulled low over his eyes he didn't look like a very promising prospect, especially with his pale, pinched face. He'd heard blue eyes and sandy hair appealed to Vietnamese women, but he'd also heard that blacks did too. He also knew that without the MPCs, the funny money, nothing was done for love. He took off his bush-hat and placed it on the bar. He brushed his hair back with his hand. Without the hat, Leonard shed years despite the lines that seemed to have been permanently scored into his face.

The older girl nudged the younger one, and she reluctantly

stood, eyes downcast, and walked self-consciously toward him in her sparkling blue mini-dress, high heels the same color blue as the dress, her legs almost spindly in the black, net stockings. Leonard wondered if she was shy or just didn't like the looks of him. He nervously licked his lips and put the crushed, empty Coke can on the bar. The girl stood in front of him, her blue eyes centered on his.

"You want good time, GI?" She sounded as if she was reading her lines.

Leonard didn't reply but his face reddened. Her voice was very soft.

"You want boom-boom? Me good boom-boom. Me number one," and she held up a red-nailed index finger to emphasize the point. She stopped the girl who was returning to her table and fired off a stream of Vietnamese at her, still in the soft, low voice.

The woman put a hand on Leonard's arm and said, "She no speak mus' Engliss'. She new. She young pussy. You like?"

Leonard wanted to put the still cool can against his face. He nodded.

"She name Mickey. Me, Tammy."

"Me, Leonard," he said, pointing with his thumb to himself.

Tammy pronounced his name several times to Mickey, her mouth twisting around the unfamiliar sounds before she could put them together. She showed a childish smile as he nodded his approval at her attempts and when she got it right.

Leonard told Tammy he wanted to stay with Mickey two nights, the limits of his pass. He raised two fingers and with truncated words and phrases and sign language made the woman understand. Mickey's head swung from one to the other as they talked, nodding in understanding when Tammy sent a burst of Vietnamese in her direction, just to let her know what was going on. After some haggling, they agreed on a price. Leonard had heard enough from his buddies to know the going rate. He would have paid anything at that point just to get in the girl's pants, but he didn't like the idea of being cheated. Tammy rattled some more Vietnamese to Mickey. She didn't appear to be overwhelmed at the offer but after a brief appraisal of Leonard accepted it. Negotiations completed, Tammy cautioned him about hurting Mickey in any way or doing 'bad things' to her. She said that Sarge would be very angry if he did. Leonard didn't ask who Sarge was. She said something to the girl and returned to her table.

Mickey pantomimed that she would like something to drink before they left. He ordered a 'champagne' for her and a Coke for himself. He figured Mickey was required to make sure he spent something at the bar. He took out his wallet to pay for the drinks, and Mickey pointed to the MPCs rather than the Vietnamese money. The bartender, an older woman dressed in a pale blue *ao dai,* served them and collected the payment from the script Leonard laid on the bar. He left the Vietnamese *piasters* for the woman.

Mickey took Leonard's hand turning it palm up, as if looking for some universal truth that existed there, which didn't require translation from English to Vietnamese. Satisfied, still holding his hand lightly but firmly, she led him out of the bar and guided him through a warren of narrow side streets and alleys: reeking with the smell of *nouc mam,* and garlic and cooking rice and noodles, produce wavering on the verge of spoilage, and rank gutters beyond purging. Vendors, men and women, stood beside their wares or squatted on splayed, sandaled feet over smoking charcoal braziers, lazily brushing away the flies hovering over vegetables or uncooked animal parts laid out on a chopping board on the ground beside them; women's faces framed by discolored kerchiefs, smiling with red betel-nut, stained smiles; men bony-legged in baggy shorts or pantlegs rolled above the knees, furrow-faced, marred by their past and the bleak future ahead of them, cigarettes dangling from nicotine-dried lips; women burdened with children on their backs or on their hips, or carrying jugs or boxes or bundles on their heads but always burdened; children, black-hair with dark-brown eyes, sucking thumbs or fists, snot hanging in yellow bubbles from button noses, holding their mothers' blouse or hand as they staggered straddled-legged along, eyes rolling gravely with curiosity at everything around them as if seeing it for the first time; a stream of people in black and white and gray and olive drab, with weary faces, too old too soon. The crippled, with one leg or a leg minus a foot or a calf or a knee, pantleg flapping uselessly or pinned at the waist, mostly in olive drab, supported by hand-hewn or government-issued crutches or canes; or sightless or with one eye; or armless or with one arm or part of an arm, the stump raw, stitches showing where the flap of skin was folded over the bone, standing, without purpose, mendicants—listlessly rattling topless Coca Cola or Budweiser cans with apathetic hope—competing with the saffron-robed monks carrying their brass begging bowls which most pedestrians ignored. Above the drone of voices, the flat, raucous bleat of a motor scooter vied with the jangling bells of bicycles for space on the crowded street—the rider with dark sunglasses and slickbacked black hair and a scent of cologne, protected from conscription by a bribe from a wealthy parent, or titled relative and his passenger also wearing sunglasses in a white *ao dai* that flowed, like her hair, behind her even though they weren't moving very fast, indifferent to the throngs they wobbled and weaved through. Leonard was vaguely aware of the people he passed, saw but didn't see or care about, had little interest in them, his interest centered on the swaying nates in blue, an exclamation mark of color he followed through the gray humanity around him. She led him to a small room, carved out of a larger room in the back of a shop that sold household goods, kitchenware, and cigarettes and whatever else had been traded with or pilfered from the U.S. soldiers.

Mickey's room was small and windowless. The only air came through the half-opened door. A GI cot took up most of the space in the room. The white sheets, GI issue, were clean. Her clothes hung neatly on hooks on the wall, and there was just enough room for a chair and small night stand. A mirror gaped at him. Leonard didn't want to think about how many men she had brought here. She placed her hands on his shoulders and pressed him to sit down on the edge of the bed. He could see his head in the mirror. He looked like he was peering over a window ledge. He took off his cap and held it loosely between his knees. His face since coming out of the field had lost some of its tightness, and the lines weren't quite as prominent. It was only his smile that saved him from the appearance of premature middle age.

She stood to the side of the mirror, her back to him, and he wondered if she was studying his face and what did she see? She undressed slowly, reaching behind her and unzipping her dress and carefully stepping out of it, barely disturbing the brownish-black cascade of hair that ended at her waist. She must have heard him catch his breath as she hung her dress on a hanger and placed it on top of several white, long-sleeved blouses. Her eyes met his in the mirror. Leonard wanted to reach out and feel the texture of her hair, put it against his face, breathe in its scent. Still with her back to him, her hands again disappeared under the curtain of hair as she unfastened her bra and hung it on a separate hook. She combed her hair, arranging it so that it fell over her small breasts. She bent forward. He could see her face and her blue eyes staring back at him while she applied a touch of gloss to her lips. Her small tongue darted from between her now shiny lips and briefly passed across them. She turned to Leonard. His chest heaved with his sharp intake of breath. He could have reached out and touched her at any time, but he waited patiently, only his eyes revealing his hunger.

She toed her spiked heels off and leaned forward and put a hand on his shoulder, her face inches from his as she peeled off her stockings and dropped them over the back of the chair. The dark fringe of her eyelashes as she bent forward hid her eyes from him, but he could smell the clean scent of her hair and see the faint line of her scalp where she'd parted it. When she straightened up without her shoes, she was much smaller. She pushed her hair back from her face. Her eyes remained fastened on the floor as she slipped her bikini panties over narrow thighs and let them drop to her ankles. He looked with fascination at her clean-shaved genital area, wanting to touch her and run his hands over her exquisite body.

She motioned for him to stand, fending off his hands when he reached out for her. She began unbuttoning his fatigue jacket. He shrugged it off onto the floor. Her fingers glided across his smooth chest and across his shoulders and down his arms. He sat down on the bed, fumbling with the laces of his jungle boots. After removing them, he stood up and looked down on the top of her head. Her hands were busy unfastening his black metal belt buckle. He stood very still as she unzipped his fly. His pants dropped to the floor without any pulling or tugging. He stepped out of them and kicked them under the bed. He didn't wear skivvies and was embarrassed at how excited he had become. She pointed to his erection and said several times, 'rubbah' and using hand signals indicated that he must use a rubber or "No can fuck," she said. Leonard retrieved his pants and took his wallet out of the pocket. He pulled out the carefully packaged protection. She took it from him and tore the package open. He stood trembling as she fitted the pale membrane on him.

Mickey gently pushed him onto the bed and sitting beside him began stroking him. Leonard closed his eyes and winced as her long nails pulled his scrotum and squeezed his testes. After running her hands along the inside of his thighs, she straddled and adjusted herself on him. He held her hips as he began to thrust into her. She placed her hands on each side of him and her sweet-scented hair fell on his face as she tried to hold his moving body in her. She rolled on to her back bringing him with her, his body slapping violently into her. Her red lips were parted, and her breath was hissing through her clenched white teeth. Her eyes were closed, and her nails dug into his arms as she held on to him. She moaned. He couldn't tell if he was hurting her, but he couldn't stop.

Moments later, they lay spent, side by side on the damp, crumpled sheets, their bodies slick with sweat. Leonard leaned over her and licked the sweat from between her breasts. Crystal beads had sprouted along her hairline and across her upper lip, and strands of her hair were pasted on her cheeks. When he began pushing her hair from her face, she opened her eyes. He lifted her hand with the long red nails and kissed it while he searched her face not knowing what he was looking for. He wiped his face. This wasn't standing in an alleyway or doorway for a quickie, listening for footsteps or a voice telling him to hurry while gum popped in his ear with indifference, nor was it unwashed bodies, underwear stained with sweat and dried gism. This was different, and Leonard was in love….

On the second day of his pass, Mickey borrowed a slightly oversized sport shirt with a Hawaiian print for Leonard from one of the girls. She wore the traditional pajamas, sandals, a conical straw hat, which shielded her face, and sunglasses. They spent the day exploring Saigon on foot, skirting places where they might come across MPs. Just to avoid any hassle. They visited shops and ate 'on the economy'—*pho,* he recognized the rice and noodles; *cha gio,* which left him uncertain—which meant that Leonard had no idea what was going into his stomach. He avoided drinking the water and any fruit that couldn't be peeled. He followed Mickey's lead when it came to the food and tried not to think that he might be eating rats or cats, even dogs.

At the end of the day, they returned to Mickey's room. She left for a few minutes and returned with a bucket of water, and they bathed each other. They talked all the time, chattering like two young high school kids. Neither comprehending the other. But communicating. Mickey showed him a picture of her brothers and sisters, and they laughed at the picture on Leonard's ID card as Mickey imitated the way he looked in the photo, pulling her chin into her neck and looking stern and flat-eyed at the camera. Leonard tried to express how he felt about her, and he knew he must be getting through to her because a look of sadness crept into her face. She became silent, turning her head away.

That night, she didn't insist that Leonard use a rubber, which was all right with him. She pointed to her pubic area and said she was 'Okay. Number one', which could have meant that she was a good fuck and Leonard would have wholeheartedly agreed. Or she was clean, free of venereal disease. Having seen other GIs, he would have preferred to avoid a dose of the clap or the syph. Although Leonard, at this point, wouldn't have cared what she had. He was in love. For the first time, he had connected with someone.

On the last day of his pass, Leonard left Mickey alone. He had an errand to do. He had seen a bracelet that she liked, and he wanted to surprise her with it. Wanted to show her how much he cared for her. He found the shop, which was easier than he expected, and with the greenbacks, cheaper than if he had paid with script. The bracelet had its own box and Leonard headed back to Mickey with his gift for her. He had been gone an hour.

She lay curled up and bleeding on blood-spattered sheets on the small bed, her clothes torn and thrown around the room. Mutely, he looked down at her naked body. He sat on the edge of the bed and raised her up and held her tightly not knowing what to do. She was trying to say something. He lowered her back onto the cot. Her eyes were puffed and starting to discolor. Her hair was matted on the side of her face. He didn't feel the tears stealing down his cheeks or his body shuddering as he looked at her bloody lips and her small white teeth now pink with blood. Leonard hadn't cried in years. About anything. She was having trouble breathing and gulped air through her open mouth.

"Sarge. Want Sarge," were her first words, muttered though the blood and pain. Leonard wiped his eyes and left to find Sarge.

III

Leonard closed his eyes for a moment to shut out the picture of Mickey on that bed in that small room, twenty years ago. The scene had been filtered by time but his rage remained. He never felt good when he thought about what had happened to her. He dragged the weight of his memories across the years to the beautiful woman sitting across from him. They'd discussed it before.

"I can always tell when you're thinking about what happened, love," she'd said.

"I don't talk about it."

"But I can tell."

"How?"

"I've watched you."

"How can you tell?"

"For one thing, you don't hear anything I say. Like you've shut out everything. Me included."

"I don't shut you out."

"You don't mean to, I know. But you do."

"Is that how you can tell I've gone back?"

"No. You start frowning. And your mouth tightens. And your eyes narrow into slits. And if you're holding something your knuckles turn white. You frighten me sometimes when I see you like that."

"I've always felt very strongly about what they did to you. I feel the same way when I read how someone has done the same thing to any woman or young girl. My god, you were so young. I'll always remember you and that day."

"I don't think about it anymore," she'd said. But he knew she said it because he felt so strongly.

He shook his head as if he had just awakened.

"I told you about the call I got from Sal late this morning," he said to explain why in midafternoon he was sitting in his recliner with his feet up, relaxed, until he had drifted back to the past.

"I just can't understand why since you just got home from your last trip."

"Yeah, tell me about it. I didn't expect it so soon after the last job. Even though it was just an overnight."

"He must have given you a reason."

"Yeah. Apparently, this situation came up suddenly, and he wanted my expertise for this one."

"Don't you think he's taking advantage of you?"

"He says it has to be done now, and you know Sal. He's not going to let this guy off the hook. No way."

"It does seem to me to be a little inconsiderate."

"The competition is heavy out there, love. I don't think he would, but he could always get someone else. Where would that leave me? Us? On the other hand, with such short notice, he'll spring for a bonus if I get the job done."

"Should I plan a side trip?"

"This one is close to home and my instructions were to make myself available afterwards—day or night. I don't know what the hell is going on. There doesn't seem to be time for anything any-more. Pressure. Everyone's feeling it."

That's what pissed Leonard off. Usually, whenever his busi-ness took him out of town, he had a couple of days to recoup, to unwind, get the competitive juices flowing again. Since they had no kids or animals to worry about, he and Mickey always planned side trips, sometimes a day or two, sometimes longer. That made up for not being able to take long vacations. Leonard couldn't afford to be out of touch for any length of time. He couldn't re-member when he and Mickey had really gotten away. By adding a few days to his short trips, Leonard was able to cover part of his expenses. He accounted for every penny he spent in his consulting business. He never tried to cheat the IRS. It was bad for business.

He got a blast when he read how some smart lawyers were doing hard time for failing to pay their taxes. Even businessmen. It was a real laugher. He made certain he didn't fall into that trap. It wasn't worth the hassle.

Mickey planned the side trips and made all the arrangements. She selected the city, the hotel, the points of interest they'd visit, and if several restaurants were noted for their cuisine, the food they'd eat. Like when they flew to San Francisco and ate abalone on Fisherman's Wharf. She also researched the night life so that they didn't waste a minute of their time, but they didn't move at a frenetic pace. They had learned to savor each moment.

If Leonard was away several days or weeks she planned her own activities accordingly, visiting his office to sort out the mail, water the plants, and dust the furniture. She let the answering machine handle all incoming calls. She checked into the hotel in the city they would visit the day before. And waited. They never went to the same city twice. There were too many places they'd never seen. What a country! They had spent several days in San Francisco, Denver and Dallas and even two days in Portland, Maine. Leonard's business took him all over the States. The demand varied.

On these trips, Mickey waited at the hotel no matter how long he might be delayed. And it happened sometimes. Although Leonard prided himself on being a good closer, not all transactions could be completed as quickly as he would like. There was always the unforeseen, despite his meticulous planning. Leonard always factored in the unexpected on these trips, allowed himself some flexibility, or 'wiggle room' as he called it. Mickey didn't know when he would arrive at the hotel until he called from the airport. He knew she would be waiting up, no matter what the hour. Mickey understood the stresses he faced in his line of work and carefully prepared for his return. She knew what helped him to unwind. That never varied.

Leonard never lost his sense of anticipation from the moment he walked through the lobby of their hotel and stepped on the elevator to go up to their room. He knew what to expect as soon as she opened the door, and even knowing that, he couldn't suppress a frisson of excitement as his hand gripped the doorknob. There was no question about it, she kept him charged up. Once inside the door and having dropped his luggage, they embraced. He ran his hands over the slight, slim woman in the silky, smooth peignoir, feeling the texture of her hair and breathing in her scent. Only when an enigmatic smile crept onto her face did he begin to undress, laying his clothes on the bed. She would have room service press or launder them by the next morning. He put his shoes side by side under the bed after wiping them with the shine cloth provided by the hotel. He was very proprietary about his shoes, which Mickey chided him about since he hadn't shown much interest in his appearance when he was in the Army. He kept them 'spit shined' at all times. Maybe, because he didn't have to.

He finished undressing in the bathroom, putting his socks and underwear in a plastic bag the hotel provided. He climbed tentatively into the steaming hot tub of water that Mickey had drawn. He slowly slid down, bracing himself, lips pursed, puffing out air for the final immersion as the water reached his neck, and his body made the final adjustment to the temperature of the bath, and he could sit back with his head against the back of the tub, and feel the sweat spring out on his forehead in tiny drops that would merge with each other and stream down his face into the pool of water covering his body. The tension began to drain from him as soon as he was under. The draft of cold air against his face signaled that Mickey had entered the bathroom. He opened his eyes as she removed her gown and hung it on the back of the door. His pulse quickened when he saw her cleanly shaved body and the firm swell of her mons.

She knelt on the bath mat, and he held his head back in the water so that she could wash it. Her nails rubbed the shampoo into his scalp, and she had him change his position so she could rinse his hair under the spigot. Returning to his former position she kneaded the bar of soap until white suds squeezed out between her red-tipped fingers. She frequently glanced at Leonard, expectant. She washed him slowly, her hands lingering teasingly as they roamed from one part of him to another, smiling as she told him what she had done during the hours or days that he was gone. She never asked him about his trip. Leonard knew she could tell from his body language if it had been a breeze, or there had been problems. He would talk about it later. When he could reflect on it objectively.

She washed his genitals, fondled them; moved to his neck where the serious scrubbing took place as she washed him and massaged his neck and shoulders, down his arms to his fingertips, but not before she tweaked his ears after cleaning them with a washcloth-wrapped finger. She took the same care with his lower body, sliding her hands over the network of purplish-white tracks across his stomach and chest. She paused at his genitals again.

"Hmm," she said. "This soldier is AWOL."

"He went AWOL as soon as he knew he had to leave his home station."

"He should know he has his duty to perform."

Leonard smiled as her fingers kneaded and pressed and caressed his flaccid member until the blood filled the muscle and it tightened, rising upward.

"Ahh," she exclaimed, "our soldier is ready to report back to duty."

"Hazardous duty?"

"Only if he doesn't perform well."

Leonard accepted this passively, a smile on his face.

When she finished bathing him, she dried her hands and wrapped her hair in a turban and stepped into the tub. Leonard pushed himself upright and began washing her legs. She held the safety bar on the wall as he soaped between her toes and squealed when he ran a finger along the sole of each foot. He kissed each foot before placing it back in the water. He slid forward in the tub and holding her buttocks pressed his face against the swollen mound between her legs. He ran his tongue into the crevice until he heard

her breath quicken and held her hands as she lowered herself into
the tub. He leaned forward, and they kissed before he continued
washing the rest of her body. This was the unwinding of Leonard,
the shedding of tension, the putting business behind him and the
renewing of the physical part of their love. The ritual rarely varied
when he returned to her after a trip.

After bathing, they dried each other, frequently kissing, ex-
tracting promises of the punishment they would inflict upon each
other once in bed, laughing at meaningless things, acting like the
children they had never been. Mickey remained in the bathroom
after they were finished while Leonard waited in bed. She varied
her makeup and perfume to fit Leonard's mood, then joined him
in bed. That ritual rarely changed either.

The last trip had been close to home. It had been unexpected,
and Leonard had not prepared for it properly, had been forced to
improvise, but in the long run it had worked out well. There was
no slack between the last trip and the call he'd received upon his
return home, and he hadn't shed the tension. There hadn't been
time to really relax, and he felt jumpy, on edge, like he wasn't sure
if he had locked the door of his office and there was no way to
check it to see if he had. Leonard thrived on arranging details,
weighing the contingencies and the alternatives and preparing for
them. The last trip hadn't given him that luxury, and with this
one so close he felt stretched. He resented it. But then he was a
realist. The business world was changing, as was his world. The
imperatives that drove decisions were different, and new forces
were at work. At least he didn't have a bunch of employees nattering
their demands nor someone hanging over his shoulder critiquing
everything he did. Of course, he had to comply with his client's
directions and his timetable. Up to a point.

If there just wasn't an element of doubt squirming around in
his head, Leonard wouldn't have felt so uncomfortable. This was
what was making him so apprehensive. Had he done something to
compromise the last transaction? Overlooked an important detail?

Why such short notice? Was he going head to head with a competitor? Was he being tested after all these years to see if he'd lost a step, couldn't close as quickly? He tried to thrust his nagging suspicions aside. Maybe, he thought, he was hitting that male crisis thing.

Well, he had to work with the available information. He'd better start thinking of all the contingencies that could occur, or at least be aware of them. There'd be a good bonus for this one if he was successful. He didn't want to think about the other possibility. The bonus would buy a few hundred shares of a hot issue he'd been following on the stock market. Mickey said she was going upstairs. She knew he'd phased out everything around him. He had to think about the information that Sal had passed on to him and how he could fulfill the contract to kill Nate Whelan, a land developer from Crescent Hills in Kaydeross County, New York.

IV

Leonard found Sarge, Master Sergeant Salvatore Perrino, sitting at the bar talking with the barmaid, drinking tonic water with a slice of lime sunk in the bottom of the glass. The ceiling fan, creaking with each revolution, struggled to push the humid air throughout the bar. The barmaid flicked a fan back and forth past her face. It wasn't doing much good. No 'hostesses' were in sight.

"Sarge. Where can I find 'im?" Leonard asked, catching his breath as he leaned across the bar.

"You're talking to 'im," the man at the bar said. He stared at the front of Leonard's shirt, took in the smear of blood and motioned him to a table. Leonard did as directed and sat down across from him.

"It's Mickey, Sarge," Leonard said as he sucked in the beer-washed air. He wiped the sweat from his eyes, gathered his thoughts. "Uhh ... I'm Leonard Grissom. I been ... stayin' with her an' she's been cut ... beat up pretty bad. Jeezuz, I was only gone 'bout an hour. She needs ya. She might be dying." He leaned across the table and added to what he thought was a question in Sarge's eyes, "I didn't do it. I was just gone an hour. She tol' me to come an' get ya."

Sarge shoved his chair back, stood and strode over to the bar and said something to the barmaid who disappeared through the beaded curtains behind her. "Tell me what happened on the way," Sarge said over his shoulder as he hurried out the door. Leonard ran to keep up with the big man, reciting what little he knew between gulps of air.

"I uhh ... just went out, like I said. Wanted to get her this bracelet … Got back an' there she was, layin' there, nekkid an' bleedin'. I din't know what to do."

"See anybody leavin'?" Sarge asked as he pushed through a clutch of Vietnamese arguing in the middle of the alley.

Leonard hustled through the narrow gap before the group could close around him.

"No, like I say, I was only gone an hour. Maybe not even that."

"She was still breathin', right?"

"Yeah, she says, 'Get Sarge.'"

Leonard was surprised that the big man moved so quickly as they weaved in and out of the clusters of pedestrians through the streets and alleys to Mickey's room. A small, thin, gray-haired Vietnamese *bac si*, 'doctor,' was already there when they arrived. He had put a towel between her legs and was cleaning the side of her face. After wiping Mickey's wound, he had her swallow a pain-killer and took a bottle and syringe from his black bag. Sarge checked the bottle. He made the 'doctor' put a fresh needle on the syringe before injecting Mickey. Leonard watched from the end of the bed.

"Antibiotics," Sarge said, standing over the old man. "He's the closest thing to a doctor we got around here. I supply him with penicillin and shit like that and morphine, and he takes care of our girls. I'm surprised he has any medicine at all. Sells what he doesn't use on the black market after he cuts it. The bastard's set up a practice of his own." The *bac si* took no notice, as if he'd heard it before.

Mickey was conscious as the old man began to stitch together the lips of the skin on each side of the long, thin slash that ran from her hairline, down her cheek to her chin. She bit her puffed-up lip but didn't cry out. Leonard pushed himself between Sarge and the bed, knelt and held Mickey's hand. The sedative hadn't yet taken hold. Her grip tightened each time the needle dipped through her skin. He was unable to tear his eyes from her swollen face and the gauze stuffed in her nose to stop the bleeding.

The *bac si* finished sewing her cheek and checked the lacerations between her legs and said in broken English and with hand signals that her assailants had started to cut her there, but he didn't know how much damage had been done. He cleaned the wound and stitched that as well. He cleaned her anus after he stanched the bleeding.

"Lucky. She lucky," the *bac si* said, pausing to look at Sarge and then Leonard. He traced with his finger the stitched line on her cheek. "He no cut nerves. Ver' good." The 'doctor' pointed to her eyes and the corner of her mouth. "Knife ver' sharp…. Make clean cut. She ver' lucky." He dressed the wound, taping the white bandages to her pale skin.

If she had struggled the wound would have been an ugly ripping of her flesh and could have put her eye out. Sarge insisted that the 'doctor' leave a supply of painkillers. He paid the *bac si* in greenbacks and patted the old man on the back. "Good job, doc," he said. After the old man left, Sarge gave Mickey another pill which she swallowed without water.

"What happened, Miko?" Sarge asked in halting Vietnamese. He sat on the chair next to the bed. Leonard sat on the floor, still holding her hand.

Mickey spoke very slowly so that he could understand. Two black GIs had done it. She recognized them from the club. They were loud and abrasive, treating the girls roughly. Leonard listened to the flow of conversation. Sarge laid his hand on her arm to slow her down when she grew excited.

"I was there the last time they showed up," Sarge said to Leonard. "Mickey fingered them as troublemakers so I kicked their asses out. They went quietly, but one of them gave Mickey the bird and then pointed it at her. She seems to think they must'a seen you and her out sightseeing today and followed you back. Came back the next day and saw you leave her. If you'd been here, you might be a dead GI now."

Mickey had her eyes closed. She reached up and fingered the bandage over her cheek. Purplish bruises and reddish teeth marks mottled her flesh. She turned her head away from Leonard and Sarge. Mickey's speech grew fuzzy as the pill Sarge had given her began to take effect. Sarge pulled the chair closer to the bed and leaned forward to hear her. Sarge translated aloud.

"They'd been drinking … She could smell it. One a the guys hit her an' she fell back onna bed an' then began ripping her clothes off. The other stuffed one a her stockings in her mouth when she started to scream."

Mickey began to sob, her shoulders shaking, the tears squeezing out from under her swollen lids. She put a fist on her forehead.

"They tore her nice dress … and threw it on the floor." Sarge put a hand on her shoulder to calm her. Leonard slumped beside the bed, holding his head, his elbows braced on his knees. She shuddered and continued.

"They called her 'Honky Ho' over and over … punched her," Sarge translated. "Did boom boom … alla time they laugh …. Stuck his dick in her mouth…. He struck her … rolled her over and … She could hear his grunts … Much pain … She passed out. Didn't feel it when he rolled her on her back. Didn't feel the knife."

Leonard looked at Sarge. He was a big man with cropped, wavy hair turning gray at the temples. He was deeply tanned. A fine brushwork of creases around his eyes and on his forehead lined his face. His dark brown, deepset eyes were too close to a narrow aquiline nose, but still gave him a distinguished, somewhat Tony Bennett appearance.

"You okay, kid?" Leonard heard a voice ask. "Ya look bad. You gonna be sick?"

"Why'd they do this to Mickey? She never done nothin' to them," his voice said from a great distance, coming through the anger that had been building through a red haze in his head from the moment he had found her bleeding on the cot. He wasn't sure if his question had gotten through to Sarge. He hadn't expected an answer. But he got one.

"A couple of tanked-up GIs, Leonard. It's my fault and they

took it out on Mickey because she fingered them, ya follow me? One of 'em musta been with her before. She won't say."

"They had no call to beat up on her and … do those things. Did they?"

"No, it happens though, kid. Somethin' sets 'em off, like any a these GIs, an inconsequential thing that builds and builds to where they see it as a major wrong against them. They gotta take it out on someone. It happens alla time in this business. No, it ain't right. What can I tell ya."

Leonard felt a calm settle on him. The red haze disappeared, and his voice sounded like it came right out of him without his opening his mouth. He knew what he had to do.

"You saw 'em before. What'd they look like?"

Sarge tried to explain to Leonard that any description that he'd give would fit any number of the blacks hanging out around Tu Do Street.

"Where do they hang out? I need to know. I need to know where they hang out."

Leonard realized that Sarge must have seen something in his face or maybe it was the insistence in his voice, or his sitting there cracking his knuckles, but before he left, he agreed to find out what he could. Leonard slumped against the wall, a hand on Mickey's arm. He opened the box that he had been carrying from the shop and slid the bracelet over her hand onto her wrist. Her steady breathing made him grateful that she was still alive. He looked ahead at what he had to do. "Just like the tunnels," Leonard said aloud. "Just like the friggin' tunnels."

V

Leonard had volunteered to go into the tunnel. This was the kind of detail that one didn't get volunteered for. It was his choice. He knew about them. Everyone did. His unit had found a tunnel, or rather, the Kit Carson scout found one. Only a few men in his company were small enough to fit into the hole, which led underground. So maybe he wasn't a real volunteer, but this was the first time in the Army anyone had given him a choice. None of that being volunteered shit. He'd gotten enough of that because he was small, like being the runt of the litter. He never understood why the big guys were always selected to be the guidon-bearers or acting squad leaders in basic training. The Army always seemed to equate size with leadership and the smarts, like size gave you special capabilities. What bullshit, Leonard thought. Still, none of the other guys, who could have, volunteered to go into the hole. Leonard didn't think of it at the time as a window of opportunity. But that's what it turned out to be.

The company was part of a search and destroy mission conducted by battalion. A VC complex had been reported in their area of operations. This meant a vast network of tunnels linking together underground bunkers, which might house a headquarters, supplies and ammunition, communications, medical facilities and even primitive factories. Suppression fire by artillery and Cobra gunships softened up the area before the company was dropped off onto their LZ by the Hueys.

The platoon began moving from their landing zone in the elephant grass, through the wet, ashen dawn, across recently tilled rice paddies and into the bush. A bamboo fence, running alongside the rice paddies on the perimeter of trees in their objective area, was the first indication of a possible VC site. They hadn't seen a village. Or people. Sergeant Cory Masterson, platoon sergeant and acting platoon leader, radioed back to the company HQ and received clearance to move forward. The battalion command and control chopper was flying in wide circles overhead, maintaining visual and communication contact with the units on the ground while monitoring the overall battalion progress. The Kit Carson scout, a VC defector, temporarily assigned to the company and attached to the platoon for this operation, found the bamboo fence and led the way through it, pointing out the barely visible tripwire stretched across the opening. The spot was marked with engineer tape. Word was passed down the column. Beyond the perimeter and inside the woodline, the platoon spread out, again, moving cautiously as they surveyed the ground and looked for more tripwires. The platoon halted when the Kit Carson scout knelt beside the barely discernible outline of a hole in the ground, betrayed by the brown grass and dry leaves that covered it. He and the interpreter went into a discussion, and they told Sergeant Masterson that the scout didn't do tunnels. That's when Leonard volunteered.

Masterson couldn't believe it when he said he'd go down. Leonard couldn't believe he'd said it. He never volunteered for anything. He didn't have to. He got volunteered for all the shit details, but he knew that it was because he was always fucking up. That's why he got all those Article 15s, company punishment. If it hadn't been for them, he would have been promoted long ago. He'd been busted to E-1 so many times he never bothered to sew on that first stripe anymore when he made E-2. He just didn't give a shit. He didn't buy into the spit and polish, nitshit stuff or kissing the First Sergeant's ass or anyone's ass for that matter. He may have been the shortest guy in the platoon, but he wasn't an ass-kisser. But he did take care of his M-16 and his bayonet. Lovingly.

Masterson wasn't much older than him and had already served a tour in 'Nam. He didn't suck up to the brass either or try to be one of the boys. When Leonard had joined the platoon as a re-placement, Masterson had told the new replacements that he was in 'Nam to kill gooks and to keep them alive so that they could kill gooks. None of that bullshit about saving the world from Communism. They had a job to do. Even if the pay sucked. Leonard had asked him one day during a break why he didn't ride his ass like everyone else did.

"Warriors come in all sizes, Leonard," he said with a distant, glacial stare. "I can count on you, that's all. I don't say that to many guys."

Masterson probably would have gone down himself except he had a platoon to run until the lieutenant's replacement arrived. Leonard wondered if that was why he had volunteered. Because his sergeant hadn't asked him. The platoon sergeant never had his troops do anything he wouldn't do himself.

"Ya know what you're getting into, Leonard?" Masterson asked when Leonard volunteered. That was another thing. No one called him Leonard until he arrived in the platoon. Before that, it had been Lenny, or 'shorty,' sometimes 'runt,' spoken in a demeaning way like he was the platoon flunky. Masterson had started calling him Leonard. Now everyone did.

"Yeah, Sarge, we wanna find out what's in the hole."

"Shit, Leonard, why you volunteering now?"

"You got someone else in mind?"

"No one wants to go down. Too many rumors about 'em. You heard the rumors?"

"Yeah, I heard 'em. They might be waitin' for the first numbnuts who volunteers."

"Still want to go down?"

"I said I would."

Masterson appeared to think it over. He looked around and hollered at his men bunching up. "Fuckin' cherries," he muttered to himself. He took it personally when someone got wasted.

"You can't fuck up down there, ya know?" The sergeant had made up his mind.

Leonard took combat very seriously. He knew that if his number was on a 122mm incoming, well, that's all she wrote. So be it. But the rest of it, being alert, tuning himself into the action, he could handle that. He could reduce the odds of getting killed. When the platoon sergeant said dig, he'd ask how deep. That was grunt work but was a good indication of how seriously he took combat. Like putting out the claymores, that was very serious shit. No fucking VC was going to sneak up on him or his squad. No way.

Leonard decided to take a flashlight, a .45, a concussion grenade, and his bayonet. He took off his fatigue jacket so that it wouldn't snag on a rock or protruding root. His tightly muscled arms and large hands seemed misplaced on his otherwise small body. He made a sweatband from his OD handkerchief and tied it around his head; emptied his pockets; put his taped dogtags in his back pocket; rubbed insect repellent on his arms and body, the back of his neck, in his ears and on his cheeks. He taped his pantlegs above the top of his boots and above his knees for the same reason he didn't wear his fatigue shirt. To reduce snags. He looped the nylon umbilical cord around his waist. It didn't matter what happened if he was killed, but he didn't like the idea of being left buried in the hole. Not in this fucking country!

The Kit Carson scout slowly pulled aside the wooden cover, interwoven with dry leaves and brush and perforated with air holes, its edges slanted to fit snugly into the narrow shaft. Several GIs stood beside the hole, M-16s pointed into the opening. Leonard felt his motor racing. It seemed like less of a good idea now. This was the critical moment if Charlie was waiting. He'd heard how they'd wait until a GI would settle into the tunnel and then they'd blast him, plugging up the hole, delaying any movement into the tunnel until the body was removed. Leonard grabbed his balls reflexively. To reassure himself. He sat on the edge of the hole. Masterson gripped his shoulder. Leonard concentrated on lowering himself into the tunnel.

"Watch your ass down there, Leonard. Good luck."

Leonard tossed him a sharp, exaggerated salute and disappeared into the dark cavity, holding several looped feet of rope in one hand. He wondered how far the air and light entering the tunnel with him would reach? If the VC waited for someone following behind the air? Could see the dark change? He crawled a few feet and sat for a couple of minutes until his eyes adjusted to the darkness. Several pencil thin shafts of light from overhead penetrated the space around him after the entrance was closed. Filling his lungs with a deep breath, more to strengthen his resolve than for the air itself, Leonard crawled forward, playing out the excess loops of rope behind him until he faced a wall of blackness. He paused again and waited, his senses stretching out in all directions around him. He felt his pupils widen to pierce the obsidian space in which he was enclosed. He listened, his hearing on full alert, reaching out for a sound, relieved to pick up a distant salvo of artillery, but searching under that for an alien sound that indicated life ahead. He sniffed the air to organize the smells in his sensory catalogue. He gagged on the fetid air, swallowing hard several times to keep from retching. He licked the air with his tongue. The taste was as bad as the smell.

Leonard's body sagged closer to the earth, his movement fluid, feral-the rhythm of his stalking synchronized to the flaring of his nostrils; his tongue tested the air, his ears and eyes strained for the sound of his prey while his hand slowly caressed the air and ground for tripwires or mines.

He unhurriedly moved forward, hands periodically checking the .45 and bayonet secured in his waistband, not slipping, the grenade snug in his pocket, the flashlight cushioned from scraping the ground in one hand. And always moving forward on all fours, careful not to scrape the ground or the narrow walls. He sniffed the air as he moved.

He was already some ways into the tunnel. Blackness couldn't hide stink. Not even the stinking air could hide certain smells. Blackness couldn't hide noise either. His eyeballs were about to burst out of their sockets. They felt like they'd been hung out to dry. He blinked several times; closed his eyes for a second and felt the fluid restored. The human smell grew stronger. He wondered if the air when the tunnel was opened had carried his smell this far. Could they smell him? His sweat? He sniffed his armpit. After a few days in the field—ripe. He couldn't feel any movement of air. How close would he get before they picked up his odor? The insect repellant? He moved slower. He reached back and untangled the rope from his foot, careful not to send any signal to the other end. He didn't need a rope flapping up and down now, dislodging dirt and slapping against the floor of the tunnel. He tensed up. Just like on ambush, with the tension building and building until Charlie stepped into the killing zone and all concentration was centered on slowly squeezing the trigger and watching the body fold or flop or jerk or judder until it hit the ground where it shook or twitched until it lay unmoving. They all died differently. He suppressed a desire to fart.

At first it was an impression of light. Leonard blinked several times to make sure it wasn't an illusion. He could smell wax burning. The voices drifted back. Leonard could almost pick out the individual words because his hearing had become so acute, like the words came out in bursts and slowed from 78 rpms to 33 1/3 when they reached him. How safe did they feel? Did they know death was just a few feet away? About to take them out? He slowly withdrew the smooth, round, black body of the concussion grenade from his pocket. He pulled the pin with the hand that held the bayonet and tried to keep the handle from flying off. It made a pinging sound as it bounced from his hand onto the ground. The voices stopped. The light snuffed out. Leonard counted and at the last second threw it around the corner into the enclosure where they squatted, curling himself and covering his ears to avoid the noise and impact of the blast. Dirt showered down on him as he hugged the floor of the tunnel. Dazed, he shook his head and quickly crawled forward, flashlight in one hand and bayonet in the other. The beam of his light picked up the three of them sprawled in a tangle of arms and legs. He shot the beam through the cloud of dust into the tunnel beyond them and listened. No one. No sound. Blood ran down their faces and from their ears. The eyes of one of the VC opened, blinked in the harsh glare of the light, eyeballs rolling from side to side. Turned his head to avoid the beam of the flashlight, his fingers skittering along the ground, groping for his weapon, stopped when he felt the sharp point of the bayonet pressed up under his chin. Leonard's light danced against the ceiling as he pushed the man's head back with his hand holding the flashlight. He adjusted the beam so that he could see the man's face, the gook's mouth shaped like an O, the perimeter quivering as if he was trying to speak and then flattening into a harsh line as understanding took hold just at the moment Leonard drove the blade up through his mouth, behind the palate into his brain. He wondered what the gook was about to say as the blade tore through his tongue. Had he formed a word; did the blade cut the word off like it cut the flesh? The other two didn't move. Leonard made sure by plunging the bayonet under their ribs and up into their hearts. The blood was sticky on his hand. He lay the flashlight on the dirt floor, its beam cut to a section of earth and the gook's leg. He wiped his hand on the pant leg of the VC. He could still feel the dried blood between his fingers. He used the hem of Charlie's blouse to clean the bayonet, running the blade through the cloth held by his thumb and forefinger. He sat back on his heels. Paused in the dim fractured light beside the bleeding bodies looking at what he had accomplished on his own, trusting his senses, killing without pity, or remorse, or regret, or conscience, or guilt. No outside message of piety had interfered, caused him to hesitate. He'd done it cleanly. As if another sense had guided his hand. Leonard had his first three kills. Not impersonal; not from a distance. He wondered why it had been so easy?

Leonard checked their pockets, removing anything that appeared official including letters. And pictures. Small, faded, wrinkled photographs, dog-eared with finger-blackened corners and edges.

Carried for how long? He stared at a photo of a young woman, smiling, her hair framing a wide-eyed face. When had she last seen her husband, boyfriend, lover? He rolled the bodies over and found a canvas dispatch bag under the first VC he'd killed. He flashed the light in the bag—papers, folded maps, more papers. He stuffed everything he'd taken from the bodies into the bag. Except the picture. He put the photo of the young woman in his pocket with his dogtags. He collected the weapons and checked to make sure the safety was on each one. He didn't need a round up his ass when he pulled them behind him. He looped a piece of tape through the trigger guards, took off his belt and pushed it through the loop so that he could drag them.

He felt a tug on the rope around his waist. They must have heard the explosion. He signaled back. He sat on the floor of the small enclosure, shined the light around the rough packed-dirt walls. He felt different. From before he went into the tunnel until now when he had to leave. It was as if he'd won a marathon that nobody expected him to finish. And he wanted to stay at the finish line and feel the elation, savor the act of completion. His moment of success. The thrust of the knife into flesh was like breaking the tape at the finish line.

He put the dispatch bag around his neck so that it hung down in front of him. He had not been afraid, and he wondered about that as he began his crawl back to the entrance of the tunnel. Fear. Not the brain-numbing, muscle-freezing immobility that choked off resolve, action. He'd been propelled by a sense of destiny. He knew fear; understood it; grappled with it; felt his body shake uncontrollably with it; and had been shamed by it. That kind of fear came from sitting in a bunker unable to move while 122 mms dropped around him, drowning out his screams of terror. But the terror vanished as soon as the VC attacked, no longer shielded by the merciless horror of their supporting fire; moved like scavengers over and under the barbed wire and through what was left of the claymores and network of grenades that hadn't been detonated by their fire support. He regained control then. His life was no longer determined by a round which had been measured and configured to reach his position if all the calculations had been accurate.

When he reached the entrance, he pushed the .45 and knife into his waistband and the flashlight into his pocket. He dragged the captured weapons forward and handed them up. Hands reached down and pulled him out of the hole. He closed his eyes against the unrelenting sunlight. He sat for a few moments savoring the clean, cooler air. He tried to rise, but his knees were weak and sore from the crawling and the tension and the inexplicable excitement he felt. Hands helped him to his feet. He wobbled for a moment in place. He loosened the rope around his waist. It slid down his legs, and he stepped out of the loop.

"Need a drink."

"No drinking fountains down there, huh?" someone said as he handed him a canteen. They laughed as he shook his head and water spilled out of the sides of his mouth. He gargled to get rid of the taste of the bad air and spat it on the ground. It still clogged his nostrils. He took the bandanna from his head, wet it down and wiped his face. He took another drink and handed the canteen back to its owner. He blew his nose and tried to dig the smell out of his nostrils. Black dirt and mucous marked his handkerchief with silvery black strands, but the smell lingered in his nose.

"Who gets this?" Leonard asked, holding out the dispatch bag.

"I'll take it, Leonard," Masterson said. He had appeared while Leonard tried to rid himself of the smell that clung to him. He riffled through it, taking out the IDs that Leonard had shoved into the bags. "Looks like one a these guys had some rank. Got caught by surprise. You have any trouble down there?"

"Stinks, Sarge. This get me an extra R&R?"

"Yeah, sure," he said derisively. "This looks like it could be pretty hot stuff. I'll call the Old Man and see what he wants done with it. I'll send you back with it. Get your gear together. You did real good, Leonard." He patted Leonard on the back.

Thirty minutes later, Leonard was back at the company and

turned the dispatch case over to an NCO from the Division G-2 section.

"It was a dry hole until we heard that you had found something, soldier," the NCO said. "Your three kills were the only ones we had for the entire operation. Wish you'd been able to bring one of them out with you."

"Sorry, 'bout that," Leonard said giving the NCO's clean fatigues and shined boots a slow look. Without saying, "Fuck you! Get real REMF."

Leonard's three kills gave him some celebrity, and his CO said he was going to put him in for the Army Commendation Medal. Leonard had gained status, but he didn't want to talk about how he had wasted the three slopes, how it had felt to push the blade into each one, quickly and cleanly. Later, he traded a radio and a watch for a Randall combat knife from a GI who'd won it in a poker game. He honed and oiled it and checked its cutting edge against the hairs on his arm. Leonard had found an extension of himself.

VI

"What was it like, Leonard, taking three of 'em out?"

"How'd ya feel?"

Yeah, how did he feel? Leonard shook his head taking refuge in silence. Didn't want to try to explain the release, the satisfaction, the discovery about himself.

"Hey, 'Killer'," someone said. Others picked it up, some saying it with friendly respect; others said it contemptuously until Leonard stared them down. He took it as an insult. He didn't think of himself as 'Killer.' Killer was emotional, irrational, uncontrolled. They waited, expecting to see Leonard the fuck-up return to form. Waited and watched. He could feel their eyes sliding in his direction, when he walked into the bunker, the chowline, at mail call, but not on patrol, not on operations where they wanted someone with his skill and fearlessness. They had their own asses to worry about then.

He didn't ask Masterson how he felt when he wasted a dink. But he wanted to talk about it. Had to talk about it. But he didn't and he couldn't. Masterson brought it up. They were on a stand-down, cleaning weapons, going through the motions of training, working on their bunkers, replacing sandbags, running no-purpose patrols at night, writing letters, listening to the Armed Forces Network, the music. And they talked about how some asshole lieutenant got fragged or didn't get fragged, but should have been fragged; spreading the rumors that grew and lost their credibility in each telling; building their personal legends by recounting their own actions during the last operation against Charlie or the one before or the one that everyone had forgotten, or if they thought of themselves as lovers and not fighters which was more often the

case after R&R or a three day pass—their physical endurance with
the broads, the pussy, the 'hoors', the cunts, the snatch. Fighting
boredom. With endless profanity-laced talk and arguments that
started nowhere and ended nowhere. Unless someone got wasted.
Then conversation ceased for a time, a short time, until Aunt Hazel or Aunt Mary or Aunt Nora visited, with each inhalation or
snort, providing new insights and clarity into their talk. And they
took up where they'd left off before, until someone else got wasted
or returned to the World.

"You okay, Leonard?" Sargeant Masterson asked.

"Yeah, sure."

"Thought somethin' might be botherin' you, ya know? You
been quiet, not hanging out with the others. Notice ya don't get
no mail."

"I ain't much good at letter writin'. 'Sides, I got no one to
write to. Nah, I'm okay."

"Thinkin' about the ones you wasted in the tunnel?"

Leonard didn't answer. Thought about it. Changed the subject. From himself.

"I guess you've offed a few, Sarge. It bother you?"

"It did at first. Because I wanted the person I wasted to be..."
He hesitated as if he'd said too much. "I enlisted to kill. Ya know
that? I came in with a rage so strong that I almost got a section
eight out of the Army. They even had me talk to a shrink."
Masterson paused, took out a pack of cigarettes, shook one out;
offered one to Leonard who refused. He took the cigarette from
the pack with his lips, cupped his hand around the flame of his
lighter, and sent a stream of smoke from the corner of his mouth.
"But they needed me, I guess. Saw how they could use me."

Leonard stared at the Sergeant with the tired eyes. I guess
when they looked at me, Leonard thought, they saw 'replacement,'
but there was something different about Masterson like he'd been
somewhere the rest of them had never been.

"I left home because my sister was murdered. Beat up and
raped. I felt I was to blame." He didn't explain. "Still do. I was

seventeen when I enlisted. I couldn't look around me without thinking someone walking the streets in Crescent Hills…"

"Where's that?" Leonard interrupted.

"New York State. The Adirondacks." His voice dropped. " I
couldn't handle the guilt trip. I volunteered for 'Nam. I thought I
could work it out here. But you know, Leonard, I haven't worked
it out yet. I never see a face when I see Charlie. I look through the
sight, line it up and gently squeeze the trigger … gently, gently
until he disappears." He raised his hand and aimed it like it was a
weapon and Leonard watched his index finger, the trigger finger,
slowly curl back to his hand and jump as if recoiling. "I wanna put
a face at the end of my sight. The face of Barb's killer. Killing gooks an'
tryin' to make it personal is no longer the same. It don't solve nothin'.

"The kind of killing that goes with calling in artillery, or Puff
the Magic Dragon, or the gunships, or the air force, that never was
personal for me. It was only when I saw the dink in my sight did it
matter, or used to, and I'd squeeze off the rounds, not firing full
automatic, killing over and over the bastard that wasted Barb, my
sister. It never goes away. But it's just a job now. Now I got to keep
you guys alive. Stay cool, ya know?"

"Uhh … how old was your sister? You don't mind my askin'?"

"Just a kid. Fifteen."

"Jeez." He looked at Masterson squatting on his heels, his arms
on his knees, his lips inches away from the cigarette, his eyes staring at something miles away in the past.

"He hurt her bad… Real bad. He raped her an' beat her and
left her to die by herself… By the side of a road … alone an'
bleedin' …."

"You ever gonna look for this guy?"

Masterson didn't answer. But let the silence grow between
them. He fieldstripped his cigarette, and they watched the red
glow of the tip fall to the ground and get swallowed up by the gray
ash and disappear.

"Hang in there, kid. There're more tunnels ahead." He rose
and left Leonard alone.

Rage hadn't driven him to kill, Leonard knew that. He wasn't convulsed by anger. Nothing personal had driven him. He thought of it as more of a newly found craft, a skill, a realization that he'd been set free. He was entering the darkness on his own. Nothing was binding him, putting constraints on him. The isolation grabbed him, left him unfettered, unrestrained. He was in control. In charge of his life. For him, the war was reduced to the black innards of the tunnel. Never had he experienced such freedom, such primal release. Cunning against cunning, strength against strength, testing one's will and resolve to crawl forward by inches, inch by tortuous inch, to lay in wait patiently while his whole body shivered in anticipation. He'd forgotten that. The exhilaration! He knew even before he threw the grenade how he wanted to waste Charlie. With his bayonet. Up close. Close enough to smell his body odors, his breath and see his face; close enough to hear his breathing as he awoke from the shock of the grenade, his sharp intake of air when he realized what was about to happen; close enough to hear the sound of his dying, of his death. He had sat in the fecal fumes the killing had released and it hadn't mattered. It was part of the killing. The wasting. The waxing. But he didn't think about this until it was over and he knew he could do this again. And again.

Leonard was the man! But subsequent operations turned up dry hole after dry hole. Others challenged Leonard's reputation. They volunteered to go into the hole only to return to the surface after so many inches or feet of moving in the unresisting, claustrophobic blackness of the tunnel; or Leonard went down to collect them piece by piece in a poncho from the inadvertent, impatient movement that set off a mine made by the enemy from one of our own 105mm rounds; or they returned to the entrance to be be lifted out screaming after the creatures of the darkness, the rats, or snakes or centipedes, attacked them. Some, at the first sign of danger or fear, returned and reported that the tunnel was cold. Only later when a sniper took out a grunt was the lie revealed. By then it was too late. For the dead GI.

"Leonard," Sergeant Masterson said, "get your gear together. They think they got a big one. They're pulling all you guys up to division for a special operation."

Masterson was there when he climbed aboard the Huey, watched him strap himself in, gave him a thumbs up, and walked under the whirling blades into the dust churned up as the chopper rose from the ground.

It was the first time that Leonard had been at a briefing. Everything in the room shone, gleamed—from the charts and pointers to the NCOs and Brass, more rank than Leonard had ever seen gathered under one roof. And RESPECT. It dripped from their words, seduced them with sincerity. Elevated them, inflated them, conned them—the dozen, scruffy, shaggy-haired, undersized boy-men—the tunnel rats, collected like so many urchins from the the different combat units, carrying with them the smell of the field, but without the weight of their previous failures as soldiers; unique because they dared to enter the black micro-world of fetid air, scurrying rats, buzzing flies and mosquitos and hidden death. They brought this into the sanitized, vacuumed, polished, air-conditioned room where operations, already planned, already decided upon were put into motion by men who viewed the black world of the tunnel rats like so many accountants who, with noses askew, measured and calculated odds and probabilities and results in terms of tonnage and bodies like chess pieces they could move around at will but now depended on these nondescript heroes to solve one of the problems that defied explanation and for which no tactics or sophisticated weapons had been developed.

The BRIEFER gave them the enemy and friendly situations, and as the officer, a lieutenant colonel, his starched collar embroidered with the black smudge of his rank, spoke, an NCO with two rockers, himself a starched symbol of the military might of the US Army, indicated with a pointer, its tip the polished business end of a 50-calibre machine gun round, the friendly and enemy positions on the wide, contour-veined, acetate-covered Situation Map.

Blue for ours. Red for theirs. The amoeba shaped blue lines dominated the map. Leonard realized that he was being read into the BIG PICTURE! He expected to hear the stiff, starched sleeve of the NCO's fatigue shirt crinkle or crack when he bent his arm to replace the Big Picture with a chart depicting their current situation. Small red circles dotted the map. Them. Charlie. Inside and outside the blue lines.

"Gentlemen." This was the first time anyone had referred to him or even suggested that he was a gentleman. Leonard knew the shit was about to hit the fan. No one talked to you like that unless they wanted something. He could feel the other tunnel rats squirming beside and around him. Heads turned slightly, making peripheral eye contact. Eyes rolled. Sighs were swallowed. A whispered "Fuck" slipped out and was absorbed by the droning voice of the briefer. "The bastards are everywhere. We can't see them, can't pin them down because they are underground. We think, and I say, we think, we've located a Military Regional Headquarters. Why not blast them out? First, they're almost under us. Second, even if we had the opportunity, the artillery and the air strikes don't do any more than dent the ground. So here's what we intend to do ...."

The grunts, in the unit they placed him with, looked like the guys in his own unit, showing the same detachment towards him as they would to anyone who hadn't cracked the code of their shared experience, or been accepted into their sodality. They hadn't assessed his ability, hadn't determined what he had brought to their unit. They knew he wasn't a cherry. He was too sparing in his movements—not wasteful, but measured, ordered, expending only enough energy for what had to be done—indifferent to them, rejecting their indifference with his 'don't give a shit' attitude. But they gave him his space because he was a tunnel rat.

The next morning, Leonard was at the hole. He went through the steps he always took in his preparations. Now instead of a .45 he carried a lighter, snub-nosed .38 in a shoulder holster. His

Randall knife nestled in a sheath strapped to his arm. He carried extra bulbs for his flashlight, which he looped to his wrist and held with his hand. A concussion grenade bulged snugly in his pocket. Leonard patted his back pocket, his dog tags, taped, and the picture of the smiling Vietnamese woman now preserved in plastic. Both for luck. After securing his pantlegs and the bandana around his head, he gave a thumbs up and with the rope around his waist they lowered him down into the guts of the tunnel. He heard someone say "… luck."

The light didn't follow him. Like a knife had sliced it off. He could almost stand in the passageway which might have encouraged him to move faster. But he didn't. Patience was both a weapon and a life saver. The tunnel bent away, took a sharp turn. He stopped, his breathing slowed. Soundless. The stench not overpowering. He waited, ears straining. He put his ear at the bend, where the dirt wall fell away; where it disappeared around the corner. He touched the wall, scanning the corner with his fingers from the rough floor to the rounded ceiling, searching for any protruding wires. He crouched to a crawling position and inched his way around the bend still scanning the ground with his fingers, the black space before him. He hadn't felt the slope in the surface. The ground was damp. He spread his body, reaching forward. His hand was in water. Stop? Go back?

Leonard lowered himself into the water, feeling for the bottom. He went under and lost his footing and his sense of direction. He touched the trailing rope and swam forward, as water filled his boots, and his pants ballooned out with the air trapped in them, pulling his legs up behind him. His lungs began to burst as he reached out, desperate to find open space above him. He burst through the water, through the layer of scum that lay like rotted skin on the surface; his head scraped the roof of the tunnel. Leonard sucked in the fetor of rot in which he emerged. He crawled up the sloped passageway, his clothes and body crushed under the putrid heaviness of the smell around him. He gagged. Swallowed. Gagged again. All thought of security left him until he heard the scurrying, scuttering, scratching movement ahead of him and the shrill, staccato squeaks of animals. A forest of sound. He flattened himself against the earth, drew his weapon. The beam of his flashlight caught the mound of bodies that moved as if trying to come untangled from the pile upon which they'd been thrown, their faces and body parts eaten away, greedily consumed by hundreds of rats that brazenly turned their red-rimmed, glaring eyes upon him; chewing momentarily stopped as did the undercurrent of sound. Rats peered out from inside body cavities, from between legs and arms and bodies; hands stripped of flesh, bone-white, pointed at him from all angles in the pile. A way station after death! A graveyard for the VC until they could be sorted out and buried properly, if ever. Not left to be part of the statistics of the enemy body count nor to become a fragment of intelligence.

Leonard slid back into the water following the rope that had sunk below him. He emerged from the water trap clutched by the stink of his trip. They waited for him at the entrance to the tunnel. And pulled him up. They backed off. Later, still carrying the putrid smell of decomposing flesh and rot in his nostrils and in his mouth and on his not yet dry fatigues he reported what he had found. Leonard thought about the three he'd left behind in the tunnel weeks before. That night when he was alone, on watch, on the perimeter he dug a small hole with his Randall knife and buried the picture of the Vietnamese woman.

VII

Leonard left Mickey sleeping on the cot. He had cleaned it up as best he could, gently lifting her slight body as he pulled the sheet from under her. He tore off a clean corner and made a pad and put it against her cheek. She moaned as he touched her face. He covered her with the top sheet. He rolled the bottom sheet in a ball with her torn clothes and threw them in a corner. The street sounds, muted to his ears, carried into the room. No one looked in on them. She was quiet. Leonard exchanged his shirt for his fatigue jacket, put on his boonie cap and returned to the club.

Sarge was sitting at a table, a cigarette dangling from his mouth, his head cocked to avoid the ribbon of smoke that drifted up to his eyes. The fan still struggled in its circular path against the heavy air. He had one hand wrapped around a glass of tonic water, a piece of lime like a bit of flotsam tossed up on the edge of his glass. Leonard went directly to his table, past two GIs sitting with the bar girls; he pulled out a chair and sat down. Sarge held up his hand before Leonard could say anything.

"How's she doin'?"

"Sleepin.' She's hurt bad, ain't she?"

"She's alive. It could have been worse. These girls get used to it."

"She ain't like the others."

"Kid, they're all alike. They end up here thinkin' it's a way out. Thinkin' some dumb GI is gonna take 'em away from all this. It ain't gonna happen."

"She's not.... What happens to her now?"

"I don't know, kid."

"She ain't got nobody to take care of her, has she?" Leonard leaned forward on the table his large hands folded, his eyes wandering across the NCO's face trying to read his expression.

"Oh, she'll make out okay. They find a way." The NCO shrugged.

"You ain't gonna help her?" Leonard leaned forward, cracking his knuckles.

"I already did all I could, kid," Sarge said, his voice indicating that the episode was closed. He started to push his chair back.

"You find out anythin'?" Leonard's voice didn't betray the turmoil inside him. But his voice had an edge to it that got Sarge's attention. Sarge sat back in his chair.

"I got a guy comin' over in a little while who might know them. Didn't take long to find this out. I already had an idea where they were from. A transportation outfit. They have big mouths. Word gets around."

Leonard sneered, sitting back in his chair, and watched the two GIs. They looked like they were negotiating a price. One of them looked over his shoulder at Leonard but quickly turned away. He faced Sarge. A feeling of calm settled on him. He knew what he had to do.

"Listen up, kid. This guy says he'll show you where they hang out. He owes me a few favors from way back. What's the point?"

"They shouldn't uv done that to Mickey."

"Hey, kid, she's just a ...." He stopped. Leonard's face tightened up, the skin stretched out over his cheekbones, a bleak stare fastened on Sarge. He reached across the table and took his wrist. He released his wrist when Sarge winced. "What I was going to say was, she's one of the girls. It's expected. Things like this happen in this business."

"They shouldn't uv done it is all I'm sayin'. I need a piece," Leonard said, as if he was ordering a Coke from the bar. Matter of fact. Sarge's eyebrows jumped up.

"You're kiddin'."

"I ain't kiddin'. I got me some business to settle. Like maybe if

I keep sittin' here shootin' the shit, I ain't gonna be able to settle it today."

"Kid, I can't give you no weapon. I give you a weapon an' you go outta here an' waste a bunch a people an' get caught, ya know what's gonna happen?" Leonard didn't respond but the expression on his face looked like it had been packed in dry ice. "They're gonna come knockin' on my door. Ya understan'? What the hell ya gonna do with it, even if I could get it for you?"

"Like I said, those guys had no call to do what they did to Mickey."

"I'll tell you what, I'll loan ya my blade for your own protection," he said as if he was trying to humor Leonard. "Ya might need it if those guys are where I think they are." He took a switchblade from his back pocket and palmed it to Leonard. "I ain't takin' any responsibility once ya leave here. Ya understan'?"

Leonard nodded that he understood. He hefted the knife and shielding it with his large hands, flicked the blade open. He ran his finger along the edge; held it under the table and stropped it on his palm. It wasn't as good as his Randall, but it would do. He relaxed, glad for this extension of himself. He couldn't explain it. He folded the blade back into the handle and put it in his pocket.

"What're you gonna do, Leonard?" Before he could answer, the NCO shifted his gaze past him and waved. Leonard turned in his seat and looked up at one of the biggest black men he'd ever seen. Up close. With one of the meanest and ugliest faces.

"Leonard, this is Staff Sergeant Richard Sanders. Call him Chief. He's part Cherokee."

The only Indians Leonard had ever seen were in pictures; they didn't look like Chief, but he wasn't about to dispute the claim. He nodded to Chief and hoped his doubt didn't show. Two large dark eyes peered at him. The whites were the color of old ivory, like they'd been cured in a smokehouse. The Chief nodded and dismissed him as he pulled up a chair.

"What's up Sal?" the Chief asked, his voice a gravelly rumble, ignoring Leonard as if he expected him to disappear.

"I need a favor. A big one, Richard."

"I figured that. You don't call me Richard 'less it's somethin' I could get my ass burned with. Like...." He looked at Leonard sitting there watching him. He stopped what he was about to say.

Sarge made a circling motion with his hand to the bartender. He waited while the drinks were put on the table, a tonic water for himself, a Coke for Leonard and what Leonard found out later was a vodka on the rocks for Chief. Chief drained his glass and began chewing the ice cubes, the sound crackling across the table. Leonard took a mouthful of soda, feeling the carbonation play in his mouth, swallowed it and pushed the can aside. He wanted to be on his way.

"I want you to take the kid to where the bloods hang out. The ones I told you about."

"What?"

"A favor, Richard. That's all I'm askin', a small favor. You know these guys so there won't be a mistake."

"You want me to be a fuckin' babysitter for this kid?"

"I'll wipe the slate clean, my man."

"Ah, shee-it, Sal. Ya know they don't let no peckerwoods on their turf." Richard tipped up his glass and crunched another ice cube between his teeth.

"They do if they're with a brother."

"The fuckin' bros gonna think I'm tired of all this slope pussy. Man, this gonna ruin my reputation. Ya hear what I'm sayin'?" He paused to let it sink in, shrugged and said, "Ah, shit, okay. But I gotta have somethin' to eat before I go out bar hoppin'."

Leonard watched while Sarge and the Chief ate. Leonard wasn't hungry although Sarge said the meal was on him. He thought of Mickey alone in her room. Sarge must have read his mind because he said he'd send somebody over to take a look at her before the place got busy.

They found the two GIs in the third bar they'd checked out. Leonard didn't ask how the Chief knew which ones they were.

Richard had taken some jibes from the brothers lounging at the entrance of each place.

Little Harlem was no different.

"Hey, brother, the slope snatch too much for ya?"

"Whassa matter, bro, ya don' like lookin' at their faces?"

Chief paused for a stare-down and shouldered his way past them. Once inside the door he scoped out the place and moved to a table at the back of the room with Leonard in tow, hat pulled low over his eyes. The bar was crowded, noisy, dark; arms and bodies jerking to the beat of the wild music, as if infected by the sound. The overhead fans barely stirred the layers of blue smoke that hovered above the heads of the black GIs and glossy Vietnamese women.

Leonard knew the Chief was fuming. He distanced himself as best he could from Leonard as they pushed their way through the crowd. He told Leonard to sit while he got their drinks from the bar. With his hat pulled low over his face and slouched in his seat Leonard didn't attract any attention. He felt the glances pass over him as they took in his whiteness but didn't stop. They'd also seen Chief.

"They're at this end of the bar. The two jivin' with the bar girl," Chief said after putting the drinks down on the table and settling himself in his seat.

Leonard didn't acknowledge that he'd heard; when Chief repeated himself, he nodded but didn't take his eyes off the two black GIs. He had to be sure. There could be no mistake about this. *I found 'em, Mickey—* the two who hurt you. He fingered the knife in his pocket unsure of what he was going to do. A burst of laughter came from the next table. At the bar, the two blacks were laughing, bent over, slapping their knees. He watched their bodies gyrating. One grabbed his crotch and shook it, which drew another laugh explosion. He watched them straighten up, heads bobbing, shoulders jerking, caught up in their own seismic energy, with the beat of the music; eyes rolling back, from side to side as they scanned the crowd; still talking and laughing. Hands drummed on the bar adding a vibrato thudding to the beat. One of the blacks picked up his drink and drained the glass, pushed himself away from the bar and headed to the toilet. Chief was watching the GIs and the women as Leonard slid out of his chair, passing behind Richard, and followed the GI as he sauntered through the crowd, still smiling.

The smell of lime and urine, sharp and pungent, hit him even before the GI pushed open the sagging door of the rest room. Leonard was a step behind him as he stepped in and straddled the hole in the floor, peeing a yellow stream almost before he got his fly unzipped. He threw his head back and let out a sigh of relief. He muttered something to himself as he hunched forward, tucked his hose away and started to zip up his fly. It was then he noticed Leonard behind him.

"Hey, whitey, what chu doin'? Ain' no room in here for you." He started to turn struggling with the zipper. His shirt was un-buttoned, hanging loosely around him. He was not wearing a T-shirt. He had no hair on his chest. Leonard pushed the switchblade under his sternum and twisted it up into his heart. He pulled the blade out as the GI crumpled to the floor, the look of surprise replaced by fear, but he was already dead by then. But the fear stayed on his face. With one swift stroke Leonard slashed the side of the man's face watching as the skin peeled back from his eye to his mouth. Watched as blood filled the crevice and spilled down his cheek. Leonard wiped the blade on a corner of the man's shirt. He wondered if the black recognized him, if he had any idea at all why he had been killed? He backed out of the rest room, pretend-ing to zip up his fly. He was colorless in the dim light.

Leonard melted into the crowd, moving slowly, inoffensively, blending with the motion of the crush of people and the smell of sweat, body deodorant, under the corona of blue smoke settled above the heads around him; his ears tuned to the high-pitched laughter of the other black GI, which cut through the music and the voices like an audible beacon that guided Leonard between the bodies. He glimpsed Richard keeping time with the music, his large hands drumming like paddles on the Formica surface. He moved behind the screen of his own anonymity, cloaked by his neutral persona—overlooked, ignored, non-threatening. He had been cool. Real cool. Hadn't let the rage take over, govern his actions. He chuckled to himself as he thought about the surprise that erupted on the black's face when he turned to find Leonard behind him like his shadow.

"What chu doin' here?" The GI had asked.

"What the fuck do you think I'm doin' here," Leonard should have replied, "I'm here to waste your ass, nigger."

But he'd been cool. Hadn't let his personal feelings interfere with what had to be done. Like in the tunnels.

He had almost closed against the black. Behind him. Separated by only one body. Close enough to sniff his musky sweat and his beer-laced breath with the reek of tobacco and the odor of Mary Jane. Close enough. Almost pressed against him like a lover, against the cheeks of his ass, his face near enough to smell his armpits.

"There's a dead guy in the crapper!" The shout cut through the clamor. A momentary hush fell leadenly on the noise; it was quickly replaced by a bedlam of sound: screams, shouts, against the beat of the music. Bodies surged toward the toilet and to the exit. People moving in different directions, elbows and hands pushing and shoving. A woman screamed. The black next to Leonard yelled. "That's my bro … lemme through." The wall of bodies didn't open for him. Leonard took hold of the GI's belt and used his forward momentum to pull himself alongside the black soldier. He pushed the thin blade up under his ribs and twisted the blade in. It stopped at the hilt having passed through a tangle of veins and arteries and tissue, penetrating the heart as the black GI turned.

"Wha' the fuck…." the GI said, reaching for the pain in his chest. Too late. Now dead, his body slowly sagging but supported by the press of the bodies around him. Falling in a heap as people stepped aside to avoid his weight. Leonard held his place as the

GIs surged past him. The Vietnamese woman behind the bar stared at Leonard as he stepped back from the dead soldier. She looked away. Leonard slipped into a group of people rushing to the exit. He didn't look back to see if Sergeant Richard Sanders was still at the table.

VIII

Sarge was sitting where Leonard had left him earlier. He stopped inside the entrance to catch his breath. Sarge appeared to be thinking; a cigarette dangled like an afterthought from the corner of his mouth. Tammy came out of the back room behind the bar followed by a GI. The soldier muttered something to her and left. Three soldiers walked in from the street and stalked up to the bar. Military script exchanged hands. The bartender took something from under the bar and palmed it to one of the GIs. Sarge pushed out a chair with his foot, and Leonard pulled the chair out and sat down. He removed his cap. He took the switchblade, wrapped in his handkerchief, from his pocket and slid it across the table. It disappeared under Sarge's hand and into his pocket.

"I wiped it off as best I could," Leonard said, apologetically, his breathing close to normal. He wiped the sweat from his face and slumped down in his chair. He wished he had a Coke, but wouldn't ask until he explained why the knife wasn't clean. He'd done it. Taken them out. It had been easier than in the tunnels. His heart slowed to its normal rhythm. He sat looking at his hands and then intertwining his fingers, cracked his knuckles. Sarge's eyes drilled him.

He took the cigarette from his mouth and butted it out on the floor with his foot. "What happened?"

"I couldn't get all the blood off without showin' it."

"What the hell did you do?" Sarge asked, leaning forward in his chair.

"I wasted them," Leonard said, as if he'd just put out the cat. "Can I get a Coke?" He motioned to the bartender to bring him a Coke. Sarge waved away his money. Leonard drank half the can and put it on the table, suppressing a belch. "They shouldn't uv done what they did to Mickey. I did it for her." He put the cold, sweating can against his cheek and wiped the moisture away with his hand.

"Where's the Chief?"

"Back there, I guess. I didn't wait to find out. Things was kinda stirred up when I left."

Sarge shook his head as if trying to understand what he'd just heard. He held up his glass. The bartender brought him a fresh drink. Leonard squirmed on his seat under the steady stare of the club owner.

Finally, Sarge asked, "Anyone see ya?"

"The woman behind the bar might uv. She didn't say nothin'. Those niggers was awful noisy. I got a problem though."

Sarge shifted in his chair, gulped down a mouthful of tonic water, took another cigarette from a crumpled pack on the table and lit it. He squinted at Leonard as he released a mouthful of smoke. Leonard turned his head away.

"I'm AWOL from my company. My pass was up today. My First Sergeant ain't gonna like that. My platoon sergeant ain't gonna like it either," he said, looking down at the table and the circle of moisture left by the can of Coke.

"Suppose I talk to your First?"

"Why would ya do that?" Leonard said, fastening his gaze on the NCO.

"I got my reasons. Let's leave it at that."

"Ya know my First?"

"No, but I might be able to do somethin'."

Sarge took a pad and pen from his shirt pocket. Leonard gave him his name, rank, and serial number, his unit number and unit location.

"I don't wanna go back."

"Mickey?"

"She ain't got nobody to look after her. I ain't never knowed anybody like her, ya know? I don't wanna leave her." Leonard couldn't meet Sarge's eyes, uncertain, as he tried to sort out his feelings. He couldn't explain how he felt about Mickey. It wasn't just because she was the first woman he'd spent a night with, or shared a couple of days with, or heard her voice before he went to sleep, touched her when he woke up in the night, heard her voice again in the morning. It was more than that.

Sarge shifted his eyes from Leonard's, and Leonard turned to see what he was looking at just as the Chief reached their table. He noisily pulled out a chair and sat down. He was breathing hard, and he was angry. Leaning across the table he said to Sarge in a loud whisper, "You din't tell me he was going to waste those two brothers."

"I didn't know it either, Richard, until he got back. He just told me." He motioned for the bartender to bring Richard a drink. Richard drained his glass and held it up for another and settled back in his chair.

"It was his decision. The two of them beat up his girl. Did a number on her. It wasn't pretty. Cut her."

"Yeah, but man, she jus' a gook. A fuckin' slope. You know, a fuckin' ho. No offense meant," Richard said. It was no secret about Ginger, Sal's Vietnamese 'wife'. He didn't look at Leonard.

"None taken," Sarge said.

Leonard's face grew hot. He fastened his eyes on Richard. He had no right to talk about Mickey like he was. He hadn't seen what they'd done to her. He wanted to ask Sarge for his switchblade. Sarge must have been watching Leonard while Richard was talking.

"He's in love, Richard. Shit, you probably can't even remember the first snatch you slept with." Sarge said in a mollifying tone.

"Tha's a fact, but he took out two bros, Sal. These are our own folks, ya know."

"How'd ya like those brothers to do the same thing to your sister or cousin? Forget them, Richard. They were bad. They thought they were bad, only this little fucker was badder. Two less for the penal system back in the World. Ya understand what I'm sayin'?"

Richard turned to Leonard. He nodded. "Sal, I ain't never seen nothin' like this. Like I never seen nothin' til it was over and people are hollerin' an' this fucker ain't nowheres to be found. I din't see 'im leave. I got outta there before the MPs come."

"Think anyone can tie 'im to it?"

"Shee-it, they was either too drunk or stoned to know what the fuck was happenin', like he was never there."

"I don't think we oughta talk about this. Let it rest."

"I done talkin' about it," Richard said. "But keep this fucker away from me."

Sarge waved Tammy over, pointing to Richard. She smiled and took Richard's hand, and they left together.

"It wasn't right for the Chief to talk like that about Mickey, to call her a …. Like she wasn't a person."

"He was uptight about your killin' the bloods. I think you shook him up."

"Uhh … I cut the one brother like they done Mickey. I figured anyone that saw that would know what happens when they hurt women."

"Very creative, Leonard. You sent a message for me without realizing it. Tell you what. You go back to Mickey tonight. We gotta get you back to your company. We'll work something out. I need you Leonard, but you're no good to me unless you're clean. Deserters eventually get caught here in Saigon, or killed if they aren't picked up by the MPs or the white mice first. Oh, one a the mama-sans took some food to Mickey and fed her. Gave her something to help her sleep."

Leonard thanked him and left. He wasn't sure what Sarge meant when he said he needed him, but he'd wait and see. He had to get back to Mickey. Make sure she was okay.

She was curled up on the cot in the fetal position. Someone had tied her hair back. The room was stifling. The single light bulb added its heat to the room. Leonard left the door open, but the air in the room barely stirred. He took off his fatigue jacket, damp with sweat and hung it on the back of the chair. He stood outside the door while he rinsed himself with the water left in the bucket. He scraped the water off with his hands. He found a towel and wet it and wiped Mickey's face. She whimpered, but didn't waken.

Leonard sat on the floor next to her bed and pulled off his boots. He leaned on the cot, his face inches from hers. Someone had put a towel under her head. He stroked the long strands of silky hair gathered in a ponytail. The sweat ran down his back. He wiped it from his eyes. She cried out several times and groaned when she rolled over onto her side and lay on her bandaged cheek.

"Chief had no right to talk about you like he did, Mickey," Leonard said to the sleeping girl. "I took care of 'em, the two of 'em. They ain't gonna hurt anyone again. Just get better."

He leaned over and kissed her shoulder. She stirred, awoke and rolled onto her back, placing her hands over her face. Leonard kissed the backs of her hands but didn't try to pull them away. She reached up and put one hand on his neck and drew his head down to her breast. He fell asleep sitting beside her bed, his head on her breast, her hand stroking his head as if he was the one in need of comforting.

Leonard awoke the next morning, stretched out on the floor beside the cot. Mickey somehow had climbed over him and had returned from having washed herself. She had carried a bucket half-filled with water for him to wash and shave with. She sat on the edge of the bed and watched him. He used seltzer water to brush his teeth. Mickey had combed her dark hair around her face. It partially hid the bandage. She had not taken off the bracelet he'd put on her arm and held it up for him to see. He watched her touch it and circle it around her thin arm and meet his eyes in the mirror.

They walked to the club to meet Sarge. Mickey wore a conical straw hat pulled low over her face and dark glasses to conceal her swollen eyes. Leonard watched her out of the corner of his eye as they walked, his hand tightly holding hers. He took short steps as Mickey duck-walked along, hampered by the cut and stitches between her legs. She stared impassively at the ground, not looking at the vendors' stalls selling rice and noodles, utensils, fresh slain animals, marble-eyed fish, fruit, vegetables, cigarettes and new and hand-crafted articles: watches, radios, items pounded out from shell casings—ashtrays, bowls, and vases. The smell of cooking, the smoke from burning charcoal permeated the air; and men and women squatted by the food stalls, spooning up their food, waving away the flies that settled on their bowls. The heavy exhaust fumes of motorscooters and minibusses weaving down the narrow streets and alleys cut through the food smells and the stench of the gutters that ran along the sides of the streets. No one showed any curiosity as the two young people slowly walked along the crowded way.

Sarge was waiting at the club when they arrived. He offered them tea and rice cakes spread out on a table. Mickey sat, head bowed, clasping her hands in her lap, a thumb touching the thin band of gold around her wrist, her eyes averted. Sarge introduced the woman sitting next to him as Ginger. Like Mickey, she was Eurasian. She wore a pale blue *ao dai* and her hair was cut short in the western style and golden hoops hung from her ears. She laid a hand on Mickey's arm and spoke to her in a soft, quiet voice. Mickey shook her head but said nothing.

"She is in no pain," Ginger said, in accentless English, turning to Leonard. She had hazel eyes that changed shades in the light, reflecting the background. Her white smile between perfectly formed lips was gentle. Ginger poured the tea. Leonard put several rice cakes on his saucer. The tea was very hot. Leonard greedily ate the rice cakes and wished he had some ham and eggs. Mickey sipped her tea but didn't eat.

When they finished their tea, Sarge began talking. Ginger moved her chair close to Mickey, covering her hand with a hand as finely boned and graceful as the young girl's.

"Ya got a problem, Leonard. No question. But not one that

can't be solved. I called your company and talked to your First
Sergeant. Seems we know a few of the same people which made it
easier to talk to him. He said if you hadn't shaped up so well and
they weren't on stand-down, he would have told you to fuck off."

Ginger translated for Mickey.

"He says you're the only one who'll work the tunnels. Says you
got a real talent. And these are his words, 'Nothing scares that
little shit. He's a fuckin' terrier down there.'"

Sarge spoke slowly for the benefit of Ginger who turned his
words to Vietnamese so that Mickey understood. To Leonard, they
seemed to speak simultaneously, without pause. Mickey nodded
her head when Sal told her what Leonard had done the night
before to the GIs who had molested her. A hint of a smile, as brief
as a passing thought, appeared and fled from the corners of her
mouth. She reached out and put her small hand with the long
painted nails over his, but she didn't look up. He put his hand
over hers. He wanted to tell her that he was sorry for what happened to her, that she had to suffer. He wanted Ginger to explain
to Mickey how he felt about her, but he couldn't get his thoughts
in order, and he hoped that his actions the night before explained
it for him. That he would do anything for her.

Sarge then began to talk about what Leonard did in the Army
and how fearless he was. Leonard wanted to walk out of the room.
He knew his face was flushed, and there wasn't anything he could
do about it. Mickey lifted her head; he could feel her eyes burning
through the dark glasses. What did she see?

Sarge explained that if Leonard didn't return to his unit, he
would be hunted down as a deserter or betrayed and possibly killed.
Then he brutally told Mickey that with her face cut up she had
lost her value to him. She would have to go out on the streets on
her own because that was all she could do. She had no education.
No skills. She couldn't go home to her village. Who would have
her? Mickey withdrew her hand from Leonard's and slumped further toward the table wringing her hands. He said he was going to
try and work out something for both her and Leonard. He then

dismissed the two women. Ginger walked out with her arm around Mickey. Leonard didn't know if she was crying.

"Kid, I think we should talk about your future and Mickey's future." He let Leonard mull that over a bit. He gave Sarge his full attention. "I have a need for what I think are your special talents. I owe you for what you done last night … uhh … taking out the bloods like you did. Ya sent a message for me, like I told you, ya know? Word gets around. Sending that message right in the middle of their turf was … uhh … an act of genius." He squeezed Leonard's shoulder. "You may not know much about this business, but survival depends on how well I can protect what I got. In other words, I've got to maintain my credibility. Ya understand what I'm sayin'?"

Leonard nodded that he understood, but he didn't see what that had to do with returning to his company or leaving Mickey or what would to happen to her. He didn't give a shit about Sarge's credibility, whatever that was. Where had she gone?

"Lemme explain," Sarge said. "If the bloods get away with cutting up one a my girls, I'd have some real problems. Like Big Time! Our competitors would say that Sarge an' his partner can't take care of their own. You marking that GI like you did was real smart. That slope who saw you probably already knew what had happened here, prob'ly heard them bragging on it as well. Word'll get around. I'd have never thought of marking the spade like you did."

Leonard took a sip of the tea. It was cooler.

"My partner and I aren't big when you compare us with some of the fatcats milking the GIs and our Uncle Sammy … uhh … but we got a niche. Ya understand? But it ain't gonna last. Guys like me an' Dao are tryin' to make ours. The rest of them, Thieu, Ky … aren't listenin' to what's happenin' in the states. Then again, maybe they're busy buildin' up a nest egg in Switzerland or southern France …. Uhh … this war is gonna start windin' down … an' people are gonna start scramblin' for whatever they can take outta here. Ya understand what I'm sayin'?"

"What happens to us? Me an' Mickey?"

"I'm comin' to that. What ya did was neat an' clean. No loose ends. I like that. More tea?" Sarge gestured towards the pot.

"A soda if I could."

Sal shouted for a Coke.

"That's another thing, Leonard. Ya don't drink an' you're not a dopehead. Mickey told me about that. Says ya never asked for either one. An' ya didn't need it last night either. I like that plus the fact you ain't afraid. I didn't expect that, ya know, 'bout you not havin' any fear."

"I gotta go back to my company?"

"Yeah, I'm getting to that. Humor me. Be patient. Like I said, I talked to your first soldier. Without my askin', he talks about your not havin' fear. He says in his twenty years in the Army, an' that goes back to the Chorwan Valley an' the Punch Bowl—they was in Korea—he ain't seen many without fear. He said if he's gonna cover for you, as a favor to me, we worked out a deal—you'd better *di di mau* outta here an'get your ass back to your company."

"What about Mickey? She gonna be alone? Ya said she ain't got no value to you. Ya gonna put her out on the street?" Leonard didn't wait for an answer, he was already trying to put together what he wanted to say, found himself choosing his words carefully, unsure if he was saying it right. "I ain't never had a girl … like someone close … I wanted to take care of, ya know, protect. They got what they deserved … the blacks. I'd do it again, whether it was them or whites, Sarge. I just can't go off an' not know she's gonna be taken care of."

"Here's what I got in mind. Listen up. I won't put Mickey on the streets. She can stay with Ginger. Help her keep things up. We got this big house. Used to be a French official's place. I sort of have a long-term lease on it. You ever been in one a these places?" He didn't wait for Leonard to reply. "I'll bring you out there some-time, show you around. Mickey can help Ginger. I know how you feel about slope pussy." He moved his chair closer to Leonard's and put his arm across his shoulders and kneaded his arm. "Why d'ya think I keep comin' back? Once you become their man, that's it. Ya follow me? Maybe Ginger can teach her some English, so the next time ya see her ya won't have to spend all your time fuckin' your brains out. There's more to life than pussy, Leonard."

Leonard wished Sarge wouldn't talk like that, even if that's all they did when they were together. Except for now with her injured. He couldn't get enough of her. And Mickey didn't object, had never pushed him away. Had tormented him with her body. He wondered if Sarge was testing him in some way, checking him out to see how much he could say before he lost his cool. He changed the subject.

"He gonna burn me?"

"Who?"

"The First Sergeant. Me bein' AWOL."

"You'll probably get an Article 15, is all. That's what the man said. But it all depends on getting your ass back to your unit."

"An' you'll take care of Mickey?"

"I'll get her off the streets. Like I said, she can help Ginger."

"I'll send ya any money I got each month if that'll help. Ain't gonna be much. Maybe, I can get me a promotion."

"C'mon, kid, I'm repayin' a favor ya did me. An' I'm makin' an investment in you. Ahh, in your special talents, ya understand?"

Leonard didn't understand what he meant by his special talents, but it must have had something to do with his wastin' the blacks.

"Ya got an R&R comin' up, right?"

Leonard said that he did, but he didn't know when it would be or what would happen after being AWOL. He was leaving any money he had with Mickey. He wouldn't be able to save much by the time it came to go on R&R. He tried to explain this to Sarge, but the NCO held up his hands.

"We want to get ya on R&R as soon as your time comes. My partner and I got this place near Vung Tau, right on the coast. I'll set it up for you an' Mickey. I been thinkin' about a special job I want cha to do for me."

"What happens when I get back to the States? I can't leave her behind."

"Trust me, kid. I've been here almost five years and I've made some connections, done some favors. Worked some deals. Got some favors owed me. We'll cross that bridge when we come to it. You can get in touch with me through your First. Like I said before, we worked out a deal. From now on, you're my main man. My ace in the hole. No one is to know about this. You don't come here anymore. This place is off limits to you until I say otherwise. I got a few things goin', but it all depends on no one, I mean no one, connectin' us, ya follow me?"

"The only thing I understand is that you'll take care of Mickey. I don't follow the rest of it; like, what do you want from me?"

"Trust me, kid. I seen ya got a skill an' ain't afraid to use it, an' ya can think on your feet. That's good. It's what I need. Not only here, but back in the World. I got plans for you, soldier, but from here on, ya gotta do what I say, an' what I say right now, is ya get back to your unit. So I can set things in motion. I'm puttin' you on the payroll as of yesterday. Before you finish your tour in 'Nam you'll have money in the bank in the Bronx. That's in New York City. You been to the City?"

"No, but you're going to have to explain all this to me. I still don't see how Mickey fits in all this."

"R&R, kid. When you come out of the field for Rest and Recreation, I'll explain it then. But ya gotta stay alive."

IX

Brrng, brrng, his phone. Leonard counted the rings as he hurried, key in hand, fumbling with the lock and entering his office. Five rings. He dropped his newspapers on the desk, sat down, and waited for the phone to start ringing again. He picked it up on the third ring. One word came over the phone and the line went dead. "Alpha." Leonard unlocked the desk drawer and took out an address book and checked under 'A.'

Alpha was a phone location at the Mall. He had fifteen minutes to drive there. The Mall was seven minutes away under ideal traffic conditions, but traffic being as unpredictable as it was on occasion, he factored in a buffer of several minutes. Road construction on the highway outside the Industrial Park where his office was located added two minutes to the trip. If he caught every light enroute to his destination, he allowed another two minutes. Heavy traffic at noon time, if the call came then, added four minutes. He figured thirty seconds from where he left his car in the Mall parking lot to walk to the phone. Fifteen minutes was sufficient time. If the line was busy, Sal would try the phone next to it.

He had two minutes to spare. He checked out the lot as soon as he turned into the Mall, watching for two or more people sitting in an unmarked car with nothing more apparent to do than sit and watch, a shopper standing in front of a store window surveilling the lot, the person reading the newspaper who too casually folds it and tucks it under his arms and stands there. Both he and Sal considered their communication system secure, but Leonard had doubts about Sal's end. How secure was Sal? Leonard stepped out of his car and locked the doors.

As he walked unhurriedly across the parking lot he watched

the reflection in the store window of the short, immaculately dressed man with the knife-edge crease in his gray trousers, the glasslike shine on his wing-tips, the Navy blue blazer with a hint of a hand-kerchief showing in his breast pocket and the Regimental-striped tie augmenting the light blue shirt he wore as he approached the phone booth. Leonard lost sight of his image and the lot behind him when he stepped into the phone booth. He patted down his thinning sandy hair. He faced so that he could see most of the parking lot while he flipped the pages of the phone book. The phone rang. He checked his watch. Good timing!

"How ya doing, Leonard?"

"Not bad, Sal. Market's flat right now."

"Ahh, who can figure with the actor in the White House. How's the wife? My old lady says she hasn't seen Mickey in quite a while. Oughta turn her loose to come down to the City. Catch a train down. Do lunch and some shopping and some gossiping or what-ever the hell women do when they get together. You know what I mean?"

"Yeah, Mickey would like that."

They always discussed this, but they knew it was just talk. Keeping the old ties. Sal had moved up in the family with his brother's help as his sponsor. It had taken a while to get made. Especially with a Vietnamese wife. And the Hmongs he brought with him made even his worst enemy hesitate about greasing him. They couldn't be bought. Hell, they didn't even understand En-glish. Sal always figured the fuzz maintained loose surveillance around him, tapped his phone lines and bugged his house. He and Sal hadn't met to talk face to face for years. The phone line was their umbilical cord. The tie between employer and employee.

"Sorry, such short notice, Leonard, you know how these things are sometimes." Not expecting a response. "We've got a little prob-lem in this burg in the Adirondacks. Would you believe that a fucking place no one's ever heard of could give me so fucking many problems? All of a sudden! Everything was going smooth, ya know? Nothin' happenin'. We built up a nice organization there ... My brother ... he's the one who set things up for you and Mickey. He's the one got me connected with one a the families. Like I told ya. They give him this area up in northern New York to develop. We had to muscle our way in because of a lot of local competition. Like what I did in 'Nam. He knew the organization I'd set up there after my partner ... uhh ...passed away. Aw fuck it, you don't remember about the ... reorganization ... because it was just about the time you got zapped. But I got Mickey home for ya didn't I? Just like I said."

Sal reminded him that he had brought Mickey out of Vietnam whenever he was about to whip something on him. Leonard knew it was coming and he wasn't going to like it, and Sal knew it. Leonard could never repay him for what he'd done for Mickey. Sal knew that's the way Leonard thought. He traded on that.

"I got this problem up there," Sal was saying. "I need action now."

"How soon?"

"Tonight."

"That don't give me much time."

"Yeah, I hate to ask you on such short notice."

Sal didn't give a shit about the short notice. Leonard knew that. After doing Sal's cleaning up for the past twenty years, he ought to know. Sal only apologized for his actions because he wanted him to feel good. Leonard didn't care about feeling good because both he and Sal knew it was just a line of bullshit. It was the results and the money that counted. They both knew that too.

"I like to plan these things out, Sal. See what the lay of the land is. Feel the pulse of the situation."

That was a good one, Leonard thought. Feeling the pulse of the situation. The only pulse he'd feel on something like this would be his own, racing out of control. It wasn't as easy as it used to be when everything he did was on instinct as a situation developed. He'd become more cautious as he grew older and the hits became more complicated. Probably saved his life a couple of times.

"This is a no-brainer; you won't even break a sweat."

"What do you mean not break a sweat?" Leonard was sensitive about his skills and disliked any implication that he wasn't a specialist; planning carefully, calculating the odds, making split-second decisions to complete the operation. His voice had hardened. Sal must have picked that up.

"Just a figure of speech. Nothing meant by it. Jeezuz, what're you getting so uptight about?"

"Sorry, Sal. Where do I make the hit and when?"

"Ramapo Service Area on the southern end of the Thruway, south of Poughkeepsie. He's got a good drive to get there so you'll have time to come up with some sort of a plan. The meet is at 2300 hours tonight. He drives a blue Mercedes." He gave Leonard the license plate number and described Nate Whelan. "He's a big guy. Tanned, fucker's always got a tan, must spend half his life under a sunlamp, dark hair graying at the temples, about your age. I got it all set up. He's fucked up the works up there."

"What's the name of this place?"

"Crescent Hills. It's west of Saratoga. Jeezuz, would you believe it? We bust our asses to get things going, latch on to a couple of bent politicians and lawyers and things are going smooth, ya know. For years. We own the town, the county. We got this Judge in our pocket and this guy, Sawyer, is handling things real well. Had a lock on the area. We convinced him of other opportunities. He brings in his son and this guy Nate Whelan who we, not me personally but the man, ya know what I mean, bring down to the City to learn how we do business and how we want it done up there. We set him up when we figure he's ready to take action. Finance his company, equipment, put up the cash so he can make a splash up there, tie him in with a friendly union which won't cause him no problems, a sweetheart contract, and all he has to do is get control of the real estate around there and start building houses. The area needs jobs so that makes him look good. He also gets the contract for building a new arterial connecting Crescent Hills with the Northway, I-87, as well as paving contracts for the entire county because old man Sawyer pushes the button on the town supervisors, knows who to pay off and who to put the heat on."

"I still don't see the problem." Crescent Hills! Where'd he hear that? He wanted to keep Sal talking. Leonard knew he'd put it together eventually. Tie it to something that was important from the past. Shit, what past? The only past he had was the Army and the fucking Bronx. And the hits. And Mickey.

"There wasn't any problem at first. We didn't have to send any muscle up there. Because he had his own muscle. It was the old man. Old man Sawyer. He put it together over the years. He had this guy, Schultz, and his brothers doing the heavy lifting. And they had their own muscle. A motorcycle gang. It was going smooth, like I said. We had a legitimate business up there. Whelan Development. We could push drug money through the company, clean it up, I won't go into that, but we were able to turn it around and use it. Had a regular fucking courier service running up there with bags of money which Nate pushed through."

"Laundered it." Leonard added. "So what went wrong?"

"Nate lost control. Al Schultz. He's our main distributor for the drugs. He owns a kennel. Uses it as a front. Uses the motorcycle gang as mules to keep the shit flowing. Also runs a dogfighting ring and pushes the shit through it. Only trouble is, he got the red-ass for this guy Masterson for some reason or other. I don't know the details. Some investigation Masterson and this reporter were doing. Schultz tried to waste him and fucked it up big time."

That was it! Crescent Hills and his platoon sergeant. What the hell was going on? Leonard refocused on what Sal was saying.

"... and the next thing I heard is that Masterson raided this dogfight, him and these Indians he'd gotten together—'Nam vets—and to make a long story short, took off with a quarter of a mil. It was supposed to finance the next big shipment of shit and included our cut as well. Whelan wants a loan to stay in business. I don't think he can handle it anymore. He not only didn't get the real estate from Masterson's old man, which is another story, but he let Schultz fuck up the works. And Whelan's got a habit. He's losing a bundle at the casinos, on the ponies and anything else he can place a bet on. I think he's skimming. The money ending up in the Cayman Islands is light. He has to go."

"It's got to be done tonight?"

"He's expecting a courier tonight with $250,000. I said I would give him a loan, this one time only."

"Why not just transfer the money to the supplier in the City. Wouldn't he wonder about that?"

"We don't want any connections being made about the lateral transfer of money from us to the Columbians. Besides, there isn't going to be any money."

"So the money is just a set-up?"

"Yeah. Right."

"Who's running the show after I take him out?"

"George Sawyer, the lawyer, the son. Junior. The old man died a couple a years ago."

"He tough enough?"

"Not like the old man. His wife is though."

"Why me?" He'd never asked that question before. He knew why he was doing it. For the same reason he always did these jobs. Sal wanted it clean. No trace. But he'd become uneasy lately, unsure if he hadn't outlived his usefulness to Sal. Wasn't sure if he wasn't going to be the one wasted. Who would be the shooter? If one of Sal's Hmongs showed up then he'd know. For sure.

"You're the best at this sort of thing, Leonard. If I send two locals up there, he's gonna get suspicious, know what I mean? Besides I can`t remember who Whelan knows and doesn't know from when he was down here. He was down here in the City for a few years. What would you do, ya see two hulks walking towards ya? You'd haul ass outta there, right? He's gonna be carrying so watch yourself, Leonard."

"Any special way you want me to handle it?" He relaxed when Sal mentioned that the mark would be carrying. He didn't have to mention that.

"No mess. The press is gonna call it a mob hit, no matter what. Just get the job done."

"Price?"

"This is my hit, ya know. Top dollar plus a bonus for it being such short notice. I may have something coming up right after this so stay in touch. Just a question of how soon. Capish?"

"Yeah, got it."

"I know it's short notice."

"It's bad though, eh?"

"They let things get out of hand. Too many people were making their own decisions. Not like the Army. Didn't follow the chain of command, understand what I'm saying? Schultz is acting on his own. Nate's letting him, and George is sitting around with his thumb up his ass. No one's in command. Not like when old man Sawyer was around."

"Yeah, Sal, I understand."

"It's not like the three of them weren't making big bucks. They only had their own expenses and the percentage they sent to us. Whelan even kept a piece of the money he cleaned for us. We fucking paid Sawyer a retainer, as well, to handle our legal problems up there. They had no complaints. Not like when we first started."

This wasn't like Sal to go on and on. Crescent Hills must have him wired. Crescent Hills. Leonard wanted to laugh. If anyone had avoided the chain of command when he could, it was Sal. He knew how to work all the angles, him and the other NCOs, the lifers, the ones in Personnel, Finance, Quartermaster; even in Graves Registration. They had their own network. Informal but tight, held in line by their own code. All of them, two and three tours because 'Nam was where the gravy train was located, making the connections when they were young NCOs in 'Nam; gaining rank because they were the survivors and moving farther and farther back from the action on subsequent tours and taking perverted pride in being called a REMF, Rear Echelon Mother Fucker, ignoring the behind-the-back comments because they wore the black

CIB, Combat Infantry Badge, sewn to their combat fatigues testifying that they'd been there and done that at some point in their careers, gotten their boots in the shit and their asses ripped while a lot of their own numbers hadn't. They developed their network during Stateside tours of duty, keeping account of favors asked and favors given, maintaining a bean counter's attention to the accounts payable and receivable and the bottom line.

Sal never followed the chain of command, not when he could get things done through the network. Someone who knew someone. Every favor asked for, gauged and calculated, based on the asker's ability to provide a favor of a higher value at a future date, if necessary. Every favor recorded and called in at a later date. Leonard should know because that's how Sal got Ginger and Mickey out of 'Nam. But they were all cutting deals by then. Phasing out their own personal retirement plans. It had cost Sal a bundle, but he had stuck by his word. A deal was a deal.

Sal must be feeling the heat, but he must have shaken his tails. He wouldn't have called if he was being followed. He didn't ordinarily talk this long. Sal must have taken some satisfaction in knowing that Leonard could be called up and would do whatever had to be done. Would obey his instructions. No matter how much flak was coming in.

"Sal, I'd better get started."

"Yeah. Love to Mickey."

Leonard replaced the phone and put his handkerchief away. Removed the black wire from the phone and put it in his pocket with the tape recorder. He drove carefully back to his office and called Mickey.

"I'll be home early. Around noon."

"Want lunch ready?"

"No, let's eat out. Combine lunch and dinner."

They had developed their own verbal shorthand.

"Had a call from our friends. They send their love."

Mickey knew that it was a business trip.

Leonard sat back in his chair. His office was small. A neutral shade of industrial carpeting on the floor. His furniture out of a business equipment catalogue—desk, chair and credenza matching in a walnut veneer. Pressed wood. Shit wood. Fake wood. But it served his purpose and was cheap. A beige four-drawer metal filing cabinet stood in one corner with two of the four drawers empty and only a handful of manila folders, carefully labeled in the other two drawers. His desk was clear, a page with the current month from the calendar under a sheet of plate glass covering the surface. He kept his pencils and pens, stapler, paper clips, rubber bands, a three hole punch, a package of tissue, a roll of stamps, a cloth to wipe his desk, in the top right hand drawer and his lunch when he brought one, in the bottom right hand drawer. The drawers on the left hand side were empty except for a telephone book and a packet of maps. The waste basket lay under his desk, out of sight. Once a week, he carried a plastic bag of papers and periodicals down to the dumpster at the back of the building, the day before it was collected. Several plants on the window ledge, each with its own schedule for watering, added some life to the bland interior. A Sears electric typewriter and a portable radio sat on opposite ends of the credenza. There were no pictures on the wall. After two years the office, still looked as if its present occupant had just moved in. He intended to invest in a computer.

No point in starting anything. He took the tape recorder from his inside coat pocket and laid it on the desk; turned it on and listened to his and Sal's most recent conversation. Satisfied with its clarity, he rewound the tape to where it would be ready for use the next time Sal called, took it out and put the tape recorder in the drawer with the telephone book.

Things were getting rough in the City. Leonard only knew what he had read in the newspapers, but it appeared that things were happening in the Gambino family. When there was unrest in one of the families there was unrest in the others. There was talk that one segment of one family had gone to the mat. Everyone was pulling in tight. The weak ones got cut away. Sal had become a captain in a smaller family, had been made because his brother

was his sponsor, but he wasn't that tight in the organization and
had to protect himself. Besides that, the FBI seemed to be everywhere. Everyone was trying to protect his own butt. Trying to
work a deal with the Feds before they got waxed. It only took a
hint of betrayal and the guy was history. Sal wouldn't pull Leonard
into the mess down there. Sal understood how to best use Leonard's
capabilities. Like tonight. The Ramapo hit. Not this gang bang
shit.

Just before noon, Leonard locked the door of his office and
went into the bathroom. The bathroom was almost as large as his
office with a commode, shower, and a wide counter that held the
sink, a soap dish, and a cabinet below the wash basin containing a
waste basket, a can of Comet and several drawers that held an
electric shaver, a toothbrush and tooth paste, deodorant, after-
shave, clean towels, and several sets of underwear and two shirts
wrapped in plastic. A small refrigerator had been built in beside
the row of drawers. A coffee pot and two cups and saucers, one of
which was rarely used, were placed on a clean towel on top of the
counter. A roll of paper towels was located to the side of the sink.
A blazer and spare trousers hung in a narrow closet. Two ties hung
on a tie rack.

Leonard spread a newspaper in front of the open doors of the
cabinet under the sink to protect his trousers, knelt down, and
removed the waste basket and the can of cleanser and lifted out the
bottom. He pried open the specially fitted tiles in the floor and set
them aside. He dialed the combinatioin of the safe, feeling the
numbers click into place, and slightly opened the door of the safe
built into the floor and secured the white phosphorous grenade.
He placed the cassette with the others in the safe. He put his
license and credit cards and other identification in a packet with
the cassettes and removed one of the remaining packets. He would
be using James Mulholland's ID on this trip. James Mulholland
wore glasses on his driver's license. Leonard took out a pair of clear-
lens glasses and put them on. The license and Mulholland's credit
cards went into his wallet. He removed half a wrapper of twenties

and put them in his pocket and recorded the amount in a small ledger under the name of J. Mulholland. He unwrapped a .22 calibre pistol that lay in the bottom of the safe, checked the safety, the hollow point rounds in the cylinder, and attached a silencer to the barrel. He rolled up his sleeve and attached the spring-loaded Randall to his forearm, comforted by the feel of the weapon. Satisfied that he had everything he needed, Leonard rearmed the grenade just before lowering the door, spun the cylinders, and replaced the floor tiles and the bottom of the cabinet with the cleanser and basket, stood and brushed off his trouser legs. He carried the newspaper back to his desk.

Leonard spread the newspaper out and placed the weapon on it. He wiped off the light coating of oil from the .22 with paper towel, dragged out a briefcase from under the credenza, and secured the weapon in clips along the inside of it. He returned to the bathroom and brought back a set of skivvies, a pair of socks, and a clean shirt wrapped in a plastic bag and put them in the brief case with a shaving kit. He sat at his desk, reflecting on the conversation that he'd had with Sal. Nate Whelan would be suspicious. Would he suspect he was being set up for a hit? Would he be wondering about the meet and why it was so late? Would he have anyone with him? Sal had said he would be alone. Why Ramapo? The meet would be in a very public area, well illuminated, even if it was late at night. Whelan would more than likely park near other cars but not too close. He'd be pretty antsy. The question that wormed through his thinking and lingered ugly and crusted with mistrust—was Nate Whelan really the target? Leonard checked his watch. He'd get there an hour or so early.

Mickey met him at the door and took his briefcase and laid it on the table in the hallway. He kissed her cheek.

"What about the car rental?"

"There's a Budget Rental, and Avis and Hertz just off the White Plains exit."

"Let's do Hertz this time. Give OJ the business."

"He does work so hard in that ad doesn't he?"

"Maybe he's running away from the women he beats up."

Leonard couldn't restrain his visceral hatred for men who beat up and abused women, especially big men who hid behind their star status as athletes or their positions in society which gave them entitlement in their own eyes.

Leonard hung his blazer in the closet and put his arm around Mickey and guided her into the living room. She took out her knitting from a drawer in the end table next to the sofa. Leonard turned on the TV to a cable station. The news.

"Where to this time?" she asked, making herself comfortable on the sofa. For a moment the only sound was the clicking of her knitting needles. And the news on TV.

"Ramapo. It's a service area on the west side of the Thruway. The meet's at eleven."

"Not much time."

"It's supposed to be a no-brainer." Leonard didn't mention his uneasiness about the hit.

"What do you think?"

"I think I'll get there an hour or so ahead of time just to safe-side it."

Mickey nodded and went back to her knitting. Leonard stretched out on the recliner bending his legs so that he wouldn't wrinkle his trousers. Right now, he wanted to enjoy his home for the next hour or so. He watched Mickey knitting. Time enough later to think about how he was going to consummate the deal.

They stopped at a restaurant just outside of White Plains. Mickey drove. Leonard had dropped his seat back and closed his eyes. She found a hard-rock station out of the City on the radio but tuned it low knowing that Leonard was shifting into a mental high gear about the job. He had gone over the meet several times, breaking it down into individual components. The most troubling aspect was going to be the actual confrontation. In and out of the service area did not present any significant difficulties. Getting close to the victim sometimes had to be planned very carefully; it could be arbitrary, unexpected variables might appear. In this operation he would be face to face with the victim. What if Whelan had someone with him? Would he be able to take them both out? What if a trooper showed up scanning the lot just as the hit took place? What if Whelan wanted to get out of his car to accept the briefcase? What if he didn't roll down his window? What if, what if? He was thinking too much. Putting in too many variables. But then that was why he was good at his job. And that's why he was paid so much. Because he could get the job done. He was still pissed that it had come up so suddenly.

From what he could remember, the Ramapo service area hugged the Thruway with a small parking lot. There always seemed to be eighteen-wheelers parked along the west side of the lot. It was the last service area before going into the City. Getting there early would give him a chance to scope it out, but he would have liked more time.

"Where do you want me to meet you?"

"At the office. I'll drop the car off at Hertz in Poughkeepsie." Leonard propped his seat back up and rubbed his eyes. "I'm going to get off the Thruway at Exit 14 and spend the night in Jersey. I'll have a few miles on the car before I turn it in. I'll pick up another car and park it behind the office. I'll call you along the way. Oh, Sal might have another job lined up."

"Soon?"

"From the way he talked, in a week or so, give or take a few days. Place called Crescent Hills. West of Saratoga and northwest of Albany."

In the restaurant, Mickey ordered for both of them. She made sure they ate healthy food even though Leonard never put on weight. He had spent a great deal of money on Nautilus equipment and a Nordic Trac exerciser. When he was home they exercised together. Leonard might pause in his repetitions to watch Mickey doing her reps, the small taut muscles moving under the smooth skin; her sweat giving her skin a polished ivory sheen. She always wore a colorful, flowered sweatband; loose strands of hair clung to her

cheeks. The scar was barely visible. Sometimes they made love on
the mat after they finished. Finding special pleasure in wrestling
to an orgasm.

While they waited for their food, he reached across the table
and held her hand for a moment, thinking about the exercise room.
The gold bangles that she wore made a clicking sound on the table
when she moved her hand. He bought her one each time they
went on a business trip. He had duplicated several of them, but
Mickey had never said anything. When the waitress brought their
food, they ate in silence. Leonard chewed his food very
slowly¾broiled chicken breast. He wasn't very hungry and pushed
his plate aside. Mickey was used to his lapses into silence and
didn't say anything. Wouldn't say anything. It came with the job.
The job with the unforeseen—the innocent bystander who suddenly appeared, forcing him to abort the hit; the cop who left his
beat to do a personal errand causing him to reconfigure the hit;
the drunk who ran a stop sign and broadsided the vehicle in front
of him, delaying the operation. Leonard talked about this after he
had shed the tensions of the action, after he had cooled his hype
and brought the adrenergic impulses to rest, under control. After
he succumbed to Mickey's care. He could evaluate, assess, cri-
tique, mull over the manner in which the operation was conducted
and executed, search for flaws, pick at it like a scab until he was
satisfied that he hadn't missed anything. They would talk about
it. She would question him; look at the steps that he had taken,
make suggestions, which he never laughed off. She had become as
wary as he, but ultimately, Leonard had to depend on his own
instincts, his ability to plan and plan well, and to react. It was the
tunnels all over again; a dark hole mined and booby-trapped with
the unexpected.

The waitress took Leonard's plate away. Mickey finished her
food and placed her fork and knife side by side on her plate. How
long have we got Miko; how long before we hit a mine?

During the past few months, a thought, like an itch he couldn't
reach, began to prickle his thinking. He toyed with the idea that

he might have become unnecessary overhead for Sal. It was a possibility. Leonard's services came high. He knew that when Sal contracted him out for someone else, he took a bite out of the fee. Like
an agent or a manager. When Leonard was doing a hit for Sal he
tried to pay below the standard price. Haggled over it. He was
bottom-line oriented. Sal hadn't tried to bargain over this hit. Why?
With the way things were on the street today, you could put out a
contract on a guy with one of the gangs that would get a kid to
carry out the hit at cut-rate prices. Put it through enough sub-
contractors, and it never got back to the original source of the
contract. There wasn't a need for the professional anymore. Look
at the drive-by shootings. It was happening everywhere. So who
was to say that X was a target? So what if a luckless passerby bought
the farm? Tough shit! If the cops caught the perp, why would they
look further? Case closed. Leonard wasn't the only alternative that
Sal had when he put out a contract. But Sal knew that he was the
most reliable on the high profile hits, like tonight. But what if one
of these days Sal had to deliver him up? To make peace among the
different warring factions in the City or to protect himself, cut a
deal with the cops? Would he do it? In a minute!

Over the years, Leonard listened very carefully when Sal called,
taping each call so that in time he noticed a pattern to the conversation: to his opening remarks, the manner in which he presented
the contract, to his closing comments before hanging up the phone.
Later, he had gone over the tapes, when he began to feel the first
niggling anxiety, the first pecking away at his self-assurance, the
first gnawing bites out of the 'trust' they'd built up between them
over the years. He picked out key phrases or variations of these
phrases that appeared in every conversation. He logged them, paying close attention to the variations, waited for them to appear
again. He was convinced he would know when he had become a
liability to Sal, expendable. A throwaway.

At first, the tapes were for his own protection, his early warning system, but later they became his ace in the hole, a bargaining
chip. If not for himself, then for Miko. The question was, how

much time would he have? How much time to get Miko out of the line of fire? That was his vulnerability. His Achilles heel. He had to make sure she was protected. She was his main reason for living. And if it came to that, his reason for dying. He had lived his life in Vietnam. Used it up. When the mine blew, he knew he had used up all his options. Mickey became his life after that.

She was watching him, and he knew as much about her now as when she was a young girl. He still couldn't read what went on behind those blue eyes that sparkled when she was happy, that veiled over when she withdrew into herself, and shone clear and bright in the normal course of their life together. She reached across the table and placed her hand over his, her nails tapping on the watch on his wrist like birds feet on a tin roof. She knew that he was getting an erection, that he was thinking about her. She could read his face.

Leonard abruptly pulled his hand away. He was losing his concentration. Mickey ordered a cup of tea. Leonard did not drink anything with his meal. Even though the meet was several hours away, nothing must interfere with the action once they left the restaurant. Mickey knew that he hadn't rebuffed her when he pulled his hand away.

They drove in silence to the Hertz Rental Agency. She wheeled the car slowly onto the lot while Leonard selected the car he wanted to drive, a blue Buick Riviera with North Carolina plates. He took the briefcase from the trunk, leaned into the car to kiss Mickey and casually waved as he walked into the car rental agency.

X

Leonard arrived early at the Ramapo service area as he had planned. 2140 hours. He parked near the rear of the lot and adjusted his mirrors so that he had a view of any cars coming off the ramp from the Thruway. Several eighteen-wheelers were parked on the west side of the lot, engines running, parking lights glowing. A cluster of cars had parked close to the entrance of the restaurant. Leonard's attention shifted to a car in the middle of the lot, the driver apparently asleep. He had not moved since Leonard had arrived. Have to watch the man when the Mercedes arrives. He bet that Nate Whelan would get there early to check the lot himself, unsure, nervous.

The rush had started; the adrenalin kicked in. Leonard was moving to the edge now, the familiar tightening of his sphincter muscles, the quickening of his pulse. All favorable signs. Familiar. Operation-friendly. He rejected an impulse to review the actions he would take, dissect them, re-evaluate them, afraid that it would bind him to a course of action that would not allow him the flexibility to respond to the unexpected. He had to trust his experience and his judgment, his ability to cope. He checked his watch: 2215 hours. He was running along the edge now, wishing for the unexpected and the chance to test himself, his reflexes. He was back in the tunnel now, back in the total experience; doing what he was best at. He willed himself to be calm. The mines were still ahead.

There it was. He knew that it would be the Mercedes because it had slowed down as it moved onto the tarmac, as if sniffing the air, alert to danger, searching for the best defensible position, gauging what might lie ahead. The lights of the Mercedes caught his mirrors, momentarily blinding him. Leonard didn't move. The driver was suspicious, moving the car around the lot as his eyes searched the parked cars. He caught the man sleeping in his car in the full beam of his headlights. The Mercedes seemed to involuntarily move away from that car, made another swing around the lot, checking out Leonard's Buick and parked under a lot light. 2245 hours.

Sal had said that Whelan was probably carrying. Leonard expected that. Still slumped low in his seat, he opened his briefcase. He wiped the .22 with the attached silencer again. It would still leave an oily stain on his shirt. He secured it in his belt, checked to make sure that it wouldn't snag when he withdrew it. He patted his sleeve where the Randall was fastened to his right arm, spring-loaded to leap into his hand should he need it. He couldn't wear gloves. That would be a tipoff. Since the arrival of the Mercedes, Leonard had transferred Nate Whelan from the category of human being to the less personal category of a name on a contract. He watched him scan the lot; move his head from left to right; adjust his rear view mirror; twist in his seat, again searching the lot behind him. The man, sleeping, had not moved. Nate Whelan fidgeted in his seat. His head swung toward any noise or movement around him—an eighteen wheeler firing up, voices from the vicinity of the gas pumps, a burst of laughter. Countdown. From the time the Mercedes had driven onto the ramp and parked, five minutes had elapsed. Twelve to go. Leonard could feel the progress of the second hand on his watch and the minute hand lurch forward as the second hand completed its revolution. He saw Nate Whelan's life fading away, the name disappearing off the contract. 2250 hours.

A group of teenagers stumbled out of the restaurant, pushing the doors wide with a thudding sound. Whelan's head pivoted in the direction of the sound. One of the boys turned back toward the closing doors and screamed 'Fuck you!' which brought cheers and laughter from the others. Despite the autumn chill in the air, they wore T-shirts, ragged torn-at-the knees jeans and baseball caps reversed on their heads as they headed for a late model, low-slung sports car. Talking loudly and laughing. One of them picked up a soda can beside an overfilled trash barrel and pump-faking, simulated throwing a pass until another boy broke from the group and caught a perfect spiral. He beat the air with a raised fist. They all cheered. Nate Whelan watched the kids. He lit a cigarette. A loose string of smoke curled out of the crack in the window. The sleeping man woke up and stepped out of his car and stretched. Nate Whelan focused on him. Leonard focused on him also and then returned his gaze to Nate Whelan. The man walked toward the restaurant. Leonard slid out of his car, briefcase in hand, closing the door quietly behind him. He adjusted the weapon in his belt and buttoned his blazer. He casually walked toward the Mercedes. It was 2300 hours.

"Mr. Whelan?"

Whelan's head snapped around as if someone had yanked on a bit in his mouth. Startled. His face going from partially illuminated into the shadow where only his chin and his shirt front showed. He almost dropped the cigarette from his mouth. He flicked the ashes off his tie with his free hand, the cigarette drooping from his half-opened mouth. He took his right hand off the steering wheel and put it on the seat beside him, his attention on the man standing beside his car. He visibly relaxed; the tension scuttered from his face when he took in the slight, innocuous-looking man with the thinning, sandy hair and wide, horn-rimmed glasses. Confidence replaced surprise, but he remained wary. He lifted his hand from the seat, took the cigarette from his mouth and butted it out in the ashtray. Leonard stood so that he was within the thin spread of the lot light.

"Jeez, you shouldn't creep up on people like that." He shifted his weight so he could see more of Leonard; his right hand back on the seat beside him. He lifted his head to talk through the crack in the window.

He'd have trouble getting that piece in action the way he was sitting. Leonard resisted an urge to touch the butt of his weapon.

He was dead meat if Whelan lowered the window and decided to take him out right there. Had he been set up for Whelan?

"Fuckin' kids, you'd think they'd be home doing homework or something." He bent his head towards the teenagers without taking his eyes off Leonard.

Leonard exhaled not giving any sign of his relief.

The kids were screaming and laughing, playing a game of 'keep away' with a hat taken from one of the girls. Their laughter and shouts resonated in Leonard's ears. The man had stopped at the entrance of the restaurant, turned to look at the noise, shook his head and went inside.

"It does make you wonder, doesn't it? About their parents. Letting kids out at this time of night."

Leonard gave him an earful of the Masterpiece Theatre diction. The wind ruffled his hair, and he patted it down. He didn't look down at the piece of newspaper that plastered itself against his leg. He shifted his weight and felt the wind carry it skittering away. Nate Whelan withdrew his right hand from the seat and ran his hand along the side of his full head of hair. Not a hair out of place. Ahh, vanity, Leonard thought. He wanted to ask him about Masterson, about the situation in Crescent Hills and why he, Nate Whelan, had to die. But there wouldn't be time for that. Not now. He wasn't paid to talk with the victim. He didn't want to talk to the victim, didn't want the voice-sound dripping from his thoughts, like so much slime as he watched the mark die. Nothing to carry away with him.

"Mr. Whelan, I'm James Mulholland. Mr. Perrino asked me to deliver this briefcase to you. I realize it's very late, but he wasn't able to reach me until this afternoon. He said this had to be done today and for me to drop whatever I was doing and ... uhh ... excuse the expression, get my ass up here. He doesn't trust everyone to ... uhh ... do these errands." He smiled indulgently. The loyal employee. Relax, Nate, it'll all be over shortly.

"I can appreciate how Sal feels," Nate said, making certain that Leonard caught the personal relationship he had with Sal.

"My instructions, sir, are for you to verify the contents here and to give him a call when you return to Crescent Hills."

Nate smiled. "Same old Sal, follow-up. He said he learned that in the Army. I follow the same procedure in my business. Give instructions and then follow up to make sure they're carried out. Properly. Makes sense. Don't you think?"

"No question about it," Leonard replied.

"You know how much is in there?"

"No sir, I'm just the ... uhh ... delivery boy, so to speak," Leonard said deprecatingly. "Your inspection will validate the transfer and of course, your call to Sal."

The teenagers were still running around the lot, hat flying back and forth through the air. A couple left the restaurant, paused to watch the kids before getting into their car. The beam of an approaching car swept across the lot, caught all four teenagers in their glare, and turned and lighted up the side of the building, came to a halt and were extinguished. Leonard didn't take his eyes off Nate. Didn't look at his watch. The minutes were ticking away.

"Why don't you hand that briefcase up with both hands? Just keep your hands in sight, okay?" His right hand held a handgun, the hand and the gun languidly draped over the top of the steering wheel. Leonard guessed a .38 Special. Playing it safe, but casual, showing Leonard he was not a novice. Was the safety on or off?

Nate pressed a button on the door, the barrel of the gun loomed up at Leonard. The window, with a faint hum, dropped a few inches. Leonard held the briefcase up to the window. When he saw that the briefcase wouldn't fit through the narrow opening, Nate lowered it a few more inches, turning in his seat so that he could take it with both hands, the .38 now pointed at the roof of the car. Leonard balanced the briefcase on the edge of the window until both of Nate's hands were on it. Shielded, Leonard pressed his arm against the side of the briefcase, and the Randall sprang into his waiting hand. Whelan's eyes widened, rolled, as he caught the flash of metal. He tried to bring the .38 from behind the briefcase, his left hand moved to push Leonard's arm away. Too late. Leonard held the briefcase. Whelan tried to shout, a denial that his life had come to this. Fear. The razor-sharp knife leaped at his throat, cutting through the muscles of his neck, the cartoid arteries and stopped in the jugular. Leonard pulled out the blade.The hemorrhage spattered against the briefcase, the lowered window, Leonard's face and hands. Leonard suppressed a desire to run, leave the blood, the mess that used to be Nate Whelan. Had to be careful. Not touch anything. He eased the briefcase out of the window. Set it beside him. Blood spatters raced down the inside of the window. Leonard wiped his face with his handkerchief. Wiped the Randall but didn't resheath it. Working swiftly. Wasn't clean. Should have been prepared for the gun. Knew it was there. Knew Whelan had it to use. Very messy. He hadn't heard the gun fall to the car floor. The mark hadn't waited. Thought he could get the better of Leonard Grissom. Hah! He didn't look at the face, had only caught the eyeballs bulging, the mouth opened in a rictus of terror, now half closed by death. The eyeballs in the dim light already clouded over.

Leonard reached in and pulled Nate by his collar, wet with gouts of blood, back against the seat. Blood pumped out of the narrow gash, spreading down his neck. He wiped his hand on Nate's shoulder. Reached in and buzzed the window down into the door. Briefcase and weapon at his side, Leonard strolled back to his car, trailing blood spots behind him. He re-sheathed the Randall. He was careful not to get blood on the doorhandle. He lay the clean side of the briefcase on the floor. In the car he spit in his hands to remove the blood, wiped them with his pocket handkerchief and covered them with his driving gloves. He could feel the blood. Drying between the Vs of his fingers, alive in the gloves, crawling over and around his hand. Beyond the Mercedes, car doors slammed and tires bit into the pavement. No one took notice of the Buick Riviera as it left the parking lot. That night in a Holiday Inn in New Jersey, after he had stopped at a rest stop and wiped the blood off the briefcase with a handful of paper towel, rubbed away the drying blood on the sleeve of his coat, and cleaned the Randall, he stood at the sink in his room and washed his hands several times, massaging the soap between his fingers, rinsing his hands and starting over again until his hands no longer felt the blood defervescing between his fingers. He drew a hot bath. The hit had not gone well.

Leonard drove to the rental agency and exchanged the Buick Riviera for a Ford Taurus complaining that the larger car was not handling properly and since he would be needing a car for several more days he'd like to exchange his vehicle for a smaller one. He paid his bill with cash and waited while the attendant filled out another contract. He collected his receipt and drove to his office where he parked in the line of cars behind the building. He went through the back entrance and out the front where Mickey waited for him. He met no one entering or leaving the building.

He leaned across the seat and kissed her on the cheek. Once out of the parking lot he put his hand over hers.

"I'm expecting another call. Any news?" Leonard turned on the radio.

"Just that it happened. No details about the victim or what he was doing there. They said there was a gun on the floor beside him. It hadn't been fired. His throat had been cut. Were you in any danger?" She glanced at him.

"He had the gun. I don't know if he was going to use it. I don't know if it was set up that way. That he'd get the money later."

"You think Sal …?"

"I don't know. No, probably not. I don't know."

"There was a lot of blood?"

"It wasn't clean. He must have been in a world of hurt to come all that way, if that was the real reason. Well, it's behind us. Sal has more work in Crescent Hills to be done so we haven't heard the last of it. Could you go to the library and find out all you can about Crescent Hills and a murder that took place there about twenty years ago? Look for the name, Masterson. I can't remember the girl's name."

"Why this interest?" She turned and looked at him.

"I don't know," Leonard said, wondering how he could answer her question.

"Did you know someone named Masterson."

"He was the brother of the girl."

"Oh."

"The girl was raped and murdered."

"How do you know this?"

"He was my platoon sergeant in 'Nam. He told me. They never caught the killer. When I heard Crescent Hills, it triggered something. I don't know why because it happened so long ago."

"What can you do about it?"

"Nothing."

"Are you going to get involved with it?"

"Maybe. I don't know."

"Is that why you want me to research the library?"

"He's the guy giving Sal the problems in Crescent Hills."

"You think Sal wants you to ... uhh ... dispose of him?"

"I don't know. I hope not."

"How old was the girl?"

"She was young, I guess. But I don't know for sure. I can't remember."

"This doesn't have anything to do with you."

"No."

"So why this interest?"

Yeah, Leonard, why this interest? Why are you even thinking about Crescent Hills other than a place where another job has to be done? Is it because of the girl or because Masterson treated you with respect, went through the same shit you went through? Sal did too but not at the same time and Sal had kept his promise. Brought Mickey and her family out. For a price. Masterson tried to keep him alive even if it was only to be able to kill more dinks. But he was always there when the shit came in. And he didn't exact a price. He didn't require payment. Leonard had a choice. When it came to the tunnels. He could have said no at any time. He hoped that Masterson wouldn't be the name on the contract.

"Ya know, I'm wondering if we shouldn't get out of this."

"What brought that on?"

Leonard could feel her eyes shift their intensity. He'd never said it openly before. He surprised himself by mentioning it.

"I don't know. Maybe, I'm getting tired. I ought to get out of this, Go away. Retire." He couldn't tell her that he was getting bad vibes about the way the situation was going; that the hit had been a bad one; that he had to improvise; that he might have missed something. He didn't tell her he had begun looking over his shoulder. She'd never believe that Sal might think Leonard was expendable. Why should he worry about Cory Masterson?

"Can we do that? Retire?"

Was that another way of her asking, "Will they let us?" He didn't answer her.

"What would you do? Where would we go?" Mickey asked.

"I was thinking about Mexico or one of those Eastern European countries like along the Dalmatian coast in Yugoslavia. We could live comfortably. I've put away quite a bit, and except for the cars and maybe the house, we've never been extravagant, bought designer label clothes and tried to outspend our neighbors with what we own, have we?"

"Skinflint," she said jokingly. Leonard knew that she could be frugal. She'd been able to stretch a dollar when they were living in the Bronx, never touching their savings, letting it grow. She had 100 different ways of preparing rice; she could make a burlap sack look stylish.

"Would they let you go?" Back to that. The $64,000 question. That bothered her too. She'd heard enough and understood enough to know that he was serving a lifetime tenure. No time off for building a real life. Whatever that was! No retirement package to look forward to. He knew the question bothered her.

"I don't know."

She parked the car in the driveway.

Leonard followed her into the house with the briefcase. He wondered how many eyes were watching them. He placed the briefcase near the door so that he wouldn't leave without it. He'd have to clean it. She was already upstairs. She had the shower running for him. Mickey would fold down the bed while he was in the shower. He put his clothes in a trash bag. Later, he'd take them with the odor of oil and death and deposit them in the dumpster behind his office

She was lying in bed when he finished showering. Her mouth was slightly open, small, even white teeth between wet, red lips, her eyes shaded partly by her thick, lowered lashes. He was bathed in her fragile scent as he pushed between the sheets. There would be no foreplay. She was already moist, knowing his need. He entered her violently not understanding why he needed her like this but careful not to hurt her even though, animalike, he gripped her soft skin with his teeth, putting her on the cusp of pain, and she sunk her teeth into his shoulder or chest to stifle her cry. Just as quickly, the thrashing of legs and twisting of bodies was over and they lay wrapped in each other's arms. He caressed her and kissed the teethmarks he'd left on her ivory skin and buried his face in her hair. He could feel her tongue on his shoulder, and they held each other as if there would not be another time.

Leonard rolled on his back. Tension gone.

"Tell me about it. How he died," Mickey whispered in his ear. "Why you used the knife." She took his hand and put it between her legs, into the soft, fleshy wetness and he stroked her as he told her how it had been instinctive, when he could no longer use the .22 because the .38 pointed with its cavernous barrel at his head looked as if it could swallow him. It was then he used the blade, knowing as always that he could rely on it. She stiffened and relaxed, but he left his hand on the warm moist patch.

The pads on her fingers traced the scars on his stomach where the mine had caught him, leaving her at the time not knowing what had happened to him. Not touching the scars with her fingernails because she had seen them at a much earlier time when the rawness of the wounds hadn't yet faded to puce but with knobs of white stitching running along the track of the injury and later when he'd been stabbed and the knife had gone through the scars, and new stitching had to be done and she had been afraid to cause him further pain although he'd said that it only hurt when he laughed which was his way of easing her concern when he came home to the Bronx and their first home together in America. He knew this because she had told him with her tears. Her English wasn't as fluent then.

Sarge had tracked him through the military bureaucratic maze from the moment he had been wounded: to the field hospital to which he'd been evacuated after the decision was made, coerced by Sergeant Masterson who would be god-damned if he was going to let them put Leonard in a body bag while there was a faint pulse pumping away, the words thundering and subsiding—'Hang on, Leonard, you little fuck, don't you fuckin' die on me, hang on,'—even though it would have been easier to let go; and then to Japan, where Sarge had found him although it was only on paper, following his trail to the World and white sheets and American voices, and Leonard all this time uncertain, when he was lucid, whether or not he would ever see Mickey again, while Sarge not using the chain of command or standard operating procedures, but talking to people he knew or to people who knew people he knew and sometimes when the chain ran out, blustering and intimidating and swearing and calling back when someone hung up and remembering the name or getting the name of the person who denied him and tracing it back until the guy understood that he shouldn't do things like that because he'd find someone who could do him a favor and set the guy right. Leonard had never connected with Sergeant Masterson to tell him that he had survived.

"I'd better go to the office now." He found her lips and held her tightly for a moment. She wiped her lipstick from his mouth. "After I clean up." He kissed her again.

"I'll see what I can find at the library. How about lunch?"

"Club sandwiches would be fine. Ham and cheese for me. If I'm not there, I won't be gone long."

The phone rang five times and stopped ringing. It was three o'clock. A moment later it rang again. A voice said ZULU. Leonard cleared his desk, putting the pamphlets that Mickey had brought in a drawer in his desk. The location of the phone was within walking distance. Leonard picked up the phone on the first ring. He clipped the mike to the mouthpiece. Switched the tape recorder on.

"Leonard?"

"He's history, Sal."

"Think he suspected anything?"

"He wasn't taking any chances. I had to use my backup." He didn't tell Sal that he thought Whelan may have considered wasting the messenger. And he didn't mention the blood. Leonard was upset about the blood. That the killing hadn't been clean. Whelan knew enough about Sal and the mob to suspect the delivery. But he'd lost the touch, his ability to recognize a set-up and how to deal with it. He wanted the money in the briefcase. And he did have the gun. His need and his ego had short-circuited caution.

"There's more to be done."

"This one didn't go off clean, Sal."

"But you wasted the fucker. You got the job done."

"Yeah, I got the job done."

"You gotta be ready for this thing in Crescent Hills."

"You said it was a bad scene."

"One of them is ready to sing. I can't have that." Leonard could feel Sal's anger through the phone. A woman moved into the telephone shell next to his. Her voice was loud.

"Understood." Leonard shifted his body so the woman couldn't see the wire.

"This one could do a lot of damage."

"That serious, huh?"

"It'll be set up for you."

"I don't like it already."

"It's the guy's wife. She's going to set him up. It's her ass too if we don't pull this off."

We?

"My ass if it gets fucked up." Leonard kept his voice low. This wasn't playing out right.

"We're talking win-win, Leonard. The only one who loses is the snitch."

"I still don't like it. I work alone. Always have."

"I need my main man on this one. In and out. I can't use anyone from here. These fuckers would stand out like a whore in a convent. Same thing for the Hmongs."

Sal was almost pleading. He hadn't brought up past history yet, thrown that at him.. Hadn't pushed the guilt trick on him. Reminding him how he didn't make that many demands and paid him well. Hadn't started to rave and rant. Sal wouldn't let it go if he refused this one. He would remember.

"Leonard, you still there?"

"How many more after this one?"

"Maybe one more. He's in the hospital. A vegetable. For now. Not sure if he'll get his voice back."

"I don't like it. You know that." The woman had hung up, glanced at him and left. He wondered if Sally at 533-4676, written on the wall with a magic marker, really did put out? If she didn't, she must be really pissed getting calls from strangers. Whose tree did she shake to get this free advertising?

"Of course I do. How many fuckin' years we been working together?"

"I don't know anything about the town. I don't like doing small towns. Too many things can go wrong. They're not predictable, you know what I mean?" He knew he was going to do it. But he had to let it all out. How he felt about this job. This particular,

planned-ahead job. Without appearing to be whining or pushing
Sal to the point where he'd hang up. Let Sal know even if it was
going to put a strain on their relationship. He rarely voiced his
concern. Always did what was expected of him. What if I'm losing
my touch? Yesterday, he was hoping to be pushed to the edge, to
test his skills, check out his reflexes. And he had been, but it
didn't turn out well. Today was different, the job was different,
and someone else was setting it up. Maybe, already turning it
over and thinking how it could be flipped to his/her advantage
with Leonard left holding his cock in his hand. It didn't smell
right.

"I hear you, but it's got to be done," Sal said. He wasn't about
to hang up.

"You can't figure people. They aren't predictable, and even if
they are, in this scenario, I still don't know what to expect. I haven't
had a chance to study the situation. How do I know some old lady
isn't sitting in her window, peering out from behind her curtains,
day after day, isn't waiting for me to come along to make her day?
Give her something to talk about. Give her fifteen minutes of fame?"

"You're right. You know your business. I can't tell you how to
do it, but this has to look right." Sal's voice was conciliatory, unde-
manding.

"You lost me."

"Like I said, this is a set-up." He went on to explain how
George Sawyer, an attorney in Crescent Hills and a partner of Nate
Whelan, would spend the last few hours of his life and how Shelly
Sawyer, his wife, would make sure he was unconscious at his desk
with a gun registered in his name in the top desk drawer. Leonard
had to make it look like a suicide.

"An awful lot depends on the wife. Can she be trusted?"

"I've known her a long time. She's a tough babe. And it's her
ass, like I said, if this doesn't go. It's a salvage operation right now,
ya understand? I don't want to lose it all. The organization there is
falling apart. She can rebuild it. I tell you, Leonard, this is one
smart babe. But she's got to come out of this looking clean.

Can't be any doubt her husband aced himself. Business setbacks, ya know."

"So I do the job. Will she hold up after?"

"Like I say, she's tough. You won't see her; she won't see you. All she's gonna do is set it up. You waltz in; whack the snitch and you're outta there. A piece a cake."

"Shit, Sal, don't put a con on me now."

"Yeah, I know, a lot can go wrong. Now you know why I need you on this one. There's extra money."

"Okay." The extra money would be, maybe, ten percent over the going price.

"You'll be getting a FedEx envelope tomorrow at your office. Should be there by noon. I'm sending the keys to the building and Sawyer's office, and the address on a sketch map of the town and a sketch of the office."

"What about cops?"

"Town's got a Sheriff's Department which is another head-ache. He was in our pocket until he fucked up. I don't know the details. I don't know who the fuck is running the show, so you got to be careful. Stay in touch when you get back. I don't know where this is all going to end."

The next morning, in his office, Leonard searched the newspapers for anything relating to Nate Whelan's murder. Nothing. It might never have happened. Maybe for Crescent Hills it happened. He didn't know anything about Whelan. Actually, he didn't want to know anything. The name on the contract was enough. Just a name. Nate Whelan had been a job. Nate Whelan bled a lot. Nate Whelan had been someone to Sal. Why did Sal have to get rid of him right then and there? Had he been expendable? Was it more than losing control of the organization? The minutes ticked by.

Mickey hadn't picked up much information about Crescent Hills from the library. Nothing about the Masterson girl's mur-der. The town was a dot on the map. A black dot connected to other black dots by veins of black lines, not large enough to be connected by a red line to anything of significance, like it had no

life, was bloodless. It had been a mill town; its history lacked history. Except for the people who lived there and what was handed
down from generation to generation. But once there, the community would have eyes and ears, would come alive, and he would be
marked, marked by the way he walked—a little too hurried, a
little too direct—by the way he talked, his accent hanging from
his words like grief at a funeral if he forgot and spoke like he normally did; his hands too clean, his face too smooth, his hair cut
too precisely. Leonard didn't like operating in small towns. They
asked too many questions. They would hear what he said and what
he said would become the topic of other conversations. And if he
didn't say anything, they would talk about that too. One person
would notice the color of his hair, another his eyes, his nose, his
height. But Leonard realized that being small town and each person vying for attention and recognition they wouldn't agree on
anything. He counted on that also.

The FedEx came at noon. Leonard signed for it, held it as if its
weight could reveal something about its contents. He locked the
door and opened the packet at his desk. George Sawyer's and his
wife's heads were circled in the photograph. They were standing
with a group of golfers. Men and women. Nate Whelan didn't
look happy. It must have been his wife standing next to him. He
didn't look at her picture. Leonard wondered if Nate took his bad
golf game out on his wife? George looked prosperous. He was putting on weight. His pants sagged and his golf shirt bulged. He was
tanned. Shelly Sawyer was a beautiful woman. Blond and tanned
but even from the picture, the way she held her head as if calculating the next move, her smile sharklike, the toughness showed
through. Did George know how tough she was? How really tough?
Tough enough to have him murdered; tough enough to partici-
pate in the murder? Was her husband's death worth that much to
her? Leonard had never spent much time considering the value of
human life. Even his own. He'd lost that in 'Nam. Every life had
so many years. Once snuffed that was it. So it was sooner than
later. It could be a car accident or falling down the stairs. One's life

may have had a purpose. One's death may have satisfied someone else's purpose. Or gone unnoticed. Nate Whelan may as well have not existed if you lived in Newburgh, New York. If he, Leonard Grissom, was going to be the one to terminate someone's life, he wanted it to be done well and clean. He'd prefer not to be caught doing it nor injured while doing it, but those things could happen. Like getting hit by a car or falling down the stairs.

Leonard went into the bathroom and changed into work clothes he'd brought from home. He wished he'd had a few days growth of beard. He retrieved his cleaned Randall fighting knife from the safe along with his taped dogtags and strapped the knife and scabbard to his arm; felt comforted having the long thin blade with him. He put the dogtags in his back pocket where he always carried them. The ones that he'd carried in the tunnels and on every job since then. He patted the pocket. Like having a rabbit's foot. He put his blazer and shirt and trousers on a hanger in a garmentbag. Mickey would bring what other clean clothes he'd need in an overnight bag. He called her and confirmed that they would meet at the Marriott in Syracuse. He didn't meet anyone as he left the building.

XI

Leonard turned off the Thruway near Schenectady. He didn't want to arrive in Crescent Hills too early but early enough to make a quick recon of the area. It would be difficult to explain checking doors in an alleyway after dark. Leonard arrived there in late afternoon. He lagged behind a school bus, eating the clouds of dust spun up by its tires from the road under construction. The road sign said: CONSTRUCTION NEXT THREE MILES. It seemed longer, but Leonard was able to get his bearings from the sketch map.

According to the sign at the construction engineer's trailer and the lettering on the earth moving equipment the Whelan Development Company was building the arterial leading into the town although construction appeared to have been halted, giving the project an abandoned look. Who was running the company now? Why would anyone want to live in such a barren and depressing place? Leonard had Sal's sketch on the seat beside him. So far so good. A sheriff's cruiser passed him going in the opposite direction, raising a heavy churning of dust in its wake; its bar light flashing. Leonard checked his speedometer. The Taurus had a light ochre coating by the time he moved off the dirt highway into the clear air over the paved roadway. The absence of foliage along the main street and the empty storefronts that stared vacantly at him made him think of an abused woman who could no longer hide her shame. He passed the Courthouse and the offices of Sawyer and Sawyer. There were several white cruisers striped in red, with Sheriff written on them, parked in front of the courthouse. Sal hadn't said the Sheriff's Department was located almost across the street from where the hit was to take place. It wasn't on the sketch either. He wondered if anyone coming out of the building across the street would hear the gunshot?

Leonard drove past his objective and pulled into a parking space. He fished around in his pocket and pulled out some change. He fed the parking meter. The meters on each side of him had expired. No one was rushing out to feed them or move their cars. Leonard wore a black Yankees baseball cap pulled low on his forehead. His slightly wrinkled, dark blue work pants were clean, though rust and oil stained. He wore a dark windbreaker with a plumbing company from Yonkers scribed on the back in yellow letters, Ace Plumbing, Yonkers, N.Y. His Adidas shoes were scuffed and had lost their original color.

At a corner drugstore, he bought a newspaper, paid the woman who told him to have a nice day, and stood on the street outside the drugstore and held the newspaper as if reading the headlines while he scanned both sides of the street. He walked around the block, slowing as he came to the alley behind Sawyer and Sawyer. He bent down, put the newspaper on the ground and retied his shoe. He picked out the doorway he'd be entering that night. The door was recessed which would be an advantage in locating it. Several cars were parked on a narrow lot across from the doorway. He resumed walking. He fingered the notched keys in his pocket. One notch, the back door. Two notches, the office door. Leonard continued his stroll around the block and checked the alley from the other end. He nodded to several people who greeted him. Friendly town. He wondered if he would recognize Cory Masterson. Out of curiosity, he stopped in a sandwich shop that advertised sandwiches, hamburgers, hot dogs and grinders. A handwritten menu, yellowed from the sun and its corners curling, was pasted in the window. A single counterman, a toothpick stuck in the corner of his mouth, stared back at him when he looked through the clouded window. Leonard went in. Took a seat at the counter.

"What'll you have, buddy?" The counterman asked, wiping off the counter in front of Leonard and brushing away a fly.

"Coffee. Uhh ... gimme a piece a that lemon meringue pie.

They hirin' aroun' here?" Leonard asked in his blue-collar voice, neutral, unaccented.

"They was 'til the owner, a guy by the name of Whelan, got hisself killed. He was the only one doin' any hirin'. Construction." The counterman drew his coffee and placed a triangle of pie and a fork in front of him. He moved the napkin container toward him and went back to wiping the counter.

"When you figure they'll be hirin' again?"

"Beats me." The counterman, a hollow-cheeked, gray-haired old guy with rheumy eyes and a gray stubble, pushed his paper cap back on his head, shifted the toothpick from one corner of his mouth to the other with his tongue.

"How'd he get killed?"

"Well, the papers says it was a mob killin'. Happened on the Thruway, down near Poughkeepsie. He was a big wheel in the town, but it din't surprise me."

"How's that?"

"He jus' shows up in town; grew up here, was away a couple a years ... lawyer ... shows up with a bundle a cash. Sure seems funny him comin' back with all that dough and startin' up his company like that. Had to be mob money behind 'im. Where else does a guy come up with that kinda moolah?" He held up his hand rubbing his thumb and index finger together.

Leonard nodded, "Yeah it soun's funny. Say, you know a guy by the name of Masterson, used to live aroun' here."

"Yeah. There's a Cory Masterson. Now there's a guy who fell into it. His old man died jus' before he retired from the Army an' left him ownin' half the county. Ya'd never think the old man had a pot to piss in. I don't mean he looked like a bum, an' always cryin' poor mouth, but he went around alla time in work clothes. Usta work as a mechanic 'til he retired. I guess Whelan gave him some trouble about the land. Lost his daughter, ya know?"

"Whelan?"

"No old man Masterson. Made all the news aroun' here. Never did catch the guy who did it. They say that's why the kid went inna Army. I think personally he just wanted to get outta this dump. How come you know Cory?"

"Oh, we was in the Army together. 'Nam."

"Well, he got shot up bad there. Didn't see much of him 'til he came home for good."

"I ain't seen him in twenny years or so. How's he doin'?"

"Lot a rumors an' stuff 'bout him an' Josh Billings. He's a reporter, tryin' to fin' out who killed Masterson's sister. Story had pretty much died down 'til Cory came back. My kid went to school with her, ya know."

"No kiddin'."

"Yeah, but that ain't the half of it. He's got things stirred up. Rumors about … Hey John how ya doin'?" The counterman broke off the conversation and moved away. Drew a coffee and slid it along the counter. The counterman held up creamers.

"Nah. Black." John said. "Still lookin' for work. Whelan's laid off half the work force since Nate got killed. I don't know who's gonna run the business now."

"We was jus' talkin' 'bout that. This man says he was with Cory in Veetnam."

"Oh yeah?"

Leonard looked at his watch and took out a couple of singles and laid them on the counter. "I gotta be movin' on. Ain't no jobs aroun' here, I guess. Jus' passin through, saw the equipment …. Well, you know…." He left it at that. The counterman rang up the sale and Leonard left the change by his plate.

"Stop back next time you're through here. I'll tell Cory you was askin' 'bout him, Mr.…."

Leonard pretended he didn't hear him and went out the door. Maybe I oughta call the sheriff and tell him I'm here Leonard thought. What a stupid ass thing to do. Leonard, where's your head? He could feel two sets of eyes on his back as he stepped out onto the sidewalk. He wondered if they would remember him on the day George Sawyer committed suicide.

He returned to his car and drove around the side streets until he found a place where he'd be able to park that night. His Taurus wouldn't attract any attention. Leonard drove to a mall he'd passed earlier once off the Northway, and pulled into a parking stall. He dropped his seat back, pulled his cap low over his eyes and reviewed the plan. Once inside the building he'd be flying blind except for the sketch. Had he made a mistake asking about Masterson?

The lights were on in an office on the second floor in the Sawyer building. The blinds were drawn. That would be George's office. He parked his car on a side street where shadows cast by the trees shielded his rental car license plates from the street lights. They must roll up the sidewalks at night, Leonard thought as he turned unhurriedly into the alley behind his objective area. He walked close to the buildings to avoid presenting a silhouette against the streetlights at both ends of the alley and moved quickly to the rear entrance of the Sawyer building. Glancing in both directions, hands encased in surgical gloves, he inserted the key into the lock. The bolt turned noiselessly. He pressed himself against the door and opened it without making a sound. He could smell fresh oil on the hinges. Good move. He closed the door behind him just as noiselessly and turned the dead bolt to the lock position. Rear secured. He stepped beside the door and listened, familiarizing himself with his new surroundings. A faint light glowed from a door at the top of the stairs. He took a penlight from his pocket and explored his narrow confines. He picked out a door under the stairs. A janitor's closet and the door was unlocked. Another door beside it; must lead to the basement. It was locked. The light went out at the top of the stairs. Someone was still there. She should have left by now. His watch showed 10:15. He carefully moved a mop bucket aside and sat down on the floor in the closet and waited. He left a crack in the door. The wind reached under the rear entrance and pushed through the space. He couldn't hear any voices. The building settled around him, and the disparate sounds of floors and walls subsiding enveloped him. The furnace in the basement rumbled alive. A vehicle crunched down the alley, the beam of a spotlight slid under the door with the wind, but quickly disappeared. He wondered if Mrs. Sawyer's car was parked in the lot across the alley. He waited. A drawer opened and closed. From the offices on the second floor.

Someone was upstairs besides George. Did George know he was going to die? When he looked at his wife earlier this evening, did he see Death's eyes? She had to have given him something to put him under. How did Mrs. Sawyer look when she watched her husband take, probably, his last drink? Was she smiling? Did she tell him how much she loved him? No one had come down the stairs. She was still there. It was 10:50. He emerged from the closet and shined his penlight on the wooden steps. Carpeted. He hugged the wall to avoid making any sound, one hand on the banister to ease his weight on the stairs. He moved soundlessly across the landing to the door of the offices of Sawyer and Sawyer, inserted the key and slipped inside. He oriented himself from the sketch he had memorized. The beam of his penlight crept ahead of him as he moved to the front of the building.

Her perfume still hung in the air, subtly. He pictured the woman from her perfume. The figure in the photo, even mixed with her sweat, matched. He passed several doors, the carpeted floor not revealing his footsteps. He glanced at his watch. 10:55. How long had she been there? He should call it off. Return the way he had come in and call it off. This wasn't the deal. Maybe Sal had expected something like this to happen. Or maybe he had planned it this way. He wanted Leonard here. A sliver of light under the door. He turned the handle and silently followed it into the room. George was sprawled across his desk, snoring peacefully. Her perfume was more noticeable now. The bathroom door was ajar. No light. She would see him if he moved to George's desk. She didn't know he was already in the room. She was going by clock time, expecting to hear him enter the room at 11p.m. Sal might have told her how precise he was. He slid along the wall to the bathroom door. He could hear her breathing. Rapid. He could smell her perfume mixed with sweat and fear, visualize her hands, perspiring, holding the gun, waiting for him to appear. Was she holding it in two outstretched hands, the weight of the weapon pulling the barrel down or making it waver? Was she a good shot? Sal would know. But had she ever shot a man? Did Sal have to persuade her that she could do it? That she could kill him and then kill George? She was wired!

"Mrs. Sawyer," he rasped, his voice gravelly like coarse sandpaper against a rough board. Flat, emotionless, deadly. "Put the gun on the floor and slide it out with your foot. Carefully."

She gasped. She had expected to hear him arrive. Had counted on it; didn't know that he was as expert in his calling as she was in hers. Didn't understand the difference, that his life depended on his skill. The door opened and a stockinged foot pushed the gun along the floor. Leonard picked it up and wiped it clean on his jacket. She hadn't even taken the safety off.

"Put on your shoes and come out here," he commanded.

Her face was ashen, tense with apprehension. With her shoes on, she was slightly taller than him.

"You almost fucked up this whole operation, you stupid bitch." She cowered as if expecting to be struck. His voice was harsh, increasing her distress. He had to keep her afraid. "Whose fucking idea was this?" He spat the question at her. He walked over behind the desk to stand near George.

She didn't respond. Despite her fear, she hadn't lost her composure; didn't break down and cry or plead. Just showed her fear. Didn't try to wipe it off or fake not being afraid.

"Does Sal know you were going to pull this?"

She shook her head, her blond hair catching the light, falling back in place when her head stopped moving, leaving several strands on her cheek. She didn't brush them aside. Stood frozen in place.

"I have the option, Mrs. Sawyer," his voice now soft and venomous, "of killing you and your husband, making it look like a murder-suicide or fulfilling my contract. According to Sal this whole operation up here has been screwed up royally. But right now,

Mrs. Sawyer, you're the problem. You've jeopardized the contract. And you've put me at risk. What should I do?" He glanced at George to make sure he wasn't stirring. Checked again to make sure he didn't cast a shadow against the slatted blinds.

She waited, her lips a red slit in her tight face. Her anxiety didn't flaw her icy beauty.

"Is your watch engraved, Mrs. Sawyer?"

She nodded, biting her lip.

"Give it to me." She walked across the room and handed it to him. He looked at the engraving, 'To Shelly. Love Dad.' "This is my insurance in case you get your story mixed up about what happened here. Your watch puts you here with me. Sal can't trust you, lady. And I can't either. You belong to me now."

"What're you going to do? What do you want? Please give me back the watch. My daddy gave that to me." It had started out with a croak, but she swallowed, cleared her throat and seemed to gain confidence. Tried to gain control. "I'll give you anything you want." She started to unbutton her blouse.

"With your husband right here?"

"It won't matter to him, will it?"

"Mrs. Sawyer, you're not worth it. Understand what I'm saying? You're a piece of work alright. Let's see how tough you really are. Stand over there."

She moved to where he pointed, in front of the desk. Stood with her hands at her sides

"Let's see if you have a stomach for this business."

He glided to where George sat, head on the desk. He checked the drawers for another weapon. George was still unconscious, breathing heavily. A ribbon of drool puddling on the desk under his mouth. Leonard looked at Shelly. She suddenly realized he was going to make her watch what he was going to do. Her face screwed up in horror. She involuntarily clutched the sides of her face. Her hands poised as if to shut out the sound of the shot. Unable to close or cover her eyes. Her mouth opened. Quivered emitting a low, keening wail.

"Watch closely, Mrs. Sawyer. This is what you agreed to do. Last chance to call it off." Tears had spilled from her eyes, but she didn't turn away. Leonard used both hands to fit the pistol into the hollow formed by George's fingers. He cupped his hand over George's and pressed it as if to cement it to the weapon. His left hand scrambled in the thinning crop of George's hair. The skull was warm. He grasped a handful and pulled his head up from the desk The head was heavy. He tightened his grip. George's mouth dropped open. Thumbing off the safety Leonard lifted the hand holding the pistol and guided it against his victim's temple. He held the pistol there, his finger on the trigger. Some primeval instinct of danger must have flickered in George's subconscious because his eyes flashed open. Shelly's hands moved to her mouth to suppress her whimpering. As George tried to move his hand, Leonard forced the muzzle of the weapon tight against his temple, and squeezed the trigger. The report was muffled. She was not prepared for the crimson gout of blood, tissue and bone that followed the round out of the side of George's head spattering against the wall, the bullet burying itself in the plaster. He watched the woman recoil and try to block out with her hands what she'd already seen with her eyes. She sank to her knees; her body rigid, convulsive. Leonard dropped George's head onto the desk and brushed his hair back in place He laid his hand with the gun back on the desk and adjusted George's finger on the trigger.

Mrs. Sawyer started to retch. Leonard went around the desk and lifted her by the arm and led her to the bathroom. He left her with her head bent over the sink and returned to the desk where he noticed the sheet of paper in the typewriter beside George's desk. It was a suicide note, made to appear that George had finished writing it before he blew his brains out. She was running water in the bathroom; she was still bent over the sink but was washing her vomit down the drain. She looked up when he entered the bathroom. The face looking at him from the mirror was bloated. Her eyes were swollen and bloodshot; spittle clung to her chin, leaked from the corners of her mouth. Her face was mottled with the intensity of her efforts. She took paper towel and wiped her eyes and mouth.

"Clean it up." he ordered, and he inspected her handiwork after she had finished and stood like an obedient child beside him. Leonard pulled the plug out of the sink to make certain no residue had stuck in the pipe. He told her to flush the paper down the toilet. He inspected the commode and the floor around the sink for any indication of her emesis.

"You're a beast," she hissed, her face twisted with hatred, tears flooding her bloodshot eyes. "An animal."

"Aren't we all, Mrs. Sawyer," he rasped. "It's a jungle out there, and we're all trying to survive. You wouldn't have been exposed to any of this, lady, if you'd stuck to the scenario. But you thought you were smarter than all of us. You shouldn't have entered my world; you'll never make it. I suggest you walk, not run to the nearest exit. And if you have any thoughts about trying to turn this thing around, forget it. You're in over your head."

Leonard followed her out of the bathroom and gripped her arm as she started to leave.

"Make sure you're not seen leaving. Your life may depend on it. Oh, Mrs. Sawyer," he said as an afterthought when he released her arm, "don't worry, I'll lock up." He didn't hear the door closing downstairs. Leonard reread the suicide note. It was a confession. George confessed to the rape-murder of a Barbara Masterson, twenty years earlier. He implicated Nate Whelan and Al Schultz. He absolved his wife of any participation in the business run by himself, Nate and Al. She only did the legal work. Neat! Remorse for killing the girl and business setbacks were the reasons he gave for taking his own life. Leonard went back and double-checked the bathroom.

He turned up the thermostat as he left, but did not turn off any lights. George wouldn't be worrying about electric bills now. He left the building as carefully as he had entered it. The operation had run overtime.

The letdown hit him as he turned onto the New York State

Thruway going west. By the time he hit the first service area he
had relaxed. He gassed up the car and went into the rest room,
checked his jacket for blood spatters, removed his cap and scrubbed
his face and hands. He put the cap back on and ordered a bran
muffin and a large coffee-to-go at the counter. He called the Mariott
from the lobby, and the clerk connected him with Mrs. James
Mulholland. Her voice was sleep-edged when she answered the
phone.

"Hi," he said. "I'm going to take a quick nap. I should be there
in about three hours. Don't wait up."

She gave him the number of the exit off the Thruway and her
room number. Leonard could visualize her relief when she heard
his voice. She would set the alarm and sleep for a couple of hours
and be ready for him when he arrived. He replaced the phone and
carried his muffin and coffee to the car. Three hours later he knocked
on the door of their room at the Mariott.

He heard the shower running. He awoke slowly, through the
sounds of the shower, the birds singing outside, the dry growl of a
lawn mower, voices in the hall, a TV blasting in the room next
door, Mickey humming a Vietnamese children's song he'd heard
many times. She'd shut off the shower, only her humming continued from the bathroom above the sound of the hair dryer. He
stretched, his whole body reaching, his middle holding it tightly
together. He grunted loudly which brought Mickey to the bathroom door, hair dryer in one hand, her other hand controlling the
ends of her hair. She had the towel tucked around her body like a
sarong. The sarong didn't reach her knees. She finished drying her
hair and retreated back to the bathroom.

"I wonder if it was her idea?" Leonard said to the vacant doorway. He pulled her pillow over and put it on top of his and lay
back.

"Whose idea?"

"The wife. Mrs. Sawyer. She hadn't left when I got there.

She was waiting. In the bathroom with a gun. Sal said she would be gone. 'Just breeze in and out,'" he said.

"Is Mrs. Sawyer beautiful?" Mickey asked from the doorway of the bathroom. She had shed the sarong. Her hair flowed across her shoulders and over her breasts. Her one leg was bent and covered the crevice between her legs.

"Seriously?"

"Seriously."

"Well, she does have bigger boobs. On a scale of one to ten, she's probably a nine, and you're… hmm… well, let's see…." With that he ducked under the covers as she ran across the room and leaped on the bed. She burrowed under the covers and thrust herself against him reaching between his legs. Laughing, he grabbed her hands and pinned them behind her. He whispered in her ear, "There's never been anyone as beautiful as you, babe." He kissed her ear and ran his tongue up her neck. "I'll call Sal later."

They lay side by side under the sheet.

"You think the husband wrote the confession?"

"No."

"Then she must have known what he did … what they did to that little girl."

"How long did she know? That bothers me. What does that make her?"

"Your sergeant, Masterson, he'll know now what happened."

"Yes."

She turned to him and drew his hand under the sheet.

"Tell me how the man died."

On their way to the dining room, Leonard picked up the *New York Times*. They waited until the waitress had brought them coffee and ordered before opening the newspaper. Mickey had an insatiable appetite for the written word. He handed her everything but the business section and the Metro Section. Neither he nor Mickey followed the sports news although Mickey knew all the teams and for some reason known only to her, followed the scores of the Columbia University football team and the Jets, both of which often left her mumbling to herself. The Metro Section in the *Times* kept Leonard abreast of the mob situation in the City although he read the headlines of *The Daily News* every morning when he picked up his papers to see what might be happening on the street. He smiled when he glanced up to see Mickey totally engrossed in what she was reading.

Was she searching for news about the Vietnamese community? The attempt by Louis Beam, the Klan and a group of Americans to drive out the Vietnamese fishermen operating shrimp boats in Galveston Bay in Texas had infuriated her, and she had gone around muttering in Vietnamese for days until she read that the Vietnamese Fisherman's Association was fighting back through the court system. Mickey had never talked about her loneliness for her country and her people. But Leonard knew when he looked in the refrigerator after a trip and saw the foods she had bought to prepare a Vietnamese dish for herself. She had located a market run by Vietnamese immigrants and overbought the specialty foods that she couldn't find in a supermarket. He never understood her loneliness especially since her family had abandoned her when she went to Saigon. Left her with only childhood memories and a sense of worthlessness. Their own early life together had been a period of struggle and adjustment. For her, it had been much more difficult because she had been deprived of having a family of her own, had been uprooted from her crumbling country, trying to understand much later in life what the war had been all about. When she dug for clues and when she put them all together it didn't balance out to anyone being right or wrong. Just dead people. Her family never wrote to her. Never thanked her for her support. Never attempted to heal the rift.

She avoided the Vietnamese groups that clustered together for a collective voice; avoided the arguments and discussions and the politics and the finger pointing and stayed away from the social clubs formed by the younger toughs whose purpose was to terror-

ize their countrymen and occasionally make incursions into the
territory of other gangs. Leonard knew she visited a local Vietnam-
ese-owned restaurant or grocery store and immersed herself, if only
for a few minutes, in the tatters of her culture, basking in the
smells and the language. She found special joy in haggling over
prices, arguing with shopkeepers, listening to their bawdy stories
and telling some of her own after they came to know her and she
them. She was especially lighthearted after such visits, telling him
of her conquests in overcoming an obdurate shopkeeper's 'final'
price, or a joke she had heard which he never understood but
smiled because he enjoyed the way she told it. He rarely ventured
into the Vietnamese community except to go to a restaurant with
her when he felt that it was time to do that. He didn't want to
restrict her or inhibit her laughter or her conversation because he
didn't understand the language and didn't want her to have to
pause to translate so that he wouldn't feel left out, nor did he want
her to feel compelled to speak English with the Vietnamese who
in turn would feel inhibited by the strange tongue that only their
children seemed to have picked up and used freely. She never spoke
about the distance between them during those moments, the gulf
that existed between their cultures which she had managed to
close because she loved him. She concealed her feelings very well.

He left Mickey at the table drinking her coffee and reading the
newspaper. He took part of the newspaper with him. They had spoken very little during breakfast, content to enjoy the food and explore
their own thoughts. She hadn't discussed what she had planned for
the rest of the day. In the phone booth, he dug out a handful of coins
and laid them on the shelf under the phone, looked in his black book,
found his number and called Sal. Someone picked up the phone at
the other end. Leonard spoke one word and gave the person at the
other end a scrambled version of the numbers he was using. He opened
the door of the booth and sat reading his newspaper. Fifteen minutes
later, the phone rang. He closed the door and put his newspaper aside
and turned on his tape recorder.

"How'd it go."

"She almost fucked it up," Leonard said, his voice low.

"What happened?"

Leonard gave him a basic outline of what had occurred from the time he entered the building until his departure. Sal listened without interrupting.

"She wasn't supposed to be there."

"You know broads, they got a mind a their own."

"Not in my business," Leonard said. "If you told her not to be there, she shouldn't have been there. You know that. She should have gotten her ass out of there."

"I understand what you're saying."

Leonard could tell from his voice that Sal was surprised by his rush of anger.

"I should have wasted her. I would have because she wasn't supposed to be there. She was going to take me out. Wanted to. You know that? Like I said, she had the gun, the one I was going to use on the husband. Why do you think she thought that, Sal?"

"Leonard, so help me, I don't know."

"She must have thought she could do it."

"She didn't get it from me. She had her instructions. She didn't follow them. She was supposed to set up the husband and get out of there. That's what I told her."

"What I don't understand is why she thought she could get away with it."

"Trust me. The broad didn't do what she was supposed to do. It's that simple."

"Being a lawyer, I guess she thought she was dealing with some of your city gorillas. It's called *hubris*. Pride. Arrogance. She can't be trusted, Sal."

"Let me handle it, ya understand?"

"Maybe you got rid of the wrong one, Sal. Maybe she's the one who's going to hang your balls out to dry."

"I said I would handle it. I know you got the red ass for the broad. This is the first time I've seen you like this Leonard. Let me tell you an' then I wanna drop it, *capish*? She was told what to do.

You're right, she could bring us all down, but that's my problem. Not yours. You got the job done, like I knew you would. Taking her out wouldn't have solved anything. You did right not doing it."

"It's your ass."

"Understood. I hear you."

"I want no part of that woman in the future."

"Sounds to me like you're trying to tell me something, Leonard. Like what you'll do and not do. I don't like that. You know that." Sal said this quietly and then in conciliatory tone, "Now you know why I wanted you to do this job. You use your head. That's good!"

He was telling him to back off.

"Did you know George, Nate and a guy named Al offed Barbara Masterson?" There was a pause at the other end of the line. Leonard thought Sal had hung up.

"Where did you hear that?"

"In the confession. Sawyer confessed that he along with Whelan and a guy named Al…."

"Schultz."

"Yeah, Al Schultz. They did the girl. Did you know about that? "

"It's history."

"They raped her. The three of them. I knew a Masterson once. My platoon sergeant in 'Nam . Said he had a sister who was raped and murdered. Didn't know who did it. This the guy?"

"I don't know. Yeah, I do know. There's a Cory Masterson, retired from the Army. He's the problem for us, but he owns the land we want. The land Whelan was supposed to get for us before the old man died. Masterson's the guy who stirred everything up. Him and the fucking reporter … uhh… Billings. Been investigating the kid's murder. Bad scene. Schultz had a chance to take him out but screwed up. The guy's an alkie, he…"

"Who's an alkie, Schultz?"

"Nah, fuckin' Masterson. They jumped him and fed him the booze. Had it all set to dump him in forty feet a water an' the fucking truck gets hung up. Ah shit, I don't wanna talk about it. Gives me a severe case a heartburn."

"How'd you hear all this, Sal?"

"The broad. She's been keeping me posted. Right from the start. What I started to say was this Masterson guy gets a bunch a fucking Indians together an' walks into a dogfight that Schultz had set up and picks up a quarter million Schultz had collected from his distributors. Schultz tried to get it back an' now he's in the hospital. A fuckin' vegetable."

"It's the same guy. Cory Masterson. They wasted his sister, eh?"

"Yeah, I just found out about it. The broad told me."

"They shouldn't have done that to the girl. Remember what happened to Mickey?"

"They were animals."

"'Cause they were black? What were these guys? One's a lawyer.... How would you describe them?" The operator interrupted and Leonard heard more coins put in the slot.

"Leave it alone, Leonard."

"This Al's in a hospital, right?"

"He's down. Not a threat right now. He was going to be the next one."

"If he talks, he can create a lot of problems."

"Yeah, but I want to wait a bit. I don't want you getting emotional about it, overreacting."

"Did I overreact after what happened to Mickey?"

"No, you were cool."

"I told Mickey she could have the scar removed. She said no. You know why she said no? She said it reminded her of what they did to her. It reminds her of what she was. I've been trying for twenty years to make her forget all that. Twenty years! Would you believe it? No woman should have to carry that kind of a burden around with her all her life. You hear what I'm saying?"

"I understand."

"I been carrying that around with me too, you know? Like no

matter what I do or how good we got it, it's still there. In her head and mine. They did it to Masterson too, Sal. They raped and killed his sister and left him with a feeling like shit. I can understand that. Carrying that around all those years. He was a good platoon sergeant?"

"This isn't your problem. It's his problem, and now that there's the confession, he ain't got a problem anymore. Ya follow?"

"All those years they … He knew someone in Crescent Hills did it."

"Let it rest, Leonard. Drop it."

"No charge for Al Schultz."

"He's under twenty-four guard. This could be tough. Wait up 'til I give you the word."

"This might make up for a few things. Mickey might feel better about what I'm doing. Might make her forget the other. Me using the blade on the blacks. Like she wants to feel it taking them out."

"She on your case?"

"Nah. Maybe I should think about retiring, after this one."

"Whoa, you never talked like this before, Leonard."

"The woman got to me. I've never seen a woman give the nod to have her husband offed. Set it up like it was a social function. It makes you think."

"You're thinking too much, kid. Let me do the heavy thinking. I need your special skills. Give me a couple of days to see what I want done."

"I need some information about Al. Room number, visiting hours, the busiest time of the day, name tags if they wear them. The broad ought to be able to get that stuff.. I'm going to be in Syracuse for a couple of days. Send the information to my office."

"I'll take care of it. Let's get together after this and we'll talk about your future."

"Sure, we'll do that."

"That took a while," Mickey said when he returned to the

table. She had finished reading the newspapers and had them folded
on the side of the table.

"We had a lot to talk about. Ready? We'll drop off the rental
car after we check out."

Before leaving Syracuse, Leonard stopped at a uniform and medical supply store, which he found in the yellow pages. He made
several purchases. From Syracuse, they drove to Geneva, New York
in the Finger Lakes Region where she had booked them into a bed
and breakfast on Main Street overlooking Seneca Lake. It was after
3pm. Tall elms lined Main Street; their branches, bereft of leaves,
reached with skeletal arms to the sky. The brown and yellow leaves
were still on many lawns; some piled high on the curbs along the
street. They passed several fraternity houses, large stately houses
with a transient, bygone appearance, like a thoroughbred horse
now pulling a wagon. Students were strolling along the sidewalks
catching the fading warmth of the final days of Indian summer.

"You wish you'd gone to college, Leonard?"

"Not after the courses we took."

"That was different. This is different."

"Hmm." He began tapping on the steering wheel. Impatient.

"I liked going to class. I liked learning. They have a men's and
women's college here."

"You were much better at classwork than I was. I didn't fit in."

She said they were approaching their lodgings, which put an
end to the conversation of what might have been. Leonard felt ill
at ease when they walked through the front door of the bed and
breakfast. It was like intruding into someone's life. An elderly,
smiling woman greeted them and had them register and showed
them to their room—someone's once-upon-a-time guest room with
a flowered bedspread and frilled curtains at the window. Hand-
woven rugs muffled the sound of their feet on the hardwood floor.
Bright scenic prints of sailboats on the lake during a previous era
decorated the walls. A wicker chair with floral cushions placed by
the window overlooked the water. She showed them the bathroom

which was the only concession to the present day with a molded
tub and shower combination and a Corian sink and counter. On
leaving them, the woman, Mrs. Everett, pointed to the the rules of
the house and a schematic diagram tacked to the back of the door
which displayed the exits from the building in the event of a fire.

Later, at dinner at the Belhurst, recommended in the brochure about the Finger Lakes, Mickey remarked how homey their
lodgings were, and speculated about families who lived in houses
with family pictures on the wall and filled with family memora-
bilia.

"Don't you feel like you've been drawn into someone's family,
Leonard? You ever wonder what its like having a family history
and family ties? Like having a favorite brother or sister you can call
and talk to about some problem that you can't tell anyone else
about?"

"We've got each other. We talk." As far as he knew, they held
no secrets from each other. With the exception of how Mickey felt
when she had a compulsion to visit a Vietnamese market and talk
to her own people. She never mentioned how she felt, only what
she did and what she talked about with them.

"You know what I mean."

"We have no families, Miko." He used her Vietnamese name
to soften what he was saying. "Your family, and excuse me for
saying this again, doesn't want you. The courts took care of my
family. They completed the process that my real parents ... parent
... had begun."

"We're a family, darling. You and I."

"You think about your family much?" He knew the answer to
that without having to ask. One look at the sadness on her face
when the Vietnamese holidays rolled around or when they cel-
ebrated traditional American holidays told him that. She didn't
carry her sadness in a shrouded moodiness. They needed each other
too much to let it dissipate into personal acrimony. One thing
they had learned was patience with each other.

"Yes, I think about them. You know that. It's just not knowing what is happening to them that bothers me. I know my mother still loves me. My brothers and sisters also. It's always been my uncle."

"They won't have anything to do with you, even after we brought them here."

"It's the only history I've got, but it's not like having real family anymore. They're more like distant relatives. I just have this emptiness inside. Like, without a family and just you and me, it's all so ... fragile."

"It's not right. I'm surprised that your older brothers or sisters haven't tried to get in touch."

"I've dishonored them."

"You had no choice. Your uncle gave you no choice."

"No, he didn't."

"Maybe it's just as well our not having a family." He didn't know where this conversation was leading. They'd floated on the periphery of it many times without coming down hard on what they could or should do with their life together. He had read between the lines. Could understand her yearnings and loneliness. The fact that he knew they existed, and he was powerless to do anything. It wasn't like a landfill that he could shovel garbage into and cover it over. There were things that were unsaid and not-discussed; things that had their own warning signs, planted on stakes in the not-to-be-trampled-on-ground between them because they had had such a violent beginning in the early days, and they'd had to learn and grow from it and cling to each other for support. Maybe they should have had kids, if they could have had kids. The blacks had torn her up badly when they raped her; had damaged her permanently, they found out later, and his anger as he thought about it was just as strong as the day it happened. Maybe having her own kid would have helped. Would it have changed the way they lived? He knew that the trips he and Mickey took after every transaction had less and less meaning. They were filling in the spaces in their lives. Like Seniors visiting a local mall every day for something to do. Or going for coffee every day at

McDonald's to fill in the time; clinging to a schedule, like a life-line. Because even with their history, they still had to fight off loneliness; had to fill in the gaps. He and Mickey filled the gaps with their reaffirmation of love after each trip because it gave them something tangible to which they could anchor themselves. A ritual to give meaning and substance to their lives. Her having a kid in the beginning wouldn't have worked. He knew it wouldn't have worked because at the time he wanted all of her attention, needed it. It was different now. They were both older and their needs had changed.

"Why don't we adopt a child, Miko?"

He wasn't prepared for the tears. A flash flood that spilled out of her eyes and down her cheeks, soundlessly, as if the tear function was a remote action unrelated to her sitting there at first, calmly. Then her shoulders started shaking, but still, no sound, and her shoulders squeezed towards each other as if they were trying to shut off her feelings. Her body jerked and her nose began to run, thin silver streams emerging from her nostrils. She took a tissue from her handbag and blew her nose. She blotted the tears from her eyes.

"Excuse me," she said and rose from her chair and walked quickly to the ladies room.

He couldn't believe he'd said that. Couldn't believe he'd just come right out and said it without thinking it through, without erecting the barriers that would have prevented him from doing anything so foolish. He'd ignored the consequences of exposing a kid to his way of life. The kid would find out; so how do you shield a kid from that? He had his office, and he could probably develop his business a little more, take some courses in the stock market. Maybe work for a year in a brokerage house. Ahh, who was he kidding. He refilled Mickey's glass. It was a New York State red.

"I'm sorry," she said as she sat down. "I don't know what came over me." She had repaired the damage the tears had done to her mascara. Her eyes were very bright. "Did you mean what you said about adopting a child? You weren't just saying it?"

"I meant it, babe." He reached across the table and took her hand in his. They held hands very tightly.

"I would like that. I feel so alone when you're not there, and I worry about you, the chances you take. You said you never wanted kids. I used to think that you said it because you knew I couldn't have them."

"No, that was never a reason. I didn't want to share you with anyone for one thing. You were the most wonderful thing that ever happened to me, you understand?" She didn't say anything, but sat with her hands in his, eyes gray in the dim candlelight. "Besides, I never thought I'd make a good father. I had no experience, no background in being a father. I'd be playing it by ear. Doing on the job training." He didn't tell her he might start thinking about what he was doing if there was a kid—wondering why it was so easy for him to kill, wondering why it didn't bother him later like her rape had bothered him all these years. Killing had been easy because it never became personal. Would he be able to do it if he had to kill someone he knew? A friend? What if Sal decided that Masterson had to go? Could he do it?

She smiled and gently squeezed his hand.

"It won't be like that, Leonard. You can get out of your line of work. We can open up a shop, or get one of those franchises. You've said we have enough to retire on right now. Why don't we? Sell the house and move somewhere else."

"It's not that easy, Miko. Sal isn't going to let me out."

"Have you talked to him?"

"I've given him some pretty broad hints, but I don't think he'll buy into it. You should remember from the old days, his own partner. You remember what happened?"

XII

Leonard's R&R came through right on scehdule. Sarge had met him in downtown Saigon near the railroad station. Leonard was dressed for his R&R: a loose colorful short-sleeved sport shirt, plain shorts and sandles, PX specials. Leonard hadn't expected to be picked up in a vintage Citroen sedan, left behind by the French. "Mint condition." That's what Sarge said as soon as Leonard settled back into the plush seat. He put his overnight bag between his feet. Sarge didn't introduce the Hmong holding the Thompson submachine gun on his lap in the back seat. Along the way, Sarge pointed out Dao's villa. Leonard glimpsed it and a guard through the iron gates at the entrance that held the high walls apart. Sarge drove them directly to his villa.

"Neat, huh?" Sarge said as they rolled through the open iron gate. A Hmong, a carbine thrown across his shoulder, a magazine in the weapon, closed the gate behind them.

Leonard agreed although Sarge didn't give him much of a chance to look at it as he whisked him through the main part of the house to a small room that Sarge used as an office. Ginger and a maid were waiting with coffee and freshly baked croissants. Leonard looked around for Mickey. Didn't see her. Sarge motioned for him to sit down at a small coffee table. Ginger poured him coffee and pointed to the cream and sugar, the croissants and a plate of sugar cookies.

"Go ahead and help yourself," Sarge said. "I wanted to give you a little background before you took off. We got a little time before you meet the convoy heading up the coast. My man, Sei, will drive you and the girl, but you can't be late. They'll drop you off on your doorstep. Remember I'd said I had a use for your special talents?"

Leonard nodded, his mouth full of cookie, unable to speak. He'd passed on the croissants.

"It was okay when Dao and I first started out in business. We both knew what we wanted. Ever wonder how I come to own a couple of bars here in Saigon?"

Leonard hadn't really given it much thought. The only thing he thought about was Mickey. He slid his eyes around the room to the open door, hoping to catch a glimpse of her, trying not to be too obvious about it.

"Mickey okay?" Leonard asked, interrupting Sarge, unable to hold back any longer.

"Yeah, she's fine. You'll see plenty of her over the next few days. What I started to say—pay attention Leonard because you gotta know what this is all about."

Leonard directed his attention to Sarge and sat with his hands folded in his lap.

"I've known Dao ever since my second tour. I was an advisor to an ARVN unit. He was a Battalion CO. Well, to make a long story short, we got to talking. They'd fucked him over pretty badly— the government. He didn't have the right connections. No relatives in high office who could nudge his career along. And he didn't have the correct religious affiliation which was another thing that worked against him."

Leonard checked his watch. He took another sip of his coffee. Added more sugar.

"He was a helluva commander, I'll say that for 'im. Took care of the troops. Didn't steal their pay or charge them for their rations like some of them fuckers. His men loved him, but that was what made him dangerous for the regime. He wasn't ever going to get a higher command."

"I thought they wanted to win this war."

"Not if it means losin' power and our Uncle keeps footin' the bill. See what happened to Big Minh."

"Big who?"

"Aw, forget it. He was a fighter. A man of the people. Anyway,

Dao got pretty bitter about being shat upon, ya know what I mean?"

"Yeah," Leonard said. He used to get bitter about the way he got treated because he was so short. But no more. He'd found his place in the tunnels.

"Dao was a Lieutenent Colonel when I firt met him. Lieutenant Colonel Ngyuen Thanh Dao. Had been one for a couple of years. All he wanted was to command a Regiment and make full bird. He figured he could retire then to his place in the south and maybe get involved in local politics. Well, he's still a 'light bird' and he'll stay a 'light bird.'"

"I don't get it Sarge, where do I fit into all this?"

"I'm getting to that. Well, after I met him again on my third tour here. By accident. We got to talking. He'd moved with his boss who was the Province Chief in Dinh Tuong Province, south west of Saigon, up here to the staff. His boss, Cao Kaac Tuong, how's that for a tongue twister, made BG—Brigadier General— and took Dao with him. Dao wanted to retire. He'd been in the shit for twenty-five years. But he couldn't. No money, nothing to speak of. Like me. He knew I ran an NCO club and supervised the EM clubs. So he suggested we go in business. That's what we did. He could get the sites—I didn't ask him how he was going to do that—'cause we thought a couple of small bars with a few girls and real hooch and real American food would go over good. Not big enough to attract a lot of attention. Eventually, we started dealing."

"Dealing?"

"Mary Jane, bouncing power, bozos as well as the artillery for the users. We deal it all. But no laughin' and scratchin' or geezin' on premises. That's when the green started rolling in. That's when Dao started getting greedy. Up 'til then, he took care of getting the girls and I took care of supplying the liquor and the food, getting the MPCs converted to green. Finally, I set up the pipeline to the states for our customers there using Graves Registration as the conduit. It wasn't big, but we had guys there who distributed the shit."

"I seen a couple a guys on patrol high on drugs. Got people killed," Leonard said.

"The users are gonna get it whether they get it from me or someone else. Might as well be me. No Lipton Tea from us, no skag, strictly high quality stuff. Just like the girls. Good quality. Clean. Right off the farm. Ginger trains 'em how to walk and dress and how to use makeup, makes sure they dazzle. Of course they know the drill once on their backs and with their legs spread. 'You want boom boom?' seems to be enough of a sales pitch. Right? We get a girl starts usin', then she babysits a young GI until she gives him wings later, then she's outta here. We don't want any bedbugs hangin' around.

"Mickey ever...?"

"Never touched the stuff. Remember, she just finished charm school with Ginger. Hadn't turned that many tricks." Sarge laughed.

Leonard wondered what the laugh meant, but didn't ask. Didn't care what Mickey had done before, but was glad she hadn't been using. Wasn't doing ... tricks anymore.

"Ginger picked it up on the street that Dao was sayin' he wasn't getting his fair share. That I was cutting him out. We'd always made it 50-50. He increased his personal security and began changing mistresses. Changed his routine. The only routine that didn't change was his work day schedule although he changed his route to work everyday. He's become very unpredictable."

Leonard waited for Sarge to continue. Instead, he lit up another cigarette and leaned back in his chair, held the cigarette out in front of him, his elbow resting on the arm of the chair, and stared at the smoke as it coiled off the ash and faded in the movement of air from the overhead fan and the breeze moving across the room through the open windows.

"Let's go," Sarge said. "It's time. We'll talk later."

He never did say how he wanted to use Leonard's special talents nor did he show Leonard the rest of the house.

"Stick this in your bag Leonard," Sarge said as Leonard climbed over the front seat into the back of the jeep to sit beside the black pajama-clad Hmong who sat over the wheel well, a carbine balanced across his knees. Sarge handed him an M-30 carbine with a sawed off stock and barrel. A clip was in the weapon. Leonard checked to see if the safety was on. It was. Sarge also put two fragmentation grenades in the bag. Just in case. Sei, a Vietnamese from the south, spoke a little English. Ginger came out of the house with Mickey, her belongings wrapped in a small bundle. She wore a light, blue scarf over her hair, her face buried inside the hollow the scarf formed around her face. She smiled and briefly hugged him. Sarge lifted her into the front seat with Sei. Sarge and Ginger, standing together, waved them out the gate.

Mickey hadn't said a word, hadn't moved in her seat to smile at him or to speak with him. The ends of her hair floated out over the back of the seat from under her silk scarf. He wanted to touch her hair, turn her head so he could look into her eyes. He tried to talk to her, but she only nodded, not moving her head, when he tried to say something. Was she feeling differently about him now?

They caught the convoy outside of Saigon and fell in behind a ¾ ton truck with several GIs sitting sideways on the bench in the back, their M-16s pointed out the sides of the vehicle. One of the GIs looked at Leonard, pointed at Mickey and gave Leonard a thumbs-up sign. Leonard returned the sign. A sergeant made sure their jeep was tucked in close to the American vehicles, ahead of a line of civilian trucks, buses and mini-busses.

When they arrived at the villa, they followed the caretaker around the house, but Mickey remained silent, expressing neither pleasure nor displeasure. Listening, not asking questions, nodding her head in occasional response. Leonard figured the caretaker told her everything she needed to know. They acted tentatively, like two kids on a first date, when they were left alone in their bedroom with only the the rattle of the shutters from the light wind which swept in from the sea. Leonard began to think that she had the rag on which didn't offer many prospects for this R&R. Mickey disappeared into the bathroom. Leonard drew the shutters apart and looked out at the ocean in the distance. The door opened behind him.

Mickey stood in the doorway in a blue-flowered bikini, her hair falling across one breast almost to her navel. She had dusted on eye shadow and painted her lips. Leonard stood open-mouthed. She sent him a shy smile.

"I learn ... speak Engliss'," she said haltingly, seeking his approval. "You like?"

Leonard wasn't sure if she was talking about her English or her bikini. He sat down on the edge of the bed and rubbed his eyes which made her smile.

"I like very much. You speak very well," he said slowly to make sure that she understood. "You are very beautiful," he added just to make sure he got it right.

She let out a happy squeal and rushed across the room, throwing her arms around him, knocking him back on the bed. They both laughed happily. He lay on his back looking up at her

She raised herself up and straddled him. Her blue eyes, solemn, absorbed him.

"I want ... sur ... prise you."

"You sure did that," he said laughing, relieved that she hadn't changed her feelings about him.

"I am very happy." She said slowly and carefully. "Now I talk to you, not just do boom-boom." No longer leaning over him, she began unbuttoning his shirt. He wanted to hold her and ran his hands along her sides, cupping his hands over her breasts and then, moving them up to touch her neck under her soft, silky hair and sliding them over her shoulders and down her arms. He made the trip several times over the landscape of her body, whispering to her about the softness of her skin, how beautiful she was, how he had missed her, and how much he loved her.

"I ver' happy ... to ... be here ... with you." She went back to unbuttoning his shirt and bent forward kissing his chest and his neck. He rolled her on her back, and she lay still, watching him shed his clothes. He folded his pants and put his shirt over the back of one of the two chairs in the room. He lay beside her under the fan, and they could smell the sea through the open window. He undid the strings of her bikini, and she unfastened her bra. He began to stroke her, careful of the deep scar that ran away from her genitals. He sat up, leaned over her and slowly inserted himself in her.

"Does it hurt? Should I stop?" She had winced, and as much as he wanted her, he didn't want to cause her pain. She shook her head, her eyes closed.

"I better. Is first time … long time… Is good." She raised her head up and drew his head to hers. He felt the fierceness of her kisses, and she laughed joyfully when his body began to slap against hers. Moments later, they uncoupled and lay on their backs holding hands, fearful of breaking the contact that joined them, watching the slow revolutions of the fan and for the first time seeing the fronds of the palm plants in each corner of the room moving lazily and the gekko, which looked down on them from the wall and the huge armoire against the wall that remained impervious to the breeze that curled around it but cooled their sweating bodies.

"Why you kill ni-gras?" She drew his hand down between her legs. He could feel the welt of the scar as she placed his hand over her wet genitals.

"Because they hurt you. They should'na done that to you." His fingers crept into her moistness. He could hear her breathing now, feel her stomach rising and falling.

"You kill Veet'mese."

"I have to."

"You kill for me."

"I had to do that."

"Why you have to?"

"I don't know."

Her breathing quickened. She pressed his hand down.

"Tell me how you kill ni-gras."

He told her, but he didn't look at her. He spoke flatly like something he had recited many times before although it had only been in his head. He had to repeat how he pushed the knife into them and how they died. Her body stiffened for a moment; she sighed after he told her about the second one again; she no longer pressed his hand. They lay there. She squeezed his hand.

"I want to marry you."

"Mar-ry. What is mar-ry?"

"You be my wife."

"I no can be... wife. No can make babies," she said reluctantly, turning her head although he saw her eyes starting to pool with tears.

"I marry you. Take you to States."

"Sarge say, GI no can ... marry ... Veet'mese girl. He say ... 'No can do.'"

"We find a way. I want you for my wife."

"You marry me ... I no can make babies?"

He drew her small body to his; began kissing her. He ran his finger along the ridge of the purplish scar on her cheek. She started to pull away.

"Make me ugly. You marry ugly woman?"

"You are the most beautiful woman I have ever seen." He spoke slowly so that she understood each word or at least the meaning of what he said. He held her tightly wanting her to know that he would protect her, but he was uncertain how he could do it but believed that it could be done, that he could do it; and she clung to him, and he felt, trusted him.

During the next couple of days they played happily on the beach, basking in the warm sun in the morning and returning to the house at midday. Leonard's fair skin reddened very quickly and Miko was very protective of him, forcing him to use lotion to reduce the effects of the sun and putting a large towel over both of them as they lay on the beach when the sun became too intense. Miko prepared a light lunch of fruit and greens and fish that the caretaker had brought and cleaned and put in the refrigerator. Except for the appearance of food on the table and their meal at

night which the wife of the caretaker prepared, they never saw the
caretaker or the Hmongs who acted as security or the VC whom
they knew watched them from a distance.

After lunch, they lay naked in bed under the sheet of slowly
moving air. They napped or talked or giggled softly as they discovered more about each other. When she slept Leonard sometimes
awoke from his own sleep to lean over her, looking down on the
thin, small face with the dark lashes and soft, full lips. Her skin
had turned olive from the sun. He wanted to touch her and more
than once, he wanted to waken her and express how he felt about
her, but he ran up against the wall of his own ignorance, unable to
articulate these new emotions.

She awakened one day toward the end of their week together
and found him watching her. He began to tell her about the tunnels, not because he wanted to frighten her or make himself out to
be more than he was, a grunt doing his job, but because he wanted
to prepare her for what could happen to him. Prepare her for one
day when he would no longer be there no matter how much he
loved her. He told her there were dangers in what he did. That he
wasn't afraid of his work, but was afraid of being taken from her.
He talked slowly to make her understand, but he talked more for
himself; that as much as he wanted her, something could happen.
He spoke without rancor or self-pity because he accepted his life
the way it was. He knew what he had been dealt. The only regret
he had was that he would lose her. He tried to make her understand that. She must have understood because she took him in her
arms and guided his head to where it nestled on her breast, and he
could feel her heart beating and her hand softly brushing the hair
at his temples and he felt less like her lover in that moment and
more like a brother ... or her child.

She seemed so young. He followed her everywhere with his
eyes when they were together, recording on the film of his memory,
the way she walked, the way she slept, the expressions on her face
when she was happy and laughing, when she was pensive, when
she was passionate so that when he was alone and away from her

he would be able to close his eyes and in the darkened theater of his thoughts be able to run the film over and over.

"You always watch me."

"Yes."

"I feel your eyes. I know when you no watch. Why you watch?"

"Because I want you so much. There are laws against what I do with you."

"What laws? What is wrong ... what you do with me?

"In the States, I could be arrested."

"Ar-res-ted? What is arrested?"

"Sent to jail."

"Why they send you to jail?"

"In the states, they say you're too young to be doing what we're doing."

"What they know?"

"They say, you're a minor. Sixteen is too young. I shouldn't do boom-boom with you."

"I'm not a woman?" she asked teasingly. "You no like do boom-boom with me?"

He looked at her and told her how much he loved her, and cupping one hand over a breast he told her, smiling, that she was almost a woman.

"You no speak true. You no love me 'cause I no have big boobs like 'merican girls," she said matter-of- factly. "I get big boobs. Ginger say, 'merican doctor make big boobs."

He laughed at her seriousness and leaned forward and kissed each breast, running his tongue over the burgeoning nipples.

"You are fine," he said, "and this is wonderful." He reached down and touched the velvety flesh between her legs and placed his hand over her pubic area. "Your sweetness here and your mouth are without exception," and he kissed her.

Sarge arrived by jeep on the fifth day accompanied by four heavily armed, pajama-clad men followed by Sei in a jeep to carry them back. Sarge's jeep had no markings, and Leonard noted the sandbags on the floor boards. A carbine with a sawed-off stock lay across his lap, two clips taped together, in reverse order, one inserted in the carbine. He climbed out of the jeep as his men jumped out and set up security around the house, nodding at the Hmongs further out away from the house. Sarge slid the piece of armor plating on which he'd been sitting onto the floor out of the sun.

"Don't want to fry my ass," he said by way of explanation. He propped the carbine next to the armor plating. "I figure with the sandbags and the plate that if I hit a mine at least I won't lose my family jewels. Runs a little sluggish," he said pointing to the jeep, "with all the extra weight. The sandbags, the piece of armor plate and my troops. What d'ya think of my private army? Hmongs. Hate the Vietnamese. They're relatives to the guys already here."

Leonard watched them squat into position, their backs against the palm trees; take out cigarettes and light up, eyes never deviating from the landscape around them. Sarge put his arm across Leonard's shoulders and guided him into the house. Mickey backed away from the doorway as they entered.

"So how ya been doin' kid? Like the house? Not bad eh? Folks treatin' you okay? No problems with the neighbors?" Sarge was referring to the VC. Leonard didn't try to respond to Sarge's questions. "I should try to get out here more often. Ginger likes the beach. Mickey, you like the beach?" Sarge didn't wait for an answer, but took in the nod of her head.

"What d'ya think about the way she's picked up English? I'll bet that surprised the hell out of you?" He paused. Leonard said that it did.

"You wonderin' about the Hmongs? I had to get them for protection which is why I wanted to talk to you, kid. Mickey, make some tea or something, I wanna talk to Leonard." Mickey left the room. Sarge sat down and pointed to a chair across from him. "No offense but I think this should be just between you and me."

Leonard said he understood.

"Remember I spoke to you about your special skills? Well, it's like this. I think my partner is going to try to get rid of me. Permanently. How do I know? Little things. He's been bad-mouthing me, ya know? Like I told you earlier—sayin' that I'm holding back on 'im; cheatin' 'im outta his full share. Won't talk to me face-to-face." Sarge looked at Leonard, his head cocked to one side, as though he was trying to assess whether or not he was getting through.

Leonard wasn't sure where the conversation was heading or how he came into it. He must have had a puzzled expression on his face. Sarge continued.

"The fact of the matter is, kid, I don't know how or when he intends to do this, but I think it would be pretty stupid for me to wait around for it to happen. Of course, he's been acting like everyone is his enemy, but I know I head the list."

"So what are ya getting at?"

"Right to the point. Good question. I want to make a preemptive strike. Ya understand?"

Leonard shot him a blank look.

"I want ya to take Dao out before he wastes me." He paused. "I wanna make a business deal with ya. I'm going to pay ya to do it, ya unnerstan'?"

"I got no use for money here, 'cept for Mickey 'an that ain' gonna do her much good if I buy the farm."

"Let me finish." He stopped as Mickey brought out the tea and placed it on a small table between them. She poured them each a cup and put two cubes of sugar in Leonard's. Sarge took one sip and set it aside. "Thanks, Mickey." He waited until she left the room. "I see us having a long-term relationship. Think ahead, kid. You expect to be here forever?"

"Only if I get waxed."

"Get positive. Long term. The future. What I'm sayin' is…. Ya know where the Bronx is?" Without waiting for Leonard to answer, he said, "It's a borough in New York City."

"I ain't never been east of Detroit. I guess I oughta go to the liberry an' look it up?"

"No jokin' kid, this is serious business. Why do you think I brought it up?"

"Ain' got a clue." Leonard wondered if Mickey was listening outside the door.

"I been lookin' ahead, like I been tellin' you to do. I see uhh … opportunity after 'Nam. I don't expect to be here a hell of a lot longer; I sure as hell don't want any fuckin' slope to be the cause of my becomin' a permanent resident. Like turnin' up one day missin', MIA. Ya know what I mean? Suppose I get Mickey out of 'Nam permanently? Suppose when you get back to the States, she's waitin' for you in an apartment in the Bronx, or Poughkeepsie, wherever!"

"You can do that?"

"Ain't gonna be easy, but it can be done. What d'ya think about that?"

"Is this part of the business deal you're talkin' about?"

"Ya like it so far?"

Leonard nodded. He didn't ask Sarge how he was going to do it. He took a swallow of his tea.

"There's more to it. I'll make sure she has enough to live on, to have bread … ahh … rice on the table. I'll also make a deposit in that savin's account I told you about."

"What kind a deposit?"

"Trust me, kid. It won't be big money. That'll come later after I'm set up in the States. It's gonna take some bucks and some pull to get both Ginger and Mickey outta here. They can stay together until I get back. My brother'll help me set things up at the other end, but no one'll know anything about it. The family don't like their members shackin' up with dinks or smokes or anyone who ain't pure Italian-American. I got a wife an' kid who I ain't seen in years. The ol' lady divorced me a few years ago, an' I been payin' child support since then. She never let me see the kid when I went home. The kid'll be about eighteen now. My daughter. I wonder how she turned out?" Sarge paused. "The payments will stop now." He swallowed the rest of his tea.

"So what do you want me to do?"

Sarge crossed his legs and slouched in his chair. Put his elbows on the arms of the chair and stared at Leonard over the pyramid of his fingers as if deciding how much more he should tell him. He straightened up and fished out a pack of cigarettes from his shirt pocket and shook one out. His fingers dug into the shirt again and came out with a lighter. He snapped the cover of the lighter shut after the first drag on his cigarette.

"Dao's giving a party. A big one. That's where his money goes. Parties, women, booze an' he's got a bad habit. Big time. He's getting unreliable, ya know what I mean? Becomin' a real schiz."

Leonard wasn't sure what Dao's problem was, but the man sitting across from him was pretty upset about it.

"He's invited a bunch a US brass, a few on the payroll, some civilians from USAID and the construction companies, some big wheel dinks in government and his boss, General Tuong. Of course, there are going to be a bunch of 'hostesses' for the brass and the civilians. You'll come in with the civilians from the construction companies. The hooker in this is that everyone is going to be searched. That oughta win some friends. I think he'll lean heaviest on the slopes because I don't think he expects any problems from anyone from the US."

"So what am I supposed to do?"

"Yeah, back to business. There's going to be a distraction. A couple of them. Outside. Everyone should be well-oiled by then. A couple of my girls are going to work on the bodyguards nearest Dao right from the start of the evening, getting them in a … uhhh … less attentive mood. When the first explosion occurs there's going to be panic. Everyone remembers Tet. There'll be an explosion upstairs as well. Ginger is going to handle that. When the shit hits the fan you take out Dao, before his bodyguards get to 'im."

"Right there in the open?"

"When else can you do it? He'll be shittin' his pants wonderin' what the hell is happening. You're only gonna have a couple of seconds or so when ya can get close to 'im. Remember, he's been in combat. He's no cherry, but he's gotten soft, ya unnerstan'? An' don't forget he's been drinkin' and no one knows how many lines of C he'll have snorted by then. His reactions will be off."

"I ain't never killed someone just … ta kill 'im."

"Ya killed the spades."

"That was different. They hurt Mickey."

"Think of it as bein' in the tunnels. Ya got a job to do."

"What if I get caught?"

"You're on your own. You don't get caught."

"Ya can't afford to let me go down, Sarge. Ya know what I mean."

"I'll be the one who pops you, kid, for killin' my partner."

Leonard looked into the flat, cold eyes of the big man.

"Seems pretty risky."

"Life's a risk. All opportunity has some risk to it, otherwise it wouldn't be an opportunity."

"How do I know ya won't pop me anyway?"

"Ya don't. It's no worse than goin' in the tunnels."

"Ain't the same."

"It's the same. It's your life on the line."

"What about Mickey? Would ya put her back on the street if I fuck up?"

"Depends. Ginger an' her get along pretty well. But I ain' in business to hand out charity Don't fuck up, Leonard, especially if you want a life with Mickey."

"I unnerstan.'"

"Deal?"

"Deal."

From that moment, Leonard realized that he had to start thinking for himself, plan ahead, look for alternatives. He had a responsibility also. Mickey. He had to do what was good for both of them. That night as they lay together after Sarge had gone, he told her what the NCO had planned for them. He wanted to make sure she wanted it also, and so he told her about the party, the risk, and what he wanted her to do. When he finished, they lay quiet, thinking, until they fell asleep.

Colonel Dao's house had once belonged to a wealthy French merchant as had many of the houses built during the colonial era. It was a two-story white stucco building with a large courtyard surrounded by a high wall. Inside the main hall, ablaze with lights and candles, ceiling fans listlessly pushed the sullen air. The wide, glass, muntin-spaced doors were open to let in whatever breeze stirred outside. The leaves of the large potted palmettos languished in the heat. Police, in pairs, leaned against the outside wall, bored and only snapped out of their indolent posture when the convoy carrying their Chief arrived and again when a similar convoy of highly polished jeeps with Brigadier General Cao Khac Tuong, Dao's boss, drove through the main gate with Vietnamese MPs in starched khakis with white fourrageres draped from the epaulettes on their left shoulders and patent leather accoutrements holding sidearms, billy clubs and handcuffs dangling from white pistol belts. They wore white gloves, shiny helmets and white-laced, glossy jump boots. They scrambled from the accompanying vehicles to take up position to protect the general. From all directions. At the main gate they watched the guests arrive giving them a cursory glance. Inside, the inspection was more thorough and seemingly unobtrusive. Americans in their starched combat fatigues were passed through with a nod of the head. Dao's security people gave Americans in civilian clothes from AID and the officials from the construction companies a quick glance and nothing more than a quick look under raised shirttails. They shunted aside the Vietnamese women, dressed in the traditional *ao dai*, and escorted them to a side room where they were inspected more thoroughly. Some of them came out giggling. The wife of the Police Chief was not subjected to what would have been a gross indignity.

Leonard watched Sarge, Ginger and Mickey pass through the doors with only a casual glance by the security personnel. He attached himself to a group of construction people queuing at the

entrance. Leonard lifted his shirt and two hands swiftly passed
down the inside of his legs. Once in the main hall he located Sarge
standing with a group of people near Dao. He identified Dao from
Sarge's description. The short, stubby Vietnamese in a white linen
suit, his broad, oily face sweating, his hair slicked back, was laughing and gesturing—the center of attention—while his eyes pierced
the room in quick watchful thrusts. In one hand he carried a white
handkerchief, with which he dabbed and patted his damp forehead. Leonard watched Dao move from one group to another, the
white handkerchief like a flag marking his position, as he wel-
comed his guests in English and French; making what must have
been off-color remarks to the Vietnamese women in their native
tongue because they laughed, hiding their smiles coquettishly behind well-manicured fingers. Leonard moved out of Dao's line of
sight, but shifted with him as though they had been choreographed
by a master hand. Attentive waiters followed the host about, frequently exchanging his empty glass for a full one. When he was
certain that all of his guests had arrived he gave a short speech in
English and Vietnamese welcoming them to his home. Then with
a smile on his broad, sweating face, he raised his hands and said,
"The bar is open, the food is laid out like a tender virgin waiting to
be ravaged; let the good times roll!" He joined the laughter of his
guests and ushered them into the sumptuous buffet spread on
tables, with white table cloths, positioned end-to-end. Candles
flickered on silver candelabras. The ceiling fans wafted the aroma
of the food throughout the room. Waiters set up white-sheeted
tables and folding chairs around the sides of the reception room
they had just vacated, and the band which had been playing soft
background music broke into a repertoire of music from the fifties
as the guests, laden with full plates, napkins and silverware, moved
to the tables. Leonard took his place in line. He had never seen so
much food. He found a place to sit with employees of the construction company and avoided talking by concentrating on his
food. Waiters poured wine, but Leonard passed it up for soda. He
stole quick looks at his watch. Several people began dancing.

Leonard was ignored by his dining companions after the initial introductions although he feigned interest in what they were saying, and nodded as though he was listening. His gaze shifted around the room as people finished eating and clustered in groups. The American brass circled around the General and Dao. Leonard glanced down at his watch. Dao had disappeared. Leonard hadn't seen him leave. He stood and nervously circulated around the room. He passed close to Mickey and Sarge but gave no sign of recognition. He took a quick look at his watch. Ten more minutes to 2300 hours.

He didn't ask himself why Dao had to die. He never considered whether it was right or wrong. Why was this any more than what he did when he entered the tunnels? He had a job to do, and he was going to do it. It could mean a future for Mickey and him. If he could find the colonel! His tension fell away when he saw Dao and the general appear through the doors leading from the main ballroom to the outside. Dao was no longer smiling, nor speaking, but listened as he mopped his face, vigorously nodding his head as the general spoke. He followed his superior like an obedient house dog as he collected his aide and bade good-night to the ranking Americans who had lined up near the entrance when they saw him about to depart.

Leonard inched his way closer and closer to Dao, weaving his way between the guests like a shadow trying to catch up with the body of Dao. Dao backed away from the doorway as the guests, some of whom followed the general out the door, paid their respects to their host. Dao watched the general's convoy disappear. Leonard joined the group nearest Dao as the first explosion erupted outside, followed by a second. Men and women turned back from the open doorway and Leonard had a fleeting impression of security people reaching for their sidearms, indecisive and turning their attention to the stairway as a third explosion shook the upstairs. Dao stood transfixed, confusion spread like a stain across his face as he turned into Leonard. Leonard shut out the sounds of voices, the shouts, the screams. The lights went out. Leonard reached behind his back and tore the knife from the tape, grabbed Dao's arm, felt him try to pull away until he drove the long slender, tempered steel blade past the silk tie and through the white shirt and the once hard stomach muscles and up under the rib cage into Dao's heart. Dao made no sound. Leonard released his arm as the colonel crumpled to the floor. Leonard stepped back and let the crowd envelop him. Someone stumbled on the body, and he could feel the people in front of him bend as they tried to maintain their balance. Someone fell under the weight of the shoving crowd. The lights went on. Several people were sprawled across the body of Dao. His bodyguards rushed to their fallen leader and pulled at the people lying on the floor. The chief of police began barking orders as policemen stood indecisively in the entrance uncertain how to stop the Americans who began moving past them. Leonard, caught up in the rush of people toward the doorway, stayed with the group until they burst into the black, brooding night. The police security had been drawn from their posts by the explosions and were spread around the grounds of the house. Leonard walked through the gate behind a group of construction personnel and broke off from them when they reached their transportation. No one offered him a ride. He had a long walk back to Sarge's house. He hated to leave the knife behind.

Leonard didn't see the Hmongs when he approached the locked gate, but he knew they were there. He could feel them. The guard opened the pedestrian gate and let him through. Sarge was waiting in the doorway as he arrived at the entrance. Mickey showed relief when he entered the room and ran into his arms. He had to unwind her arms from around his neck. Ginger smiled. A Hmong appeared with a can of soda; Sarge motioned Leonard to a chair. Except for several pieces of thick bamboo furniture the room was austere. Several large palm plants broke the plain symmetry of the space. A sand-colored fiber rug muted the sound of their footsteps. Leonard led Mickey by the hand to the rattan couch, and they sat down. He wiped his face and pulled at his shirt which stuck to his body from the long walk. He took a long swallow from the can of Coke and put it on the floor.

"Any problems getting back?" Sarge said, sitting down across from Leonard and a smiling Miko.

"I stayed in the shadows and ducked any a the white mice all the way."

"I was watching until the lights went out. That was a nice clean hit."

"We gotta a deal now?"

"A deal."

"Including everything we talked about?"

"We gotta deal, Leonard, just like I said." Leonard sank back into the cushion. He held Mickey's hand. She sat on the edge of the couch, her blue eyes searching his. He wondered what thoughts were going through her mind when she knew he was going to kill a man, could see the victim. He tightened his fingers around hers, and she responded.

"I think he knew in that split second when he turned into me that you had gotten to him first."

"Suppose all the lights didn't go out?"

' "It would have been the same. He was dead as soon as his security took their eyes off 'im."

"Miko got the lights?"

Leonard nodded. He didn't tell Sarge that he had expected him to waste him as soon as he took care of Dao. Sarge had never mentioned shutting off the lights. He had the feeling that Sarge was standing near him when he moved toward Dao. He turned to Mickey and smiled. They would take care of each other.

"That was a smart move."

"This makes you the Boss man?"

"Yeah, Ginger's brother is ready to move up now. He'll front for us. He knows a lot of the right people. US and Vietnamese." He looked at Ginger and gave her a wink.

"What happens when we pull out?"

"The organization will remain. The bars may close. We expect them to close, and the hostesses will probably be re-educated."

"The VC going to go along with all this?"

"The VC are very grateful for the support Dao gave them, and I expect that Ginger's brother will arrive at an accommodation with them. At least a temporary one. We may get a smaller cut, but, hey, that's the cost of doing business."

"I gotta get back to the company tomorrow. I 'preciate using your place. It was real nice."

"Part of the deal, kid."

"I wanna a house like that someday where we can move around and not bump into things." Mickey squeezed his hand. He would do whatever it took. "Got a question, Sarge. Did you and the Colonel shake on the deal you made with him?"

"Yeah, Leonard. Just like we did. Gentleman's agreement, ya know? Why?"

"Just wonderin'."

"Don't think too much. I said we got a deal. Trust me. Don't forget we're Americans. We gotta stick together, right?"

Leonard and Mickey spent the last night of Leonard's R&R at Sarge's house. Three weeks later, Leonard stepped on a mine.

XIII

The first words Leonard heard were 'Dust-off, dust-off.' The earth had stopped exploding around him and settled into a sullen silence. He didn't remember being lifted up or being slammed against the ground. Only fighting to breath. The pain was beginning. He called for the medic. Not because he was afraid to die, but to stop the pain or at least put a clamp on it to keep it from spreading because when he reached down to cover the pain with his hand he felt grit mixed with blood where his stomach was supposed to be. He thought he was going to die.

"Leonard, gadammit, open your eyes. You fight this, Leonard. We called for a dust-off. It's on the way. Obie's here an' he's gonna help you." It was Masterson. His platoon sergeant. The voices came from far away. He wanted to tell them to talk louder, but he couldn't raise his voice. He could barely open his eyes. Barely keep them open. He wanted to sleep.

"I'm gonna give you somethin' to ease the pain, Leonard," Obie said, his black face hovering over him. He didn't feel the morphine enter his arm.

"They hurt Mickey, Obie. Had … to … do … it. For her!"

"Don't close your eyes, Leonard. Talk to me. Who's Mickey?"

The voices bunched up on top of each other and he couldn't separate them out. White face, black face, black and white voices. White and black voices.

"Shudda … stayed … tunnels. Quiet … Black."

"Open your fuckin' eyes, Leonard. Hear the chopper? Your taxi's here," Masterson said.

"Wha … 'bout others …? They comin'?"

"It's okay, everythin's gonna be okay," Obie said. "Stay with me, Leonard. Here hold this in place."

The black medic lifted his hand and put several first aid pack-ets on his stomach, and placed Leonard's hand over them. He could hear the chopper now. It stirred up pieces of brush and dust, and a rush of humid air and grit against his face told him the chopper was on the ground. He tried to focus his eyes but couldn't keep them open. He felt himself bobbing like a cork on water. Masterson held his arm until they reached the medevac.

"Chauffeur's here. Listen up, Leonard. You're gonna make it, ya hear?"

Masterson's voice was the last one he heard. Lift off!

"How'd you get here, Mickey?" He heard his voice, clear and distinct. But she didn't answer. Her face floated over his. The scar on the side of her face split open and he stared into the gaping crevice that grew and grew toward him. He couldn't reach up to close the wound. He wanted to tell her that Obie wasn't like the ones who had cut her. Told her Obie would close her wound. He didn't know how. The trees rushed past them, and Mickey's face disappeared and a gray canopy of clouds replaced her. Leonard didn't see or hear anything for a long time after that, and what he did see and hear when he finally realized that he was not going to die was closely bound up with pain and relief from pain for several hours at a time, but never continual, because the interludes of pain returned to be doused with a shot of the latest, approved painkiller; and he was never sure if the blood going in equaled the blood taken out of his arms; he was never sure which tubes did what¾the tubes attached to a needle taped to his arms and gave him nourishment although he hungered for a thick juicy ham-burger or the tubes draining his stomach or inserted into his nose. The world became clearer when they removed the canopy fitted over his upper body, and he could see the doctors and the nurses whose faces were no longer blurred and who pulled and prodded and pressed and took his pulse and put a hand against his forehead and wrote things on charts about him. He lost track of time and who he was and where he was and if Mickey had ever, in fact, existed. He probably knew it all the time, but when he reached the point when he could vaguely understand what was happening, he knew he had to live.

He awoke one day, and the day sorted itself out from the moment he opened his eyes. Everything around him was clear and distinct. He was alive. He had made it.

"You were a lucky young man," the doctor said, a Major with the gold oak leaf on one collar of his shirt and the gold caduceus on the other; an enamel name plate over the left pocket of his long starched white coat and a pen hooked over the edge of the pocket. The Major's name was Mulholland. He had just removed the bandages from his stomach and the nurse was about to replace them.

"You should be dead by all rights. You were a 100-1 shot. It's been touch and go for a few weeks now, but I think we're out of the woods. I'd like to take credit for the surgery. It was a pretty good job. But a lot of the credit should go to those guys who got you back into treatment as quickly as they did. Actually, you've been given a second life."

Leonard stared up at the doctor for a moment, nodded his head in agreement, closed his eyes and slept.

Leonard had not heard from Sarge or Mickey since returning to the States aboard a hospital aircraft. He was assigned to Madigan Army Hospital in California. His mail caught up with him in California. Sarge tracked him down using his own network. The letter was stamped with the postmark of the APO in 'Nam and then Japan before arriving in the States. The letter was brief and said that everything was going smoothly as far as getting Ginger and Mickey out of 'Nam. He gave Leonard an address for his apartment in the Bronx. And the name of the bank where his money was deposited. He told Leonard that he should keep a low profile, underlining the word low. Leonard wished there had been a note from Mickey even if Ginger had to write it. He missed Mickey. Now he had to beat the drugs they'd been giving him.

XIV

Leonard and Mickey arose early the next morning, took a short walk along the broad sidewalks looking down at the lake, glaucous under the curdled clouds. Hand in hand, breathing in the lake-scented air. They returned to their lodging for breakfast, paid their bill and left.

"We're going to Crescent Hills, Mickey."

"I thought we'd be going home."

"I have something I have to do."

"Does Sal know?"

"It's gotta be done, Sal knows that. I do it now, or I do it later. The woman almost made me abort the last hit. She's Al Schultz's attorney, and I can't have her involved in this next one. No matter what Sal says, I don't trust her. Something else. George Sawyer confessed to the rape and murder of the girl. Barbara Masterson. Masterson's sister. The three of them did it. Whelan, Sawyer and Schultz. Ironic isn't it, me being the one to take two of them out but for a different reason. I want to do Schultz, not because he screwed up Sal's operation, but because he raped and murdered a young girl. Masterson talked about it in 'Nam, always thought it was someone from Crescent Hills. It ate at him, Mickey. He thought that he should have been able to prevent it. How, I don't know. Reason I remember it was because it was the closest he ever got to talking about himself, his past. He was a helluva platoon sergeant. She was just a young girl, Mickey. Younger than you were."

Tears were forming in her eyes. She blinked them away.

"You understand why I have to do this?"

"There will be more risk in this one," she said.

"I didn't want to involve you, but I don't see any other way.

Schultz is the last of them. Sal would go off the deep end if he knew I was doing Masterson a favor. This thing has to be done now, before the woman gets involved." He outlined his plan to her and what actions she was to take if he was apprehended.

At three o'clock, a BMW pulled up to the entrance of the Kaydeross County Hospital. Dr. James Mulholland leaned across the front seat and kissed his wife. He followed the people into the hospital: visitors, people arriving for appointments, and shift personnel. He walked past the reception desk. An elderly heavy-set woman, sitting at the desk, looked past the person standing in front of her and broke off her conversation when she saw him.

"Good afternoon, Doctor," she said effusively. Dr. Mulholland smiled at her, nodded and went to the in-patient desk. Later, when questioned, Agnes Ball remembered that she always smiled and greeted the physicians and nurses when they arrived. She said that she felt it cheered them up to get a friendly greeting, put their day on an upbeat. She said Dr. Mulholland looked like an owl with his large horn rimmed glasses. No, she couldn't describe his features except the white coat he wore seemed too big. He did smile at her. Had she seen him before? No, but then she only worked three days a week. She *was* a volunteer, you know.

The woman at in-patient smiled at him when he approached. "Good afternoon, Doctor."

"Good afternoon. Has Mr. Schultz been moved yet? I understand that he may be moved to Albany Med."

She looked in the register.

"Oh, that awful man. I always said those Schultz boys wouldn't amount to much. Always in trouble. I don't think any of the nurses would go in his room if he wasn't a quadriplegic. Just looking at him, they say, gives them the creeps. He's still in 321." She started to look for Dr. Mulholland's name on the physician's roster, but as she told the deputy sheriff later, it was break time; she had already worked thirty minutes beyond her break; she was dying for a cigarette. When another nurse, her friend Kathy Boylen, told her she was going for coffee, she forgot about the doctor. She did remember that he had a pleasant and cultured voice. He looked like a professor with his large horn-rimmed glasses. No, he wasn't very tall.

When the nurse at the in-patient desk proceeded to take her break, Dr.Mulholland walked away. He paused at the hospital directory and noted several names before following a nurse and several visitors into the elevator. The nurse glanced at him, gave him a quick smile, but didn't study him or try to make conversation. She got off at the second floor. Dr. Mulholland followed the visitors past the check-in on the third floor. The deputy was sitting with his chair propped on two legs against the wall; his hat, a can of Pepsi, and his hand-held radio were on top of a clipboard on the floor beside him. He was reading a paperback. His eyes jumped off the book whenever a young woman or a nurse entered or left one of the adjoining rooms. He didn't return to the book until the woman disappeared from sight.

"How's the patient doing?"

"He ain't goin' nowheres," the deputy said with a dry chuckle. The deputy was a large heavyset, young man, not long past youthful acne which had left its scars on his face. His uniform was wrinkled, and sweat stains darkened his shirt under his arms. "Geez, I can't unnerstan' how anyone would wanna go on livin' like that," he said, motioning with his thumb over his shoulder.

"Hmm, yes. Seems like a heavy burden."

"The sonabitch, 'scuse my French, deserved it. Those Schultz brothers was bad actors. Even the dummy, the retard," he said as if that explained it all.

Dr. Mulholland looked at his watch. "Doctor," and he gave the name of the chief surgeon, "asked me to look in on Mr. Schultz. Wanted an outside opinion. Would you check to see if my name is on your list of authorized visitors? Mulholland. Dr. James Mulholland."

The deputy let his chair drop onto all four legs and with a grunt bent over and picked up the clipboard. He made a production of checking out the names. He laboriously went down the short list, his lips moving as he read off each one to himself.

"No, your name ain't on the roster, Doc."

"Damn. Don must have forgotten to call it in. I won't be back through here for another week or so, and I told him I would stop on my way up to Rochester." He looked at his watch. "I'm on a pretty tight schedule, so Don's out of luck. Well, thank you, deputy...." Leonard sighed, shrugged and turned as if to walk away.

"Ahhh... I'm not supposed to let anyone in to see the patient unless he's listed here. Seein's how you're a Doc, an' you was ast to do this, I can't see no problem you lookin' at 'im. I gotta keep the door open. That way, it won't be like I'm not maintaining security, ya follow me?"

Deputy Blanchard handed Dr. Mulholland the clipboard and watched the left-handed doctor sign himself in. Blanchard thumbed the doctor into Al Schultz's room. He stood outside the door watching as the doctor read Al's chart. He replaced the chart and walked around the bed, lifted Schultz's hand and proceeded to check his pulse. The doctor looked back when he heard the deputy talking. He dropped the patient's hand.

"Hi Bill, what're you doin' here?"

"Hi Linda, long time no see? What's it been, two, three months? Ain't seen you out at the Ol' Red Barn. What cha doin' here?"

"Oh, it's my mother again. Been here about a week. What's goin' on? I saw the deputies sittin' out here the past couple of days, but they didn't look like they'd answer any questions. So what's goin' on?"

Out of the corner of his eye Leonard saw the girl peer around the big deputy. He still filled the doorway, but he had his back to the room now.

"You didn't hear about all the excitement out at the Masterson place?"

"Is that the Army guy who's been stirring everything up around here? My mother says nothin's been the same since him and that old man, Josh Billin's, started diggin' up all that stuff about a murder twenty years ago."

"That was Masterson's sister. Schultz, Nate Whelan and George Sawyer raped and murdered that girl."

"Oh."

"It was in all the papers."

"Oh, I ain't got time to keep up on everythin' that's goin' on aroun' here. Besides, who needs it? Got enough of my own problems with my mother in here."

"Well, they was bad actors, real bad. Say, you still hanging around with Joey G.?"

"An' that's another problem. Nah, we split up a couple a weeks ago. Had a big fight, ya know. Told 'im he ain't cheatin' on me no more."

"Geez, I'm sorry to hear that. You an' him was pretty tight for...."

Leonard could tell from the sound of her voice that the girl was standing in front of the deputy. He pushed back Al's eyelids. His eyes had rolled back into his head. He was out of it. Leonard wanted him awake. Schultz must have sensed someone was in the room after he felt the fingers on his eyelids. Leonard pinched his cheek. Schultz opened his eyes. They widened as Leonard drew the icepick from his sleeve. He wanted him to know fear, the same kind of fear that Miko and the Masterson girl had experienced when they had been attacked. He paused as he placed the point of the icepick on the cartilage leading into the ear canal. Schultz winced.

"This is for Miko and the Masterson girl," he rasped as he penetrated the wall of the ear canal and plunged the sharp, steel point through the tympannic membrane, and the small cavity of the inner ear and into his brain. He felt cheated as he pushed the weapon deep into Schultz' skull and saw a slight smile struggle through the bearded man's face. Al Schultz had wanted to die.

Leonard took a cotton swab from his pocket and pulled the point of the icepick through it. He stuffed the cotton swab into

Al's ear and arranged his long hair to cover it. He replaced the icepick up his sleeve. He tucked the sheet around Al's neck, and when the deputy turned back into the room after agreeing to give Linda a call, he feigned writing on the chart at the foot of the bed.

"Any chance he's gonna walk again?"

"No chance, deputy. No chance at all." With that he replaced the chart and faced the deputy who stood leaning against the door frame.

"Must be tough knowin' that you ain't gonna enjoy the natural things in life anymore."

"I wouldn't worry about that. He got what he deserved. Thank you … ahh …Deputy Blanchard. You saved me some time today, and I appreciate it."

"That's okay, Doc, I know how busy you folks are. Glad to do it."

Later, the deputy would say that he considered himself a good judge of people. He described the doctor as being short, sandy-haired, in a white coat with a stethoscope hanging around his neck. Even wore a nametag. Said: Dr. Mulholland. Hey, the guy looked like a doc, talked like a doc. What more do you need? Not like some of these jokers walking around in Reeboks and baggy pants and beards and ass-wiping long hair pinned back in a ponytail. He even wrote like a doc, and the Deputy who by now had smudged any possible fingerprints handed the clipboard to the investigator who saw a vague, scrawled signature.

Leonard had just left Deputy Blanchard slumped back in his chair with a sigh as he returned to his paperback when a large officious woman came bearing down on him. Name: Ms Snyder. Title: Nurse Supervisor. She called him as he pushed through the exit and entered the stairwell scrambling down the stairs two at a time. He heard her shrill voice calling to him from the top of the stairs. He pulled a plastic shopping bag from around his middle and stuffed the white coat and stethoscope and the horn-rimmed glasses into it as he moved down the stairs. He followed the signs directing him to the lobby and slowed to a casual walk as he pushed through the doors into the reception area. A screen of visitors stood in front of the information desk, and he walked out of the hospital. Mickey, who had been watching the entrance from the parking lot, drove up alongside of him. He climbed in and fastened his seatbelt.

"Don't panic, but we'd better get out of here," Leonard said as he pounded his fist against his knee.

Mickey drove out onto the highway, careful not to appear in a hurry; patient as she fitted the car into the stream of traffic passing the hospital.

"People must be getting out of work," she said to fill the void made by Leonard's anger. Once they were moving steadily forward, she reached out and patted Leonard on the arm. He didn't react.

"The bastard wanted to die," he said angrily. He stared into space, unfocused, seething inside. "The bastard wanted to die," he repeated, "and I helped him. I put him out of his misery."

They could hear the sirens now. Two Sheriff's vehicles, sirens screaming, bar lights blinking, flashed past them, going in the opposite direction.

"I think we better head for the Northway, honey," he said. He pushed his anger aside when he realized that it might upset Miko. The car surged forward as they passed through the dust of the arterial and out of the 45 MPH speed zone. Leonard dropped his seat back while the tension flowed out of him. He had not wanted to involve Mickey. But he had done it for her. She had understood, probably even better than himself, why he felt as he did about the Masterson girl. In his mind he could see a child, hands tearing at her, striking, beating; stifling her terror as their bodies inserted themselves into her, shredding her virginity, plowing through it like a farmer with a runaway tractor gone amok. Until they killed her. No matter if she had lived, the scar would remain, seen by her withdrawal from the people around her, her wide-eyed fear at being touched, unable to love.

Schultz had cheated him though. Had gotten the last laugh.

He had wanted Schultz to show fear; wanted to see him plead for his life with his eyes; wanted him to know why he was going to die. Instead, an assisted suicide.

"Almost home." The words filtered through to his groggy brain. He sat up, disoriented. Listless. He opened the window to bring himself around, drag himself into the present. He saw the familiar streets.

"Sorry, you had to do all the driving. Geez, I must have slept a couple of hours."

"I like to drive, you know that. You needed the rest."

"I don't know why, but it took more out of me than I thought. I had to do it. I know the woman would have set me up. I know it. I should have left Schultz alone. He was dead already."

She turned onto their street. Leonard could hear her sigh of relief. He knew he would be hearing from Sal.

Leonard was late getting to his office. He and Mickey had lain awake the night before discussing the baby she wanted so badly. Despite Leonard's reservations.

"You're not worried about bringing a kid into our world?" Leonard asked. They lay on their backs, eyes staring at the darkness, conjuring up the life a child would have with them.

"We can give him a good home."

"Him?"

"A boy. I would worry too much about a girl. Worry about...."

"I know, babe." He took her hand which lay next to his. "I would worry too. I think a boy would be better also."

"How are we going to get this baby?"

He hadn't thought about that part of it, and now he had to wonder, although it wasn't a new thought. Hadn't he been kicking himself time and again for making the suggestion? How the hell was he going to make this happen? There would be too many questions if he went to a legitimate organization. Sure, he could call himself a consultant and supply tax records, and a bona fide history, but someone might start digging, want to know more, want references, work history— names, places, the source of his income—would possibly be prowling the neighborhood asking questions, wanting to know what they knew about him and Mickey. He knew there were lawyers who could expedite the process, but he didn't want to give them any leverage over him, nor did he want to pay out the kind of money they'd demand.

"I don't know," Leonard replied.

"I don't want Sal to help us with this."

"He could make it move faster with his connections. Then no one would know."

"Except Sal."

"Yes."

"He'd use the baby against us, Leonard. He'd find some reason to hold it over our heads."

Leonard knew she was right. When he finally drifted off to sleep he knew she was still awake making her plans for their son.

It had only taken Leonard a few minutes to reach the safe phone after he had left his office. The phone had begun ringing as soon as he entered his office, and once he had the location code word he hurried to the strip mall and waited, newspaper in hand. He looked around at the collection of stores-a laundromat, a drugstore, a convenience store, a liquor store, two vacant store fronts, and litter. The BMW looked out of place among the pickups, and battered station wagons and vans. He picked up the phone on the first ring. His tape recorder was set.

"Leonard?"

"Yeah, Sal." Leonard dispensed with the pleasantries. From the sound of his voice, when he verified who was on the line, he knew that Sal wasn't going to waste any time on the amenities.

"What's going on? How come you don't answer your phone?"

"I was late getting in this morning. Sorry."

"Sorry, my ass. Suppose this was an emergency? What the fuck am I supposed to do?"

"I had my own emergency to take care of," Leonard said, on

the verge of telling Sal to get off his back.

"Ya didn't answer my question. What's going on?" Louder, insistent, petulant.

"I don't follow you. What's going on where?"

"Like you're taking things into your own hands. Like all of a sudden you've decided to start making decisions outside the ... uhh scenario."

"Jesus, Sal what're you talking about. Clue me in will ya?"

"No one gave you orders, ya know, to whack Schultz.. Uhhh ... did I give you orders? Did I say, Leonard, go ahead do it on your own ... uh ... without checking with me? Did I say that?"

"No, but you wanted him offed. You said so. So what's the problem? He's history. You got no more problem with him."

"Ya don't understand. Ya shudda waited."

"Aw shit, Sal. So I chose the time and place. The last time it was set up for me the bimbo almost screwed it up. Who's to say she wouldn't try again? Who's to say she didn't have her own plan? You as much as told her what was going to happen when I asked you to get the information about the hospital for me."

"I keep telling you that was uhh ... an aberration. It wouldn't have happened again."

"You don't know that, and I sure as hell didn't know that. Only the broad knows what she was going to do."

"Trust me, kid. It wouldn't have happened like that."

"What the hell we arguing about? You're the boss. I know that. Aw fuck, maybe I'm getting too old for this shit."

"What're you tryin' to say? This isn't the first time you been talking like this. I don't think I like what I'm hearing."

"The broad's got me spooked. Like somewhere along the line there isn't any control, like maybe something's going on I don't know about, you know what I mean? I feel like I gotta watch my back more carefully now. You see what I'm getting at?"

"Back to the Sawyer dame again. Forget it, ya hear. It was a mistake."

"Maybe she didn't think it was a mistake. What she was going to do. Like you might be covering her ass."

"What d'ya mean by that?" Sal's voice had dropped a notch, came through the receiver softly tinged with warning. Leonard knew he was overstepping his bounds. Questioning Sal's judgment.

"No trust. Yeah, that's what it is. No trust. I gotta trust you when you give me a job to do. I can't keep asking if there's something I don't know. Like did the snatch think she could freelance her instructions, stretch them to fit the situation?"

"Ahh, Leonard, What the hell's got into you. Not getting enough pussy? You ain't been around lawyers like I have. They think their shit don't smell. They think they got all the answers. She ain't been in the real world. Our world. Trust me Leonard. I need you. You're my main man, you know that."

"I work alone. I haven't let you down have I?"

"You read the Albany papers yet?" Sal asked, moving away from the subject they had been discussing. "Made the front page. 'Key Witness Rubbed Out.' And underneath, 'Mob Hit Suspected.' The only lead they have is a description of the perp which could fit any number of guys. He's short, tall, thin, heavyset; wore horn-rimmed glasses and talked like he had mouthful of something. Like he was from Boston or was a Brit. All depended on who was being questioned."

"What did the deputy say?" Leonard opened his newspaper, found the article and his physical description. It didn't match. The only thing they got right were the horn-rimmed glasses. And the accent.

"They have him working with an artist. Trying to get a composite sketch of the killer."

"The deputy was trying to get a piece of ass with a girl he was talking to and make brownie points with the physician, me. I don't know what he could add. They shoulda canned him right after that. Anything with the woman?"

"The woman?"

"Your girlfriend, the lawyer." There was silence at the other end of the line. Leonard had meant it to lighten up the bad feelings which hung like a black cloud between them. He knew it was a mistake as soon as he said it.

"Be careful, Leonard," Sal said, not attempting to conceal the menace in his voice. "She's holding up her end. Has filed a complaint on behalf of the brothers, who incidentally are in jail waiting on an indictment for a hit-and-run murder and trying to ice this Masterson guy. They've fucked up everything. You coulda been caught Leonard."

"Goes with the turf. I felt a lot safer knowing the woman didn't have a part in this."

"Well, you took him out; I guess that's what counts; you didn't get caught."

"Funny thing...."

"What's that?"

"He didn't try to alert anyone. Didn't try to make a sound. He wanted to die, Sal. When I told him he was going to die, he smiled, just before I put him down. Like he was saying 'Fuck you!' Like he didn't give a shit about the girl or dying."

"What girl? What the hell are you talkin' about?"

"I did him for Miko and the kid. The one they raped. The three of them:Whelan, Sawyer and Schultz."

"Jee-zuz, you losin' it? That Masterson thing happened twenny years ago. Fuckin' Masterson's the one got this whole fuckin' thing started. Him and that ol' fuck Billings. The two of 'em. I told you that."

"Masterson was straight up, Sal." He didn't owe Masterson anything, but he did. He'd given him respect. Treated him right. Valued him for his ability. Judged him for himself. He didn't get much of that from anyone else. He felt good about the three hits. He'd taken them all out without knowing what they'd done to the girl until he read the confession. The last one, Al Schultz, was his choice. Relieved Masterson of the burden. Repaid him. He had no regrets except he'd remembered that Schultz wanted to die.

"He might have to go, Leonard. You might have to take him out."

Leonard didn't say anything. He couldn't. He should have expected it, and he guessed that he had been expecting it. Now he was where he never wanted to be. In the tunnels having to make a decision as to which branch to take, left or right. Leaving the tunnel behind him unsecured no matter which branch he took. Or go back. There was no going back with this.

"Leonard, you hear me? I said you might have to take him out."

"Yeah, I hear you. I don't get it."

"Sawyer's up to her ass in alligators tryin' to get a handle on things. She don't need any more hassles."

"Why now? Why not before all the trouble started?" Why not back then when I wouldn't have remembered? When the name wouldn't have meant anything? Might not have meant anything? But he knew he would have remembered and at the last minute. Would he have been able to pull the trigger? Would he be able to pull the trigger now?

"I didn't know what was going on at the time. Not until it got out of hand."

"When do I do the job?" Leonard asked.

"Gotta wait until things cool down. Won't be for a while, but he's gotta go."

"Mickey wants to adopt a kid," Leonard blurted out. There it was. He had to get it out. He held the phone away from his ear. Prepared for the explosion.

"What?" The sound burst through the phone. Incredulity. Disbelief. "She wantsa adopt a kid? Where the fuck did she come up with that idea?"

"She never talked about it. I mean, after all these years, she says something. Before that never a hint. I thought I ought to tell you."

"She know what that means? How're the two of you gonna raise a kid?"

"We could do it," Leonard said resentfully. "She was feeling down. You know how women get sometimes, and I found myself saying maybe, we ought to adopt a kid. Jee-zuz, you'd a thought I hit her or something because all of a sudden, and we're sitting in this nice restaurant …, all of a sudden the tears burst out. No sound. Just the tears running down her cheeks like there's no shut-off valve. They just keep coming and coming and her not making a sound. She left the table. You know what, Sal? Those fucking tears were tears of joy. So how do you figure? She was happy!"

"That's the reason for all the talk about retiring?"

"Yeah, that's part of it."

"You'd better talk it over with your cunt, Leonard. You know I need you. A kid will sidetrack you, take your mind off your job."

"I hated to bring it up," Leonard said, his anger barely under control at the way Sal referred to Mickey. Sal was baiting him. Looking for something.

"Say you did retire. What would ya do? You got no uhh … marketable skills. Your skill is killin', Leonard. You're a fuckin' gun for hire. You're my gun. I own you Leonard. I own your whore, the fuckin' two a ya. You understand?"

He wasn't going to be able to hold it back. He felt it building in his head, a red storm cloud of anger, rage. If Sal had been standing in front of him he would have killed him. Slow. Make him eat his words. Make him gag on his own blood. Control. He fought for it, but his anger was a car that hit a spot of black ice, spinning, uncontrollable. He hit a dry spot in the asphalt of his anger and held back. Not yet. Don't blow it!

"Okay, Sal. Maybe I'm in that mid-life crisis thing, you know?" He tried to lighten the tone of his voice, shunting the anger aside. Putting it on a siding to be rolled out later. He would have killed Sal. Control. The red rage had faded leaving behind a drumming in his head.

"You an' your ol' lady better do some serious thinking. Like what would she be doin' if I hadn't gotten her out of 'Nam? Her an' her whole fuckin' family who don't give a shit about her. She'd be a bent over, syphilitic, ex-whore, old before her time if she was able to survive."

"You don't have to bring that up, Sal, like we don't know what you did for us." Like we don't know how this hired gun saved your ass by zapping your enemies and how you contracted me out to others. How much did you hold back on those hits, Sal? How far would you have gotten if I had missed on any of those hits? "It's just thinking about the kid. You know how one thing leads to another."

"Don't go off half-cocked. Maybe we can work something out. I won't deny you an' Mickey that. But remember, you an' me got this thing. It's what brought ya all ya got. Ya understand? Ya understand what I'm sayin'?"

Leonard heard the click of the phone and then the buzzing. He reached into his pocket and turned off the tape recorder.

XV

Leonard remained at Madigan Army Hospital for several months after 'Nam. After the mine. Where he learned how to walk, eat, and breathe again and adjust to a missing toe and the missing end of his little finger on his right hand.

Sal stopped on his way through to Fort Dix where he intended to retire from the Army. He brought Leonard up to date on the situation in 'Nam as the US began withdrawing its forces.

"The whole situation's fucked up, kid. Everyone's scrambling. No one wants to be the last to leave."

Leonard, pale and hollow-eyed, scuffing about in issued slippers and ass-showing gown which left his legs only partially covered, sat in the patients' lounge listening to the big NCO talk, eyes shifting to anyone who approached them, his voice low, conspiratorial.

He heard how Ginger's brother had taken over the operation, but no one knew what would happen when Graves Registration pulled out, and they had no way of getting the drugs to the states. Sal's brother had been made, and because of Sal's operations on the west coast, looked for a great future in the family. Sal went on and on, and that's when Leonard had to ask about Mickey.

"Everything's gonna work out kid. Din't I tell ya that. When ya outta here?"

"Prob'ly in 'bout a month."

"No sweat. She should be already there waitin'. Din't I tell ya that was part of the deal?"

"Yeah, Sarge." He wanted to hear more about her, wanted to know if she was okay, but he didn't want to push it.

"We're gonna be a team, kid. Here, let me write down the

address. When ya get into Kennedy, ya can ask how to get into the City. Don't take no fuckin' taxi. It'll cost ya."

The week before he was discharged from the hospital and mustered out of the Army, Leonard received a telegram from Sal that said: 'She's here. Everything AOK.' Leonard qualified for a disability pension for not being able to eat all the things that he used to eat, and to breathe properly and for the loss of a toe and part of a finger. He missed not being able to eat the things he liked though; the other losses he could put up with. Leonard selected the Bronx as his home of discharge. The Army provided him with a ticket to JFK. Leonard collected the pay that had accumulated while he was in 'Nam and in the hospital, along with his mustering out pay and his discharge. He now had the most money he'd ever had in his life. He checked his duffel bag which contained his worldly possessions including a new knife with a scabbard that he could attach to his arm and boarded a flight to New York.

No one met him at JFK, but he didn't expect anyone. Leonard found his entry into New York challenging although he didn't push and shove his way off the plane nor rush to get to wherever he had to go in the Bronx. One reason was that his duffel bag was too heavy. He thought that once he left the terminal he would be on the streets of New York. Actually he was on Long Island but the airport seemed like a suburb of something, and so he dragged and carried his duffel bag until he realized that he was hungry and bought a Nathan's Famous hot dog and a Coke and watched the baggage-laden people, scurrying down the long corridors. He stopped at a gift shop and paid too much for a sterling silver bracelet with the Statue of Liberty and Empire State Building charms on it for Mickey. He had it wrapped and went into a cubicle in the men's room and deposited it in his duffel bag. He took out his knife in the thin-skinned scabbard and strapped it to his arm. Over his shirtsleeve. So that he could reach it easier.

He found an information desk and asked one of the women behind the counter how to get to the Bronx. Leonard—short, pale-faced, cap askew and a row of military ribbons pinned like an

afterthought over his left breast pocket—saw her face change from
a look of annoyance to one of compassion. She took the time to
explain to him what he should do and directed him to the shuttle
bus, telling him how frequently it ran and cautioning him about
holding on to his wallet whereupon Leonard took it from his back
pocket and put it inside his blouse beneath his ribbons. She also
warned him about the panhandlers. He thanked her and smiled
when she smiled.

Arriving at the terminal, Leonard again asked for directions
showing the information clerk the address in the Bronx, but ending up more confused. Shouldering his duffel bag, he saw a cop
standing outside the entrance and walked over to him. He dropped
his duffel bag onto the pavement.

"Say officer, could you tell me how to get to the Bronx and
how much it costs?" The cop's eyes gave him a once-over, but returned to the ribbons on his chest.

"'Nam?"

"Yessir. Just got back. Never been here before."

"See you got the CIB and the Purple Heart."

"Yessir."

"Was in Korea, myself. 187th Airborne."

"Yessir."

"C'mon, we'll see if we can't get you home a little faster."

Leonard followed him over to a taxi stand. The cop slapped a
meaty hand on the roof of the cab and leaned down and looked at
the driver.

"My ol' Army buddy here wants to go to the Bronx. I told
him about what it costs if you take the most direct route. I told
him to give me a call at the precinct if you charge him much more
than that." The cop wrote down the cab number and asked and
received the driver's name.

"Get in," the cabbie said.

"Thanks, officer." Leonard said to the back of the cop who
returned to his former position. Leonard wrestled his duffel bag
onto the rear seat and climbed in after it. He settled back and

listened to the cabbie's monologue about driving in the city—the traffic, the potholes, the pedestrians and then about the Mets, about the City administration, about the cabbies who couldn't speak English and didn't know fuck about the City, and the other drivers who were out there to keep him from making a living. Leonard hadn't called the apartment because he didn't have a phone number. Didn't know if she had a phone. Would she be home? Did she still feel the same way about him?

"This is it, soldier," the cabbie said, breaking through his thoughts. "Watch your ass, kid. This is a bad neighborhood." Leonard paid the driver and pulled his duffel bag onto the curb. He scoped the street, his duffel bag at his feet beside a mound of trash and dented garbage cans. He glanced up at the three-story, crumbling brick building that looked like it had been dragged kicking and screaming from the past into the present with only hard luck and hard wear in between.

Two blacks and a Hispanic slouched on the stairs leading up to the scarred door of the entrance. Radios or TVs mixed with children crying, shouting, laughing, screaming and women cursing at men swearing—the only life in this non-life of poverty and despondency and surrender.

"Hey man, you, peckerwood! You's in da Ah-my?" A voice shouted at him.

Leonard didn't say anything, still looking up at the facade of the building. He wondered if she could feel him down below on the sidewalk, know that he was home?

"Hey whitey, you din't hear me talkin' to yas?"

A tall, thin, black youth sauntered towards him, his hair, a black burr with a yellow plastic comb rising out of it. An oversized Raiders jacket hung loosely around his spare frame.

"I hear you, man." Leonard said, shifting his weight slightly so that he was standing less on the edge of the sidewalk.

"Why you ain' sayin' nuffin when I ax you a question?"

Leonard watched the other two teenagers sit down on the steps, stretch their legs out to get comfortable while they watched the small drama unfold. Movement stopped on the neighboring steps. One of the teenagers, laughing said, "Ax 'im how many those kongs he kilt." That drew laughter from the other two.

"Yea-hh, how many a those kongs you kilt, sojer?" The youth bent forward, hands on his hips.

Leonard saw a corner of a curtain pull back and a wizened black face appear and stare down at him. He let go of his duffel bag making certain that it wouldn't fall into the gutter. The curtain dropped back into place.

"I live here, man. I don't want no hassel."

"What hassel? The man says we is hasseling 'im. Is we hasseling 'im?" The two teenagers made some derisive comments. "Who the fuck is you to say, we's hasselin' you? We's jus' axin' you some questions. Fren'ly like. You tryin' to start some honky shit, man?" He moved toward Leonard.

"Look man, I want no problems, ya hear?" Leonard spread his hands out, palms facing the black youth.

"Man, you's the pro'lem," the youth said as he stepped into Leonard, their bodies not quite touching, spraying Leonard with spittle. "You's one a those whities who ...."

Leonard suddenly stepped into the youth and grasping him by the belt, shoved the blade up under his chin. The boy's body jerked. He froze in place. His mouth hung open.

"You crazy, man," he squealed bringing the other two to their feet.

"They move, you get cut," He brought another squeal out of the teenager as he nicked him with the point of the blade.

"Hey, bros, cool it, unnerstan'? Mothafucka's crazy," the black said, wide-eyed, his fear showing, a lip-wiping swab of his tongue, sweat popping out across his forehead. He put a hand up under his chin. Looked at the stain on his fingers.

"This prob'ly won't mean shit to you asshole, but start lookin' over your shoulder 'cause if I'm hasseled by anyone, you're my man. You're the one I come lookin' for." He released the kid, who shifted his shoulders, threw his chin up and strutted away, waving his friends to follow him.

"That man, he crazy. Crazy!" Certain that he was out of reach, he turned and pointing his finger at Leonard, snarled. "You's dead meat, mothafucka." And with that he turned and juttered and jived away, the three of them shouldering other pedestrians aside.

The apartment was on the third floor at the back of the building. Leonard set his duffel bag down when he reached the third floor landing. He'd bluffed them. He'd barely made it up the steps. He wasn't breathing. He was wheezing, overworking the one lung that was left. When he caught his breath, he dragged the duffel bag by the shoulder strap along the hall to her door. He knocked softly, unthreateningly, more of a tap with the joint of his index finger locked in place with his thumb. Not hard or loud enough to cause her alarm.

The dead bolts clicked back, and the chains clattered against the door as she dropped them until the next to last chain. She opened the door a crack, one eye looking over the last chain that remained. Eye suspicious; it widened, and he heard her sob as the eye disappeared, and the last chain was removed. She threw the door open and leaped across the threshold into his arms. They held each other wordlessly, confirming body feel, corporeal presence, wait-ending reality. Her heart was beating wildly, he could feel it through the rough texture of his can't-wait-to-be-shed uniform. Her face was wet with tears that seeped between their cheeks. He lifted her back inside the door, his face still pressed to hers, reached down with one hand, pulled his duffel bag in and kicked the door shut with the back of his foot, holding her off her feet with his one arm. He heard dead bolts sliding into place and a chain locked into its receptacle. Her hand was on the back of his head, her fingers combed through his hair, his cap at his feet, while she validated his presence. Putting her down he stepped back, held her at arms length so that he could see all of her. The tears streamed down her face. He took out his handkerchief and wiped her cheeks. Her lips trembled. She took his handkerchief and blew her nose. He took her in his arms again.

"Sal say you come home. Not say when. I am hap-py," she said and burst out crying, the tears now accompanied by wet sounds and shoulders shuddering.

She seemed even more childlike with her tears like drops of clear crystal on her eyelashes and lodged in the corners of her eyes.

"I've missed you," he said, unable to explain the sickness he felt when he didn't hear from her, the terrible loneliness of knowing that she was somewhere in the World, and he couldn't see or be with her. He kissed her open mouth, tasting the salt of her tears on her lips. Moments later, she was leading him around their furnished apartment, the furniture once worn and stained and scratched and torn from previous tenants, which she had cleaned and patched and mended or covered. He could see where she must have worked a long time to remove a stain from the pale blue wall-to-wall carpet in the living room because it not only was lighter than the rest of the carpet but had no color at all. She had bought flowers and plants which offset the sparseness and general seediness of the rooms. Vegetable tins with incipient sprouts and leaves lined the window sill in the kitchen. She had managed to build a barricade against the smells that had leached through the hallway from drunks urinating against the walls or on the stairs or kids getting sick, and the odors of cooking and living which had followed him into the room when they stood in the doorway, and once in the room and isolated from the hall, disappeared against the barrier of cleanliness she had erected. The rooms smelled clean from detergents and fresh paint.

"I'll bet you got the cleanest windows in the Bronx," he said as they stood, arms around each other, staring at the bland wall of the building across the alley. He told her how nice the apartment was, and she laughed happily, hugging him, and he vowed to himself that he would some day take her out of there, one way or the other.

Later, after eating and talking and letting the spaces when

they had nothing to say, remain unfilled because they had not developed enough of a history together to feed those empty slots with small talk or any kind of talk beyond saying over and over how much they missed each other, she would tell him what it was like being alone. Her words came out slowly as she thought out each sentence before she spoke, and her hand covered her mouth when she thought she had made a mistake and giggled nervously looking at him. He encouraged her to talk, warm with the sound of her voice, content to sit on the plastic-padded metal chair in the kitchen with its faded linoleum where feet over the years had worn several paths, watching her eyes and her mouth as the words flowed in cadence with the fluttering of her hands as she spoke.

Later, when he had to say something because she asked, he talked about his flight home and the confusion he experienced at the airports and the people who helped him find his way to her and how he never expected the cop to be so helpful. He didn't talk about his wounds and the hospitals nor what it was like. Or that he never expected to see her again. Only that he was glad to be with her. And he didn't talk about 'Nam except when he woke, later, in the darkness, with what he still carried in his head, unable to let it go until it crept up on him during the night when he was most vulnerable. He didn't tell her about the incident on the street when he first arrived at their new home.

She drew a tub of hot water and helped him undress. He put his uniform with its ribbons askew and underwear and socks in a trash bag, which he would throw out the next day. She gasped when he lifted his newly issued OD colored T-shirt, the smell of newness mixed with his sweat, over his head and saw the mauvine lines crisscrossing his stomach down to his groin and when he took off his pants, resumed their tracking on one thigh. She traced the scars with her fingers as though touching a piece of rare china, tears forming in her eyes. She ran her fingers over the smooth, still reddened joint where he had lost part of a finger. Later, she would trace the the scars again with her lips and tongue, and he would stroke her head, feeling the texture of her hair like a tailor with a bolt of fine cloth. They climbed into the small tub together, her legs over his, on each side of his body, their genitals touching. She leaned into him, soaping him down and scrubbing him with her long nails telling him he was too thin but saying, as she stroked his erection that she was glad that it hadn't lost any weight.

Mickey had pulled the sheets down on the bed. They were clean and fresh, and he wondered if she ever used the bed, or waited for him so they could use it together. She stayed behind in the bathroom while he lay in bed, aching for this woman whom he had thought he'd lost and was with again. When she came out, her dark red lips parted in a smile, her eyes lightly shadowed, no longer a look of innocence on her face, she crawled under the sheets and laughed joyfully as his body rode hers. When he lay back spent, she took his hand and placed it between her legs, and he told her again about the blacks he had wasted for her. Soon, she was sighing with pleasure.

Later, they sat at the narrow, Formica-topped table in the kitchen, Leonard in clean OD shorts and T-shirt, barefoot, and Mickey in a flannel robe that dragged on the floor, her tiny feet in a pair of shower clogs. She had made tea and she apologized for not having a meal ready for him. They ate cheese and crackers, and Leonard said they would go out for supper. She told him that she only went out to shop at a local grocery.

"Sal been around?"

"No. Ginger help me get settled. Buy food. Cleaning stuff. I don't see her no more."

"They give you money ?"

"Man comes, same time every month. Put money under door." She told him how much she was given, and added happily that she had saved enough to buy a small black-and-white TV with a 13" screen. She led him into the other room and showed him how it worked. He looked at it and was proud of her because she was so elated that she had saved enough to buy it. And he was ashamed because he had not been able to send her any money and had to depend on others. She turned it on and ran through the channels until some of the channels became fuzzy and only the voices came out clear, or there was no sound at all, only static and blurred white lines. She said that Ginger had given her a radio to listen to. She used them both to learn English. Mickey pointed to their phone and wrote the number on a piece of paper which he folded and put in his wallet. She said the phone was in his name.

Mickey showed him around the neighborhood during the next few days, and they discussed what they had to do since Sal would not be sending any more money now that Leonard was home. They would have to get jobs. They were going to have to assimilate themselves into the life around them without attracting attention. For Mickey that meant learning to speak flawless English. For him, it meant getting an education and not talking like a bum.

They must have been tracking him for some time, from doorways, alleys, inside storefronts. Had seen him and Mickey leaving each day for their jobs in a fast food restaurant, coming home together, rarely going out at night. No one bothered Mickey when she went out alone. Rumor had it that she was protected. Everyone saw the car pull up once a month and the big guy in the leather jacket walk in and minutes later, come panting down the stairs from the third floor. So they must have been waiting.

When it happened, when they did make their move, Leonard knew he had become careless. He had gone out to the local grocery for ice cream. Sometimes that was all he could eat or wanted to eat because that was all his stomach would hold. Mickey locked the 'gates' when he went out the door and down the stairs and knew the approximate time when he would return. Leonard left the store that evening, ice cream in hand, lost in thought, thinking about how much it would take to move Mickey out of this neighborhood, but unable to think beyond his next paycheck. Unwilling to tap their reserve or the money in the bank. Anxious for Sal to tell him what he wanted, fuming at the lack of communication.

He wasn't ready for them. The scuffle of their feet didn't register.

They grabbed him from behind just as he passed the alley outside his apartment building. One on each arm. The tall thin black directing them back into the alley, out of sight. They ran him in, feet dragging, unable to kick out. He knew it was the two spades and the spic because it wasn't enough that they had caught him, had his arms pinned back, but had to rub it in; had to let him know that *they* were doing it to him, losing that fraction of a second to gloat between bashing him, spraying his face with a saliva of hate until he sagged, unable to move his legs. They dropped him, bleeding, semi-conscious, onto the garbage-strewn pavement wondering who would take care of Mickey. They took up with steel pipes what they'd started with their fists, losing some power because in their eagerness for him to know his assailants they banged each other's pipes or struck the ground to avoid hitting each other; taking their time, certain that he would never be in a position to revenge himself on them. He crossed his arms over his face, rolling from side to side, unable to kick or use his legs, but making himself a difficult target; peering between his forearms through swollen eyes as the pipes tattooed his arms and body, his legs, a rhythmic pounding, conjuncted with a cacophony of curses, taunts, and other revilements reflecting their hatred. He covered his head with his arms when he could no longer hold them up, the blows dancing around his skull, against his shoulders until his attackers grew tired and took a moment to heap more invective on him. Then they began kicking him with their feet which was less severe because they were wearing soft Adidas or Converse shoes and not heavy, steel-toed work boots. But the law of averages was moving in Leonard's favor. They had waited too long; hadn't finished the job cleanly; had become emotionally involved. A shout echoed against the walls in the alley. The tall, thin black stopped. Leonard knew it would be him because he had been disrespected on the street in front of friends and people who had feared him, and he had lost his dominance over them. He had to be the one to thrust the knife into him and wipe away being dissed, wipe away the white disrespect. Leonard felt it cut through the fabric of his

clothes and the wall of his stomach and come to a stop where it
hung up between his ribs, forcing his assassin to struggle to pull
out the blade and in completing the act was caught in the white,
dark-penetrating column of light probing forward, backwards and
sideways into the alley. Bouncing off the tired brick walls and the
littered asphalt. Coming to rest on the alley drama. Doors slamming. Pipes clanking to the ground. Heavy footsteps slapping
against the pavement toward him—footsteps, slipping, sliding,
stumbling away from him.

Hands rolling him over on his back.

"Better call the meat wagon, this guy looks bad." A hand against
the side of his neck checking his pulse. Footsteps moving away.
Returning. A hand tugging at his wallet. Voices, distant, hollow,
talking through a tube. Not with it. Gut hurts. Burning. Won't
ask. God. Never asked before; not a beggar … Oh, Mickey…

"It's on the way. You check the kid out?"

"Set of military orders. Just a second. Got a set of dogtags in
his back pocket. Taped up. Ex-GI . Welcome home, hero."

"You make the perps?"

"Brothers. Probably a drug deal gone bad."

"Guy prob'ly brought the habit back with 'im."

Leonard lost consciousness.

He struggled up through the mind-numbing, pain-diminish-
ing haze of the sedation. He'd been through it before; knew that
he would live; hadn't begged to live; knew he was in a hospital.
Even before he opened his eyes; knew what he'd see; and what
he'd soon feel when he explored the extent of his ability to move.

"How'd you find me?" Leonard asked, reaching out his left
hand with its plaster cast, not yet introduced to the full extent of
his pain because the pain hid behind the sedation, waiting.

Mickey sat close to his bed, reading a book, in English. Relief
lit up her face as it moved from concentration to puzzlement to
elation and to tears at the sound of his voice. She was pale and her
eyes were swollen and raw-rimmed with dark pouches under them.

Her head dropped forward onto his hand, her hair spilling across the white sheet.

"I worry. You no come home." Her voice muffled from talking into his hand. "Police call me," she said, raising her head, her eyes awash, her hair lifted up from the sheet to around her face leaving behind gray spots on the white from her tears. The slender fingers of her free hand pushed the hair back from her face. She wore the bracelets he'd given her months before. "They find number you write for phone. Tell me where you are. You be okay, policeman say."

"How long have I been here?"

"Two- three day. They say ver' bad. No one tell me nothin'. I ask. Nice nurse tell me you be okay. She say you tough guy."

"Not my time yet, babe," he said, smiling and squeezing her hand with his fingers. "You call Sarge?"

"No. You say, no call Sarge for any reason. When I find you, I wait."

"Mmm, you did right." He drifted off, holding what he could of her hand with the tips of his fingers as if holding onto the drifting log of his life.

Mickey arrived at the start of visiting hours and stayed with him until they ended. When he woke up at various times, Leonard worried about her traveling back and forth, especially returning home at night and insisted she take a cab. He knew she had money because they had hidden what he had brought with him when he was discharged. They had agreed to use it for a rainy day. Well, they were in a flash flood now. One day, when she came in, her face drawn and sad, she said they had lost their jobs. He told her if they were careful they could make the reserve last. He reminded her that they still had the bank account they could fall back on. He worried about how long they would keep him in the hospital. He worried about her. He never worried about himself. What had happened had happened. Life was a matter of survival of the fittest, not necessarily the smartest or the strongest, but for those who could adjust to a dog-eat-dog world, aware that life played no favorites. When your time was up, that's all there was. Or would be. Accept it. That's why they sold insurance policies, wasn't it? They bet you were going to be around a long time before they had to pay out. And because they knew you might be worried about leaving someone behind. Leonard's life had been spared. Twice now. He hadn't asked for it. Hadn't begged for it. Hadn't made promises to an unknown concept, which he knew or at least expected he couldn't or wouldn't keep. He didn't want any favors. Besides, he hadn't done anything with his life which would give him the right to ask. But he was glad he was alive.

Sal moved them out of the apartment to a slightly better neighborhood. Ginger had made the arrangements. Leonard hadn't seen Sarge since he'd arrived in the Bronx. He realized that he was now an employee, a tool to be used by Sal when he was needed. Ginger and Mickey sometimes met in the oriental section or Little Saigon as they called it, where they would be inconspicuous and an occidental would stand out like a Black in a Wasp congregation.

When the cast came off Leonard's arm, he made his decision. He'd received no instructions from Sal. Nor did he ask for any. He returned to his old neighborhood. No one paid any attention to him because they saw only a bundle of rags sitting in a doorway or shuffling along the street peering into gutters, turning over the trash in the sidewalk waste receptacles, trudging through alleys lifting the lids of the garbage cans, looking back over his shoulder, concealing whatever he took out of them in the folds of his clothes. He stepped into the gutter when brash and loud teenagers swaggered along the street. He didn't look at them. Gave no reaction when one reached out and shoved or pushed him. Shut out the curses they heaped on him. At night, he huddled in doorways, clutching a brown bag twisted around the neck of a bottle in two begrimed hands. He never begged and always found a bit of loose change in his pocket to buy a box of milk and a hard roll. Leonard became part of the scenery. Eventually, he located the teenagers, followed them. They became accustomed to seeing him like they saw the garbage cans in the alley or piled on the curb, like the dog shit smeared across the crumbling, gray sidewalks, or the smashed bottles at the base of a wall or the graffiti sprayed on the face of buildings like war paint—if they saw him at all.

While Leonard was still in the hospital, the police had sent a detective to question him. His stabbing had aroused some interest in the local press because he had been wounded in Vietnam. He achieved momentary celebrity as a war hero and was just as quickly forgotten when a reporter found that Leonard appeared almost inarticulate and wouldn't take a stand about the US position on Vietnam. The detective kept using the term perps for perpetrators, which confused Leonard at first, and was satisfied that the stabbing was not connected with drugs or gangs, but was a random stabbing. Leonard couldn't describe his assailants; the detective thanked Leonard for his time and left. He didn't leave a forwarding address with the police when he moved. They put the telephone in Mickey's Vietnamese name when they began living in their new apartment.

Two months after he left the hospital, Leonard wasted the tall, thin, black teenager. He took him out at one-thirty on a Saturday morning as the brother was walking home, a boom box on his shoulder, next to his ear; the music shattering the otherwise quiet street. One block from his house. Almost on his doorstep.

"Remember me, asshole?"

The brother stopped, annoyance wrinkled his forehead like a slept-on quilt, his eyes glazed from a 'one for the road' pop.

"What chu say?" he asked the small ragged figure who had materialized before the white-showing, widened eyes of the youth. Leonard thrust the gun into the teenager's stomach as he pulled himself against the black with his other hand; firing so quickly that the muffled explosions were one drawn out burst. The radio crashed to the sidewalk.

"Ya kilt me, man," the boy groaned, a look of defeat on his face as his eyeballs turned up into his head, and he crumpled to the sidewalk. Leonard turned off the radio. He glanced up and down the street and stepped back into the alley. No one appeared to have heard the weapon firing, but then, they'd heard such things before. Better to leave well enough alone. Not get involved.

He took out the other two in the following week. Same way. But it took longer. Because they stuck together like Siamese twins. Leonard, the small 'homeless' man, disappeared from the neighborhood soon after. He wondered if anyone noticed. Leonard didn't bother to read the papers. It might have been a line or two. He didn't tell Sal about the hits.

XVI

A week after Leonard wasted the three teenagers, Sal called and suggested that they meet at a nearby McDonald's. Leonard waited beside the entrance. Sal pulled up in a beige Buick. Leonard srolled over to meet the big man. The Hmongs jumped out of the car ahead of Sal and casually walked in different directions, surveying the area. Leonard recognized them from Saigon, but they didn't speak to him. Sal looked the same. Still tan and fit. He threw an arm around Leonard's shoulder and guided him into the restaurant. He wore a knee length, black leather coat and except to push open the door, didn't take his other hand out of his pocket until they were inside. His eyes swiveled back and forth, never resting, like he was expecting to see someone he knew or like a politician honing in on the next hand to shake. Two of the three Hmongs followed them inside. One remained with the car. The Hmongs went to the counter, one at a time, ordered sodas. One of them took a soda out to the man at the car. They took seats facing the window.

"Jeez, you're looking great kid," Sal said. He paid for their two frozen yogurts and took them on a tray to a booth by the window.

Leonard still hadn't lost his hospital pallor. He was just regaining strength in his left arm. The bruises had healed, and he was moving easily without any aches or pain.

"Ya should've called me. Sorry, I couldn't get up to see ya when ya was in the hospital, but you ...uhh ... know, I don't want anyone to ... uhh ... connect us, ya know what I mean? Couple a spades, huh? ..." Before Leonard could respond, Sal went on to discuss how the brothers were taking over the neighborhoods and how he could see their militancy in 'Nam. "I read about the killings of the three spooks in the papers. Cops leaned on some of our people trying to tie it in to a drug deal. Funny no one knew anything about it. I figured it was you 'cause I read about how ya got mugged. It was your style to take 'em out. I'm not gonna ask you where ya got the piece, that's your business. Ya could have fucked things up, kid. If ya got killed or caught. G'dammit, I got a lot of bucks invested in you an' you can't be goin'... What if I needed ya? You got a responsibility to me. You an' your woman both. You owe me, ya unnerstan'? I didn't bring her an' her whole fuckin' family out an' set you up just so's you could run off..." A crimson flush broke through his tan. Sal spoke softly, punching out his words until Leonard interrupted.

"They cut me bad, Sal." Leonard said, quietly leaning across the table their faces only inches apart. "I tol' 'em before about hasselin' me. I din't need that shit from those teenage dirtbags, ya know what I mean? Besides, I couldn't a done anythin' for you when I was laid up. What could I do then?"

"The thing is, I got a job for you, an' when ya was in the hospital ya weren't any good to me. Ya weren't worth shit to me. You understand? Not worth shit. An' then you disappear for a couple a months. Mickey says she didn't know where ya were. No one knew where ya were. An' I got uhh ... this contract that has to be filled. I took it because I was countin' on you to be available. An here, I read, you're in the hospital, not good for shit, an' then ya take off without lettin' anyone know where ya were. Times runnin' out now. I got pressure on me, right from the man himself. Maybe I pull this thing off, I get more opportunity, a bigger slice of the action. You benefit too, kid. But ya gotta be ready. Like I gotta know even when you take a shit ... like you're gonna be indisposed. I gotta know that."

"You want total control."

"Ya got that right."

"They thought they killed me, Sal. I gave 'em a split second before I wasted them so they'd know I kept my word. The first one seemed to know it was gonna end like it did. It was on his face. He

knew there wasn't a fuckin' thing he could do about it. The other
two was surprised it was happenin' to them ... like they wasn't
accountable ... like they had this right."

"Okay, it's done. I'm not sayin' what you done wasn't right, I
mean, they did, like ya say, cut ya pretty bad. An' we know bein'
juveniles they won't serve no hard time. While you got the problem of havin' your gut opened. Nah, what cha done was right, ya
unnerstan', but I got people dependin' on me to get things done
for them. It's not like 'Nam where I had my own setup. This next
transaction'll give me a push up. I gotta produce; show 'em I'm
the guy who can deliver."

"So what do you want me to do?"

"Patience, kid, I'm gettin' to it." He took out a cigarette from
a crumpled pack inside his coat and lit it, sending a cloud of smoke
out of the corner of his mouth while he threw a glance over both
shoulders. "I volunteered to ... ya remember what we said in the
Army, never volunteer for nothin' 'cause ya knew it would be a shit
detail whether it was in garrison or in the field. Well, it's the same
in the real world. Ya volunteer an' ya know you're gonna catch
shit."

Leonard began to lose interest. He'd finished his dish of yogurt and wiped his mouth with a napkin. The Hmongs hadn't
changed position except to take sips of their sodas. They were carrying. Leonard knew that, but the anoraks with a Bronx cement
company inscribed on the back hid their weapons.

"You gonna eat that ice cream?" Leonard asked. Sal pushed
the untouched plastic cup to him, and he began eating the yogurt.

"Listen up, Leonard." Sal lowered his voice, his eyes moving
again like a direction finder. "We got this Borough DA up for
reelection. He took on a couple of new assistants because of the
rumbles about corruption, and fixin' cases an' pledged to clean
house, attack organized crime and clean up the judicial system.
All the usual bullshit. One of these new ADAs began making noises
to the press about how his boss is draggin' his feet on pushing for

indictments on a couple of bent judges. The opposition party began sucking up to this guy. Maybe thinking of running him against our man. This could cause problems for the family. They got a lot of money invested in our guy."

"So what d'ya want me to do?"

"We want ... I want cha to take this guy out. If we don't, then it means big trouble for all of us. If he keeps it up, he's gonna have the Feds breathin' down our necks. Shit, he might even get elected."

"A DA is pretty important, ain't he?"

"Yeah, pretty important. We just don't want this guy to get any more important. We wanna get the message out, ya know what I mean? That we got reach even if they ain't sure we did it."

"I ain't done nothin' like this before, Sal."

"I know, kid. But if we just take him out on the street, the DA will have to do somethin' about it. So it's gotta seem like ... uhhh ... an accident. Like it can happen to anyone, anywhere."

Sal went on to explain where the victim lived in the 'burbs.' He had staged a couple of burglaries and break-ins in adjoining neighborhoods as a cover. They didn't want cops crawling all over the target area. The neighborhood the ADA lived in was quite affluent and had paid security patrolling by vehicle. Sal told him the address and the best way to get there.

"Mickey drives, right?"

"Yeah, Ginger taught her and helped her get her license. She's pretty good. We appreciate the car you gave us. 'Course it's parked inna garage most a the time."

"Thank the asshole who left his keys in it. It's in good condition; didn't look like much when we got it, but with the dings out of the fenders, a paint job as well as new papers.... What can I say, it's a car. You got a week to do the job. But ya can't make no stupid-ass mistakes. Here's his daily schedule, time he leaves his nest, work hours, and when he comes home. There's also a couple of pictures so you'll recognize the guy. We know he's the guest speaker at the local K of C annual banquet. That's firm. You may have to improvise, but we gotta get to this guy, ya unnerstan'?" He slid an envelope across to Leonard. Leonard dropped it inside his shirt.

"He got bodyguards?"

"Come on, kid, this ain't 'Nam."

Leonard didn't ask why Sal had his Hmongs. Instead he asked if he was going to be paid for the hit.

"Big bucks. If you get 'im."

"Suppose I get caught?"

"You do the time. No help here. Don't get caught. You keep your mouth shut an' we'll do all we can to help Mickey, other-wise…. But there's a limit. Five thou to do the hit. Part in cash, the rest will be an insurance check to your account. You keepin' up your savin's account?"

"Sure Sal, I remember what cha said about savin' for my old age." He didn't mention having to touch his reserves because they lost their jobs.

"Your new place okay?"

"Yeah, it's fine."

"You have to make it look like a random robbery when you take him out, ya unnerstan? Incidentally, he's a bachelor; lives alone, no wife, no kids. An' no fuckin' dogs. I'm countin' on ya not to fuck this up." Sal slid out of the booth, nodded to the Hmongs and left with a wave of his hand. Leonard drank the melted yogurt from the cup, wiped his mouth with his napkin, picked up their tray and emptied it into the trash receptacle. On his way home, he stopped at an appliance store and bought a tape recorder and batteries. The clerk showed him how it worked.

Mickey picked her way through the traffic. Leonard acted as the navigator

"Someday, babe we'll have a house like these folks. It may take a while, but we'll get there." Leonard couldn't see that far ahead, but put it on his wish list.

Mickey nodded, concentrating on driving, her eyes glued to the traffic in front of her. They drove past the mark's two-story

brick house with a patch of lawn cover and a tiled sidewalk leading
up to the front door. The next evening they drove back to the
'burbs' where Mickey let him out, several blocks from the house.
He slid into the alley behind the ADA's house and concealed himself along a line of bushes for a couple of hours trying to get a make
on the security patrols. The house itself must have been on light
timers because the ADA hadn't arrived home yet and lights were
going on in different parts of the house. Except for a stray dog that
sniffed and growled at him and might have pissed on him if he
hadn't prodded it with his knife and sent it yelping away, he remained undetected. A neighbor putting out his trash cans stood
within two feet of his position. Leonard held his breath and didn't
move until the man left.

The night of the banquet, Mickey, again, dropped him several
blocks from his quarry's house. Leonard hurried under the canopy
of maples, his movement shielded by the shadows and cars parked
along the street. He slowed whenever he approached anyone walking and pleasantly greeted them. He didn't see their surprised
stares as they turned and looked at him. He turned into the alley
behind the ADA's house and moved to his pre-selected position
just as a pair of headlights sent twin cones of light against the line
of garages at the entrance of the alleyway, settled on the concrete
passageway and slowly moved toward him. A third beam shot out
from the side of the windshield on the driver's side of the car and
thrust and probed the darkness and bushes in the backyards behind the houses. Leonard lay still, not looking up at the lights
which passed over him and came to a halt as the car stopped. He
turned his head slowly. The spotlight made a careful inspection of
the yard behind the ADA's house and moved on.

Leonard lay prone against the fence, under privet bushes whose
branches lazily swept against the top of his head as he prepared
himself for a long wait. He hadn't wanted to take a chance on the
ADA arriving home early. He lay with his head on his arms. The
hard scabbard of his knife pressed into his other arm with the
weight of his head. He didn't try to push what he had to do from

his mind. He had to think about it, wanted to think about it, wanted to create his own scenario, place the victim and himself in the context of what was about to take place; he moved the figures across the stage of his thoughts, the one character, a photograph, entering his house, pulling his world in and around himself, safe, unaware of...? While the other character, a smudge, which followed the ADA about the room like a shadow waiting to strike. Leonard didn't think about right or wrong, had no problem with what he was about to do. Would not let it float up later to chew away at his thoughts because he had taken a human life. What would worry him, nag him, would be if he didn't do the job clean. Left the victim with pain and alive. People should expect to die. They knew they were going to die. Even knew that they wouldn't or couldn't choose the time. Death was always a surprise. Even when it was expected.

The garage door opening jarred him awake. The car swung wide; the beam of headlights swept over him as it made the turn into the garage. Leonard had a view of garden tools: rake, hoe, spade, limb saw, rope neatly coiled, ladder, evenly spaced along the wall. And on one side of the garage a polished, gleaming yellow Corvette. The ADA was driving an official vehicle. Leonard saw that from the license plate. The blast of light against the far wall went out and in the light from the ceiling, and as the garage door began closing and before it shut off his view, Leonard saw that someone else was in the car, and they were embracing.

Sal hadn't said there would be two people. Leonard glided across the alley and pressed himself against the wall of the garage. Car doors slammed. Voices. Laughter. Unsuspecting laughter. The side door to the garage opened and closed. Sensor lights flooded the space between the house and the garage as the two men walked toward the house, their voices—murmurs and suppressed sniggers as they lurched, their arms around each other, to the back door. Sal hadn't mentioned the sensor lights either. Leonard moved, eyes on the two men, preparing himself for even a casual glance from one of them, preparing to freeze in place so as not to disturb their peripheral view, crouching along the side of the yard, pressing himself into the bushes that hid him from the neighbors on either side, closing the gap between the two men as the screen door of the porch rattled shut, and they entered the kitchen.

The flood lights went out as Leonard crawled beneath a line of interlocking branches of yews planted along the back of the house. Buried himself in the evergreen scent. He waited until his night vision returned. For what? He couldn't take out the two of them. He'd have to wait until morning. What happens if the two of them leave together? What would be the possibility that the ADA was armed? If he takes the ADA out in the garage, that would leave the other one in the house. Would he check to see why the ADA hadn't driven away? If he did check, that meant Leonard would have to take him out when he entered the garage before he recovered from the shock of seeing his friend sprawled out—dead. Too much like a hit, if he didn't get caught. If they left together, forget it. No way he could do the contract. He could abort now or play it by ear. He would be ready for a third option if it materialized. He stopped thinking about the things he couldn't control. He'd wait until morning. He pulled the windbreaker over his head and nestled into the soft ground. If he wasn't at the rendezvous at 1a.m. Mickey was to drive past and return the next morning, after the ADA normally went to work and wait at a Dunkin' Donuts which was located several blocks from the drop-off point. When he walked by she was to circle the block and pick him up. She would worry. He hoped she would be able to sleep.

The sun rose over the garage but didn't penetrate the yew branches. He was stiff. He straightened his legs one at a time, slowly, so as not to disturb the bushes. He shook his arms to restore the circulation. He flexed his fingers until they shed their stiffness. Voices filtered out from the kitchen. A radio voiced the news. The smell of brewing coffee drifted from the kitchen. He waited.

The kitchen door opened and footsteps creaked across the porch overhead. The screen door screeched open. Pause. The door still open.

"I'll call you from the office, luv. I may be late."

The other voice through the open kitchen door told him not to worry. The screen door slammed, and a pair of shined black shoes stepped down inches from his face and clacked along the sidewalk to the garage. Leonard didn't stare at his back, afraid that the very weight of his fear of being seen would cause the mark—force him—to look back The garage door scraped open on its rollers and closed with the same grating sound behind the ADA's official car as he backed into the alleyway. The rattle of dishes and running water filled the quiet morning stillness. The radio no longer played. Silence from inside the house. Leonard wondered if the guy was sitting at the kitchen table, maybe reading the newspaper, sucking up a cup of coffee. The sun was up over the garage, and he felt its warmth through the bushes. He didn't move. It wasn't the stiffness that still lingered in his body from laying in one position all night nor the dampness. He couldn't move. His heart pounded. He wanted to sink into the ground and become part of the warm earth that was nurturing the bush under which he lay. For a moment he thought it was holding him. He turned his face and smelled it and the vegetation. The tunnels had never had a clean, earth-smell, but were always dank and rotted, the air laden with the odor of human excrement and decay. The pressure in his bladder forced his decision. He had to move. But hesitated, hoping for a noise or movement in the alley which would delay what he had to do. Quiet. He breathed in the clean, earth-smell one last time.

Leonard slowly crept from under the bushes and rose up beside the screen door, brushing himself off as he moved, taking the steps along the outer edge to avoid their groaning under his weight. He stopped as the spring on the screen door began to screech as he opened it. Waited. Listened. He wedged himself through the narrow opening, guiding the door closed so it wouldn't slam. He moved across the porch, stepping carefully to avoid any creaking boards. He stood with his back to the outer wall of the kitchen and listened. He drew his knife from his sleeve and unconsciously stroked the narrow, steel blade. The adrenalin pumped through his system, bringing a rush. Nowhere to go. Just do it. He tested the door knob. It turned smoothly in his hand, and he opened the kitchen door, expecting to see a man sitting at the table—prepared for it, disappointed that he wasn't when he stepped inside, disappointed that he wouldn't be forced to make a split-second decision. No one. No threat. Leonard moved from the kitchen through the dining room, focused on the beat of the music coming from above him, which grew louder as he located the stairs to the second floor. He moved cautiously up the carpeted staircase, careful not to touch the balustrade nor the pictures lining the wall. The beat of the music came up through the floor, he could feel it underfoot. Same kind of music the nigger was playing when he took him out. A shower door slammed. The music grew louder as he approached an open door. The bedroom. No need to hide his movement. The bedclothes on the king size bed were thrown back. Shiny, red, satin sheets. The master bedroom. Leonard moved toward the bathroom, the door partially open. The sound of the shower, a voice muttering or was it singing? A gray silhouette moved behind the opaque glass. The rush of water failed to drown out the sound of music. He was a big man. He was a big, gray, faceless man. Leonard tried to estimate the position the man would be in when he opened the shower door. How quickly would he react when the door was opened? Or would he stand locked in place or try to defend himself ?

The drum of water against the door masked the turning of the handle. Leonard felt the handle disengage. The man had his face bent under the shower spray, letting the water beat against his shoulders and neck. He turned his head, eyes blinking, smarting from the soap when the music entered the shower stall. He raised his hands to wipe his eyes. Leonard widened the door, felt the spray on his own hand and face and on his leg as he stepped into the shower, thrusting and twisting the blade into the tanned, muscled body, into the stomach, under the well-developed pectoral muscles of a body-builder's chest, covered with tightly curled blond hair that receded into a thin line that entered the bush of pale hair, partially covered with a mass of white suds around a large erection from which the rapidly disappearing suds hung like spanish moss. The man dropped one hand to stop the blade which had already completed its course. The hand fell on Leonard's arm and slid off as the crumpling body pulled its hand with him onto the shower floor. Leonard hadn't looked at the man's face as the blade went in.

He stepped back out of the shower. Water began to accumulate and turn pink as blood flowed out of the body which clogged the drain. He shut off the water and repositioned the body to allow the water to recede. He used the towel hanging outside the door to wipe up his footprints, wipe off his blade and threw it on top of the body. He turned the hot water back on and watched the steam fill the shower stall. Before leaving the bathroom, he relieved himself and carefully wiped the bowl before flushing the toilet paper away. He checked to see if he'd tracked any dirt into the bathroom.

The radio continued its beat while he searched the bedroom, careful to wipe anything that he touched. The man's wallet and a watch inscribed on the back lay on the top of the dresser. A gift from the ADA. He took that and the money, a hundred bucks or so, and credit cards and the guy's driver's license from the wallet. In the top drawer of the dresser, he found a box with men's jewelry. He dumped the contents of the box on top of the dresser and selected what he thought might be valuable pieces. He dumped the other drawers onto the floor. Going through the closet he found a thin photo album on the shelf. The album contained pictures of the ADA and his lover in a series of nude poses. Thumbing through the album, Leonard found other pictures of the ADA with other men. He lifted his windbreaker, sucked in his gut and pushed the discovery inside his belt at his back. It rode over his butt.

Downstairs, on his route through the house, he pulled out

drawers in the dining room and scattered their contents across the floor. He wanted to take several prints that hung on the walls in the living room, but thought better of it. Leonard hated to break anything. It was a very nice house.

Leonard set the lock on the kitchen door and pulled the door closed behind him. The phone rang inside. He walked to the garage and took a rake from the wall and departed through the side door, the rake over his shoulder. Leonard pushed his baseball cap onto the back of his head and sauntered through the alley, whistling tunelessly. A delivery truck passed him on the next block, and he waved. The driver waved back. Before leaving the alley three blocks away, Leonard pushed the rake under some bushes.

Mickey picked him up fifteen minutes after he left the alley and passed the Dunkin' Donuts. He opened the bag she'd saved for him and drank the carton of milk and ate a cream-filled donut. Later, on a side street three miles away, Leonard threw the watch, jewelry, license and credit cards down a storm drain while he checked his tires. He pocketed the money. Over a hundred dollars and change.

XVII

Leonard stood at the phone booth and waited. Mickey had parked the car at pole G on the mall lot according to Sal's instructions. He'd left the trunk unlocked. Mickey disappeared inside a nearby drugstore within sight of Leonard. He picked up the receiver on the first ring.

"Leonard?"

"Yeah."

"Sal. It came over the news.... They all heard it ... and ... uhh they called it a.... They like your work, Leonard. The queer is still walkin' aroun' but hey, you destroyed his image. He won't show his face. Our man is breathin' easier. You cut the balls off the opposition."

"I haven't heard the news yet."

"No one's sayin' much. What's to say? The newspapers are gonna be playin' this up, I tell ya. No one has come right out an' said the guy was a fairy, but his boyfriend was in the shower and only one bed slept in? C'mon, gimme a break."

"There were two of them. I couldn't take 'em both out. They say anythin' about who did it?"

"The word on the street is that it was another neighborhood robbery, gone bad; the guy was unlucky. Wrong place; wrong time."

"I had no choice, Sal."

"Well, the heat's off. Uhh ... you're gettin' a bonus for this one. Looks like they're gonna be givin' me a bigger piece of the action upstate. So you did me a favor, kid."

"I left a package in the trunk. Your name's on it. Didn't like leavin' the trunk open though."

"You where you can see your car?"

"Yeah, some guy jus' put somethin' in the trunk. He has your package."

"You should be able to go back to your car. Jus' make sure he don't get a good look at ya. The 'insurance company' will be sendin' a check to your account. Uhh ... Leonard take Mickey out an' do some shoppin'; buy her somethin' nice, ya know what I mean? Gotta keep 'em happy. But be ... discreet. Don't flash your dough. It arouses suspicion, ya unnerstan'?"

"Yeah, Sal, I'll be ... discreet."

That had been the turning point, Leonard remembered. They'd opened the package left in the trunk of their car and counted out $1500 in used bills onto the kitchen table. Later, with the money still sitting on the kitchen table they listened to the six o'clock news.

"The string of robberies in the Wakefield section of the Bronx took a tragic turn today when the body of a man was found murdered in the home of ...."

Leonard and Mickey sat tensely, hand in hand on the sofa.

"This is it," Leonard said.

"Shh," Mickey admonished him.

"..., the Assistant District Attorney. The victim, a white male, has not been identified pending notification of the next of kin. The police aren't releasing any details at this time only to say that they are working on the case and expect an arrest will be made shortly. We'll bring you further details...."

They listened again to the news at eleven, waiting to hear of any leads that the police might have released. The reporter hinted at some compromising photos that were in the hands of the cops .... "Assistant District Attorney Halloran has been very critical of the way the DA's office has been waging its highly publicized fight against crime. It's not known at this time what effect this latest information will have on the upcoming elections, but it is rumored that Halloran will withdraw his name. He has not been available for comment...."

Leonard shut off the TV. Relief swept over him. They sat, neither speaking. Mickey turned on the sofa toward him, one leg tucked under the other. She shifted so that she was looking directly at him. She had something on her mind, the way she hesitated before she spoke, stutter-stepped around it, anxious, taking a deep breath, going squinty-eyed, measuring him, her lips losing their soft fullness as they tautened into a thin, determined line. He wanted to laugh, but didn't. She'd have that same look when she was dredging up a word to fit into a sentence, to express an idea, a word that she tried to shift from Vietnamese to English. But this was more serious. She was going to have all the words in place, the thoughts ready to lay on him.

"Leonard, why do you want me in nice things?" she asked.

That was easy, Leonard thought. He'd told her what Sal had said about taking her out shopping and buying her some nice things. He said he thought she should have what other women have, like what they saw in the fashion section of the newspapers.

"Because you are beautiful and I want you to have them. Why?"

"But it doesn't mean anything if I wear nice clothes and look nice, but people think I'm a peasant."

"Who said you're a peasant? You're no peasant."

"I feel like a peasant. My parents were peasants, uneducated, barely able to read and write. Rice farmers, remember? And I was a whore with a nice dress, but still a whore. Remember?"

"Don't talk like that babe. That's behind us."

"I still feel that way. My uncle won't let my family forget it. Who will our friends be five, ten years from now? Other ignorant people in nice clothes? What do we know about what is happening around us? What do we know about anything?"

"Ahh, we'll do all right. Money comes in, we'll do fine."

Leonard wondered if this was all about wasting people? For pay. Geez, he couldn't even remember how many so far. What was it seven, ten, fifteen, counting the ones in the tunnel? But the kills in the tunnel didn't count. He had a license to do that. Uncle Sam paid him for that. Gave out medals for that sort of stuff. And

Mickey had grown up with death around her: relatives, friends killed by one side or the other in the name of principle. Death was as common for her as roadkill on the highway. His killing had gotten her and her family out of 'Nam. He didn't understand the problem. She sat not speaking. She waited until he was looking at her again, not panning the room with his eyes, uncomfortable with her assessment. Eyeball to eyeball.

"Look at us. We've got money now, but we're nothing. A Vietnamese immigrant and an ex-GI. No jobs because you were in the hospital."

"You know why I was there. I had to do it."

She put her hand on his and squeezed. "I know."

"And I owe Sal for getting you and your family out of 'Nam. I owe him for that. I guess I'll always owe him. Ya understand?"

She smiled wistfully, her hand still on his.

"I think we can do better for ourselves, honey."

"Okay what do you think we should do?"

She must have been thinking a lot about it because what she laid out was as tough as basic training. There was no slack. She wouldn't allow slack. The goal was five years to make the turnaround. She started by enrolling in a high school English course and made sure he continued his education. He took a basic business course starting with bookkeeping, primarily because it ran at the same time as hers. From there it was ancient history, European history, American history. Unfortunately, this was all being done while holding a day job in a nearby restaurant—Mickey waiting tables and Leonard doing dishes and pots and pans; pearl diving he called it. They received one free meal on the job which cut their expenses and cut down on the cooking that Mickey had to do.

Sal expected him to drop everything when he had a business transaction for him. Random killing was Leonard's specialty. On subways, city streets, buses, airports, unexpected hits; unorthodox modus operandi, silent; tough to pin on the mob. Sal joked about how he'd arranged the contract for his ghost killer to execute. Yeah, a mob killing made to look like a random killing. Could happen to anyone in the City. Any city.

"Kid, ya can't expect to keep making the hits looking like a sad sack. Ya gotta get some style, ya know what I mean? Pretty soon, you're not going to be able to get near these guys we want to wax. No one lets a bum near 'em, especially now, when a derelict seems to be the primary suspect in these killings. The fuzz is startin' to put this together, ya know. Think all these wipeouts may be by the same guy. Ya hear what I'm sayin'?"

Leonard agreed.

Mickey took care of the style. Cajoled him into buying decent clothes. He felt like he was always wearing his Sunday best, but like everything else, he got used to it. Especially when they went out together, and he'd see the appreciative stares that his wife received. Mickey had style!

The only problem was that the jobs for Sal took a couple of days, sometimes longer. Especially when he had to track the mark in an unfamiliar part of the City or in another city. Learn his schedule, his routine, his habits and find the gap when his guard was down. When he felt most secure. And then he had to be able to fade away, unseen, unremembered. Leonard couldn't hold a day job.

"Babe, I can't keep up with all this. Job, school, Sal. We got no time together. Weekends we got to study. Every spare minute we got to study. This has been going on now for a year and half."

"I know, honey. You've got the credits and I'm just about finished with the courses I've been taking. Passed my GED. Why don't we apply to a college?"

"College?"

"We can do it. I'll keep working."

So they went into phase II of their plan. Leonard struggled with his accounting course and took a couple of fluff courses over the months, to help himself to learn to speak and express himself more clearly. Not working a steady job gave Leonard more time to study. Leonard picked up a copy of the *Wall Street Journal* that had

been left on a desk in one of the classrooms and found the world of
the stock market intriguing. He stopped by the library every day
and read it section by section.

"Why don't you invest in something?" Mickey said one day
when he mentioned that several stocks had jumped so many points
overnight. "Let's use that money in our account."

"Oh, I don't know. Think I should?"

"It'll make money won't it?"

"What if I lose it?" He wasn't as aggressive spending money as
he was in making a hit.

"Let's think long term, Leonard. Wasn't it Sal who said you
have to plan for your future?"

Since they took many meals at McDonald's, Leonard's first
investment with a local broker was for 100 shares of McDonald's
stock. They watched it every day at first, watched it fluctuate in
price from week to week and eventually edge up beyond what they
paid for it. The stock split, and Leonard had to to do some research to find out what it meant. He also put some money in
several blue chip stocks and bought several hundred shares of
Chrysler when it hovered around $4 a share. He had a gut feeling
about that even though it looked like it was going under. That's
when he began looking at the management teams that ran companies. Could turn companies around like the Italian did with Uncle
Sam's help. He became a player.

Those were tough years: learning his craft, doing contracts for
Sal, more studying month after month, separation from Mickey
for days, sometimes weeks. No let up. Mickey kept their focus.
Leonard began to consider himself more than just a tool that was
at Sal's disposal, but an asset, having some value to Sal. He began
to rethink their relationship. He needed Sal just as much as Sal
needed him. But Sal'd had a partner in 'Nam and had made the
decision to terminate him when the need arose. That was something to consider, Leonard thought. Even though he owed Sal for
what he'd done for Mickey and him. He was already taping all of
their conversations. Was it out of fear or was it to have as a bargain-

ing chip so he wouldn't end up like Dao? The only thing he feared was something happening to Mickey in all of this. The tapes would be for her too.

Leonard never got his degree, but he knew he'd changed. Developed? Gained confidence in himself. Yeah, he'd grown. He'd become more professional. Planned the hits more carefully, never taking anything for granted; reviewed each hit for a developing pattern that might betray him; and always made alternative plans in the event that he had to abort the original one. The ability to kill cleanly, suddenly and silently, with little or no pain to the victim gave him a feeling of pride in his craftsmanship. Also, discovering that he had grown intellectually, could express himself clearly and logically on a range of subjects even though it sounded like he had marbles in his mouth gave him a sense of satisfaction. He owed that to Mickey. Her encouragement and drill sergeant attitude. Sal had been amused at the change. Had commented on it several times. He hadn't been amused when Leonard moved them out of their second furnished apartment to another, more upscale, including the rent, without getting his approval. Sal had lost sight of him for a short time, but Leonard quickly resumed contact after they'd gotten settled.

"What're ya doing, Leonard. Sneakin' around. I told ya, didn't I, I need to know even when you take a shit. Didn't I tell you that?"

"Yeah Sal, you told me."

"How many times I tell you that?"

"A few."

"A few? What're you a retard? Ya got no memory?"

"Sorry, Sal. I heard about the place and took it on the spur of the moment. It was a good deal."

"You know what is a good deal? I know what is a good deal. A good deal is when I know you want to move, and I know where you're going. That's a good deal."

"I understand." What the fuck, Leonard thought. He wanted to tell Sal that he wasn't a kid or his fucking flunky, but he didn't.

"You're getting away from your friends, kid."

Which was true, Leonard realized, if getting away from his friends meant away from the combat zone—from street rage, ethnic rage, class rage. Away from the addicts, the drunks, the hookers and pimps, the homeless bums; the screams of abused kids and wives and groans and curses of streetwise adolescents. Away from the tension and stress of walking down into the dark caverns of the subway tunnels or tripping along garbage-strewn streets late at night. Away from the turf battles of blacks and whites who waged a guerilla warfare against the cops, against other ethnics, against each other, against the 'haves', all of whom had staked out their territory for selling drugs or protection or whatever the scam of the day happened to be. He was no longer willing to be held hostage by circumstances.

"You got my phone number, Sal. I'm as far away as your telephone. I figure it this way. I distance myself from you and that makes it safer for you, right? I don't bring any heat on you. And I still do the job."

"But you don't go sneaking off again. I might think you're trying to bug out."

"You know I wouldn't do that."

"You're my ace in the hole, kid. Up 'til now you done real good. An' I been taking care of you, right?"

"That's something we ought to talk about."

"What's to talk about?"

"I think we ought to agree on a price before each transaction, ya know? We're both in business so we ought to talk about it businesslike. Ya know what I mean."

"Fuck! I been taking good care of you. Haven't I? Ya got nothin' to bitch about, have you? Ya got a complaint?"

"I've been doing contracts on guys that have no connection to you. Shit, Sal, you didn't even know that creep in Philadelphia or the bum in Newark. You're subcontracting me out. By the time I take care of my expenses, my bottom line has shrunk to zip." Which wasn't exactly true, and they both knew it. But it showed Sal that he was no dude to be jerked around because he didn't know the score.

"Ya sayin' I'm holdin' out on you? C'mon, kid, how far back do we go? What is it since I set you and Mickey in that first apartment? Five, six years?"

"From what I read in the *News*," Leonard replied, ignoring the nostalgia, "the rumor is that you're a real comer in the family, the guy they go to when they want someone removed. The Mr. Clean of hired killing. You got a real rep, Sal, and from what you tell me, you're the guy they turn to when they want to get control of a new area, branch out, like in upstate New York."

"You know me, Leonard. I exaggerate sometimes. I think you're getting uppity on me. Maybe all that education you and Mickey are getting has screwed up your head."

"Ahh, come on Sal. Look at this way. I'm an investment. You got any lawyers or accountants that you can hire to wax a 'competitor'? And whom you can trust? Shit, if they could do that, they'd nudge you out of the picture, guinea or guinea. It's all bottom line today, Sal. And I want to grow my bottom line."

"You're pushing me kid. You're cutting into my end."

"You give me a transaction, I take the risk. I fuck up, I take the fall. So what have you got to lose? Squeeze someone else. I'm not a kid anymore."

"Yeah, you've grown up. Maybe too fast."

"But I'm still your main man, right?"

"Still my main man, kid, but don't forget you're still just a punk."

XVIII

Leonard went to his office the next morning. His conversation with Sal the day before and his own physical description in the newspaper had jarred him. There was no way anyone would recognize him from that, but nevertheless he'd never experienced being fingered before. The mail lay spread out on the floor inside the door. Stepping over it he placed a cup of Dunkin' Donuts coffee and his newspapers on the desk. He then went into the bathroom and filled the coffeepot with water and measured the coffee into the basket adding a partial scoop to give it some bite. He picked up the assortment of bills; advertisements; windowed and windowless envelopes; insurance offers (3); once in a lifetime offers if he acted right away; envelopes with confidential printed on them—white envelopes, brown envelopes, letter-size envelopes; business-size envelopes, sorting through them as he returned to his desk. Normally he would scan the advertising, but this morning he threw them in the wastepaper basket under his desk, retaining only the brochure about Mexico. He didn't open his bank statement. He knew to the penny what his account held, nor did he open the literature from his broker. Everything else went into the basket, file thirteen.

He took a sip from the syrofoam cup. Driving to his office that morning, he had speculated about buying into a franchise. He wondered how much longer he could stay with his present business. Having an enterprise like a franchise would give him and Mickey something they could build together. Like a Sir Speedy. They would be working together.

"How long do you think we'd be able to work together?" he'd asked her once after she opened the subject about buying a franchise.

They had just finished eating supper in the kitchen. Mickey was clearing the table while Leonard poured her cup of coffee.

"Don't you think we could do it?" She stopped, dishes not yet put in the rack of the dishwasher.

"I don't know."

"Why, don't you think we can work together?" She turned to him, still holding their dinner plates?

"I didn't say that," Leonard said, not looking up as he poured his cup of coffee.

"You said yourself that we would be building our business together."

"Yes, I did, but that was before I began thinking about it." Leonard replaced the coffee pot on the counter and sat down.

"What is there to think about? We start a business and we build it together. Side by side." She finished putting the dishes in the dishwasher, turned it on and sat down across from him.

"Day in and day out. Have you thought about the long hours we might have to put into it?"

"I can do it. You don't think I can do it, do you?"

"Yes, I think you can. I didn't say you couldn't. I never even thought it. There's no doubt in my mind." He'd seen the look of determination mask her face. Eyes narrowing. Mouth tightening. Chin thrust slightly forward.

"Well, then I think we should start a business."

"We should give it more thought before we make a decision. But you're right, we could do it together. But it would be hard work."

Leonard knew he had to give it more thought. They would be seeing each other differently. Now, they had their lives compartmentalized. He had his office and occasional out-of-town business. She had the house and her books. She was picture perfect when he came home or met her at a hotel. He had never seen her doing housework or laundry, even back in the Bronx, although he knew she did it herself even though now they could afford hired help. He had never seen her in soiled clothes with her hair messed up and her makeup smeared and her nails chipped. When she wore 'work clothes' it was for comfort. They were always clean and smelled fresh. Leonard didn't like to get his hands dirty and left it to Miko to call in a repairman, electrician, gardener or handyman. He never worked around the house, never did odd jobs with the exception of using the tools at his workbench to alter a weapon or hone a blade or work on a timing device. He kept a collection of knives in the basement in a locked wooden case. His pistols were maintained, cleaned and oiled in a separate secure box under the basement floor. All were throwaways. Why change it, Leonard thought. If it ain't broke, don't fix it. He knew they lived a charade, a make-believe life gleaned from magazines and their own dreams of the kind of life they wanted.

They had too much to remember not to want to live with what they had. They didn't need to see each other in work-induced sweat; arguing over every slight; haggling over every penny, but it was tough. Especially during the adjustment. To each other. To their surroundings. To their life. But they'd made it. Withdrawing into their own agreed upon space of silence until time eroded their potentially festering, possibly explosive differences and brought them back to their need for each other, to the realization that they couldn't, didn't want to, make it alone. Reconciliation was tentative, ending in an exhausting frenzy of lovemaking that left them with sweating bodies in a tangle of damp sheets. And without the unspoken words and phrases which could be dredged up and bitterly hurled again during later moments of acrimony.

Leonard filled his styrofoam cup with fresh coffee from Mr. Coffee—*Thank you, Joe, Joe Dimaggio.* Leonard started to turn to the business section of *The New York Times,* put the newspaper down, swiveled his chair to stare out the window. Why would she want to adopt a kid now, he wondered? How could she want to start a business with a new kid on her hands? Maybe one that cried a lot or was sickly, one she had to spend a lot of time with? They had each other, a nice home. I should have kept my mouth shut. He slapped his forehead, remonstrating with himself. They were doing okay, he said to himself. At least he was. It was the tears that did it. They'd gushed out like they'd been sitting there dammed behind her blue eyes for years, waiting for the right words from him. And he'd pressed the right or was it the wrong button? It would have been okay if they were sad tears, like those you shed when someone near you dies. Although it had never happened to him. Yeah, people died but it meant nothing to him. Not even in the Army. Not even when it was a 'buddy'. The guy's number was up. He could handle that. He'd seen her cry when she was sad, not often, but when she'd try to talk to her family in California, and they'd hang up on her. Considering her the dishonored one, although the help she gave them wasn't rejected. It was like they expected her to keep paying retribution all her life for the dishonor she had brought on them. They never objected to the money she sent them. She cried when she saw something sad on TV about the abuse of kids or kids with AIDS. Those were tears of sadness. Of frustration. He could handle that. The moments would pass.

But her tears in the restaurant were tears of joy. Honest to God tears of happiness. Like he'd promised her something deeply felt, truly personal, not like a piece of jewelry. They were more binding, connected to him, not something he could expect to pass off. Basic goodness tears. Leonard stood, walked around the desk, cup in hand, trying to thrash out an answer in his own mind. He slumped back into his chair. Why would she want a kid now, especially now that he was thinking about retiring, and not knowing how he was going to do it and not wanting to put that on her, his not knowing how the fuck he was going to get out from under Sal and still protect her? And a kid? Jee-zuz. He didn't know how they could handle it all. Why would she want to adopt someone else's kid? Not knowing what was in the kids genes. Shit, they could be adopting a Charlie Starkweather or Charles Manson. It would be a crapshoot. He … they wouldn't be getting papers attesting to the kid's lineage, his pedigree. A lineage they could trace. What would it be bringing with it as it grew older and developed from a cute easily managed bundle to something with a mind of its own, its own agenda? Kids become teenagers. Who needs those kinds of young shits on the streets nowadays? Who needs them at home? It's in the newspapers all the time. A kid waxing another kid because he wants his Raiders jacket or his Nike shoes. What if the kid turns out to be one of these animals?

Miko wants a kid. She'd never shed her family ties. Couldn't, it's part of her culture. Shit, he didn't need a family. Who'd have wanted to belong to his family? Drunks, woman abusers, kid abusers, ne'er-do-wells, dirtbags, scumbags, nothings; foul-mouthed, foul-minded, skanky. He couldn't call up an image, a face to relate to. He didn't try very hard. They weren't worth remembering. He'd never needed a family. He never even thought about it. Not until Mickey came along, that is; she's family. He needed her. Sal used to be family in a way. He used to think that no one did as much for Mickey and him as Sal. But Leonard knew he'd paid for it. Sal was more like a banker or a loan shark, holding a debt over his head, so he'd keep up the payments. He was Sal's handyman, that's all. The only difference was he was well paid. That's where it stopped. It didn't go beyond doing a job and getting well paid for it. And worrying about his ass. It's different between Mickey and Ginger though. They got their culture and that thing between women, whatever it is, that makes them more responsive to each other's needs. The culture is the bond though.

How do I share her with a kid? Leonard asked himself. How can she feel something for a kid who's not hers? Back to that again. How could he feel anything knowing it wasn't his, didn't have his genes, his blood? But then would he want a kid with his genes? Would it grow up like him? Would it spawn others like him? Well, she would never have kids of her own so that took care of that but still didn't solve his problem. Aw shit, he thought. It won't be the same, but he had to do it, no matter what. Perhaps it would make up for all those years that she had to avoid her people, her culture. Leonard could always tell when she visited the Vietnamese market. He never questioned her about it when she returned home, withdrawn, with the smell of *nouk mam* and garlic on her clothes, in her hair, on her lips. She'd made a nostalgia trip. She never complained. Was just withdrawn for a short time until she got over it and returned to their life. Leonard knew he had to do it for her. That would be a real gift. A killer's gift of life.

The phone rang. It would be Sal. He let it ring to make sure. He could imagine the phone, as if it had a life of its own, jumping in its cradle.

"Grissom Consultants."

"I need you for a quickie, Leonard."

"What's up?"

"The lawyer. She's got a hair up her ass since Schultz. I think she's running scared."

Leonard didn't say anything.

"Kid, you there?"

"Yeah, Sal."

"Well then, say something for Christ's sake."

"You said you think she's running scared."

"She's coming down here."

"You said she was tough. Remember you said that?"

"I know what the fuck I said."

"Scared bimboes don't sound tough to me."

"Fuck off, Leonard."

"She's in over her head."

"She can handle it. Right now they got pressure on her. Billings, he's that old fart I told you about. Him and Masterson. Billings don't think it was a suicide."

"She shouldn't a been there. She shoulda got out according to the plan.If she hadn't been there she wouldn't have seen what she saw."

"Fuck, that's history. Forget it."

"What do you want me to do?"

"She's coming tomorrow by train, an'll be leaving the day after." He must be talking at a safe phone and in a hurry because he rarely ever called Leonard at his office to talk or give him instructions. Sal told him where she would be staying and when she would be leaving, the train she'd catch. Leonard made notes.

"She's running scared. But I gotta see her. Calm her down. I can't have her running down here every time she starts to panic. I'm not her fuckin' father."

What the hell did that mean, Leonard wondered.

"I warned you about her," Leonard said.

"It's not your fuckin' business. Understand?"

Leonard didn't reply. He didn't know what went on between Sal and the woman. He didn't care. Instead he asked, "You said you had a job for me."

"I want to throw a scare in her...."

"I thought you said she was running scared."

"I know what she wants. I'll take care of her. But I want to keep her wired, ya understand? She has to know we can find her anytime, anyplace. No rough stuff. A threat. She's got to be more afraid of us than the State and the Feds." The receiver went dead, Leonard had his marching orders. He called Miko and told her about Sal's call. Told her he wanted her to go with him.

"Think she'll show up for breakfast?" Miko asked.

"Who knows?"

They'd arrived early to catch a glimpse of her. To get a fix on her. They'd parked the car near the northernmost stop of the subway, in the Bronx . Mickey had worn low-heeled shoes and matched Leonard step for step as they moved through the subway system, and rode the swaying, early morning train into the City. Leonard carried a shopping bag, holding it against his side when they had to stand and putting it between his feet when they were able to sit, staring straight ahead or crisscrossing the line of sight of other passengers who likewise never met anyone else's eyes but angled their gaze off to the side or over the head or shoulder of other passengers or stared vacantly at the advertisements over the windows or kept their faces buried in their newspapers as the train flashed by stations and people standing and waiting for the next train. He held Mickey's hand and they communicated with hand squeezes when a person attracted one or the other's attention—either because of their clothes or their condition or their appearance Their faces never betrayed their reaction. He lifted the shopping bag over the turnstiles, and held it close and let Mickey precede him through the horizontal barred exits that funneled pedestrians like cattle out into other people entering and leaving the subway stop, past the panhandlers and the entreprenuers selling things you'd never need and through the jostling crowd, up the stairs and out on to the littered streets of the City and into more people with the glazed, unidirectional stare of New Yorkers hurrying into their future but never catching up to where they were going or escaping from where they'd been, but settling for a stop along the way at a job, or a cup of coffee or a newspaper or for no reason at all.

"Does she even eat breakfast?" Mickey asked as they settled into a booth along the wall where they could watch both the life on the street and the entrance from the lobby into the hotel coffee shop. Leonard had bought a *New York Times* at a newsstand before entering the hotel and passed her the front pages and the sports section while the waitress poured their coffee and took their order. He waited until the waitress left.

"I have no idea, but there's no reason we can't have ours. We know when she has to catch her train."

Mickey ordered for both of them when the waitress returned. English muffins and poached eggs. They ate while each of them burrowed into the news, never taking their eyes off the entrances into the restaurant for any length of time.

"Is that her? Looks like her from your description. She's very attractive," Mickey said nudging Leonard with her foot.

"That's her. Seems to me she's weathered a bit. You see love, that's what happens when women have their husbands killed. One day they're young and beautiful and whammo, they have their husbands killed and it shows up the next day on their faces." He folded the newspaper so that he could watch Mrs. Sawyer. Mickey gave him a kick under the table.

Shelly Sawyer paused in the doorway; her eyes travelled across the dining room, over them, as if she expected to see someone she knew. The navy blue suit and pumps accentuated her blond hair and her tan. She wore pearl earrings and a string of pearls. She held one hand on the strap of her shoulder bag and waited for the waitress to show her to a table. She had the imperious look of people who expected to be waited on.

They watched her sit down, but she didn't pick up a menu. She put her handbag on the floor at her feet. The waitress turned her cup over and poured her coffee. Shelly Sawyer spread her napkin on her lap; opened a package of sweetner and stirred it into her cup. She didn't look at the menu but gave the waitress instructions which she wrote on a menu pad. Shelly sat sideways to them and Leonard examined her profile and was close enough to see that her face showed some slippage and that her hand shook a bit when she stirred her coffee. She glanced at the other people sitting at the tables around her and threw another quick glance at him. Their eyes met. She shivered and gripped the table with both hands. The waitress, returning with her order, blocked her view of their leaving. Leonard left a tip beside his plate and out of sight at the cash register, paid their check and moved outside. They watched her, from near the exit to the street, take a deep breath and turn to look again and then twist in her seat and turn from side to side as her eyes searched the dining room. He knew she recognized.him.

"Why did we leave so quickly?"

"She recognized me. How? I don't know. Maybe from a description in the paper. Maybe when I was standing in the light just before I wasted her husband. She got a good look then."

"Think she'll call Sal?"

"I don't know. It doesn't matter. We'd better hurry so we can pick her up at the station."

He waited for her outside the terminal, watched her as the cab pulled up to the curb and as she leaned forward to pay the driver.

Watched her long sleek legs step out of the cab, an overnight bag in one hand, one hand on the door, her handbag swinging from her shoulder over the gutter as she stepped out onto the sidewalk. She walked to the entrance where a ragged, unshaven derelict peeled himself away from the wall and approached her. She appeared startled when he stepped in front of her and held out a grubby hand, and ignored the "…. fuckin' bitch" that trailed after her as she pushed into the crowd through the doors into the terminal. Once inside she found the location of the track she'd be leaving on and headed for it.

Leonard, now in tan workpants, a windbreaker, Adidas shoes and a baseball cap pulled low over his eyes, angled toward her as she hurried to the steps leading down to the platform where she would board her train. He took her arm as she reached the top step. Her hand reached out for the railing as he shoved her forward but without releasing her arm. She gasped. Her overnight bag bumped against his leg. She had a firm hold of the railing. She tried to pull away but he increased the pressure on her upper arm.

"You're hurting me," she cried. Heads turned to look but continued on.

"Don't say anymore Mrs. Sawyer and don't look 'round. Keep walking. One step at a time," Leonard rasped. As if to encourage her he bumped her again, and held her up as she started to lose her footing.

"What do you want?" she asked, turning her head. Her face strained and pale.

"You better watch the steps, Mrs. Sawyer. You could break an arm or a leg … or smash your face if you fall … head first." They were taking the steps very slowly, people moving around them down the stairs.

"Tell me what do you want?" she croaked, the words coming out like dry leaves that someone was walking on. "I'm going to scream. Leave me alone."

No one turned, no one paid any attention to the small, slight man helping the lady down the concrete stairs to the platform below.

"I can find you anywhere, Mrs. Sawyer. Whether you're here or in a hospital. Al Schultz wanted to die. Do you?" He increased the pressure on her arm; she stopped and went up on her tiptoes; her eyes widened and her mouth spread open in silent agony, and then he released her, turned and went back up the stairs two at a time. He didn't look back to see if she had stopped to rub her arm or tried to catch sight of him as he disappeared. But he imagined she did.

Mickey waited for him beside a newsstand and followed him out carrying the shopping bag.

XIX

Leonard studied the artist's conception of James Mulholland that stared back at him from the front page of the Albany paper. Close. Too close. The horn-rimmed glasses made him look like an anorexic owl with his thin nose, high cheekbones, humorless mouth and his hair slicked back from his forehead. The description was close: thinning sandy hair—combed straight back for this job—height five-five to five-seven. The weight was way off. They'd seen a butterball, a tub wearing a white coat, not aware of the blazer Leonard wore under the lab coat which hung below his knees. Did people see a killer's face? He saw himself in the sketch. Who else saw Leonard Grissom? Mrs. Sawyer must have. Why else would she have reacted as she did in the restaurant? She must have had a local paper with her or seen the sketch the police might have shown her as Al's attorney. Or had it been from the night he killed George Sawyer?

Would his neighbors take a look at the picture and say, 'Doesn't that look like what's his name next door or so and so down the street?' Or would they care? Or would they even look at the sketch? Would anyone associate his recent absence with the murder of Al Schultz, miles away? Would they remember how often Leonard was away? The trips he took? Would the headline over his picture, HIT MAN, be enough to cause an anonymous caller to contact the police? Then the line that set him on edge. 'He spoke with an English accent.' That could be a giveaway. It marked his break with the past, with his origin. People might not remember anything else, but they'd remember the accent now that it could be associated with a face.

The deputy remembered. It must have been the stupid deputy

and the cruiserlike supervisor sailing up the corridor toward him. They'd come up with the description of him. The deputy remembered the accent; the head nurse must have filled in some of the details of his description. She could have grabbed him if he hadn't burst through the exit to the stairs. He didn't like the idea of hitting a woman, but he would have if it meant avoiding capture.

He knew that he'd hear from Sal. The North Country was Sal's territory. Word would get out on the street. They'd know things were going sour there. Because the money was drying up. Sal would be behind in his payments. Which meant the vultures would be circling. Sal'd be scrambling to put his organization back together using the Sawyer woman. In the meantime he might feel that with Leonard's picture in the paper, he would be drawing more heat. Someone would make the connection that Leonard had to be Sal's man. Sal's 'ghost' killer. He'd deny it at first, but would give him up if it meant his own ass. Put out the word that Leonard had been the one who had whacked certain wise guys with close ties to other elements in the family. Put out the word that Leonard had gone ballistic, out of control. Had become a liability. Leonard could see himself becoming the poster boy for all the mob shooters. Or would the man give Sal the job of finishing him off? How much time did he have? Sal couldn't just come out and admit he'd used Leonard as his own hit man. He'd have to cover his own involvement. Leonard knew too much about the way Sal did business. Sal wouldn't want anyone else to pick him up or take the chance of his going to the feebies. Leonard knew he'd brought his problems on himself. The usually cautious guy had taken matters into his own hands, hadn't listened to the danger signals, or was it the exhilaration of running the edge? The rush that came with beating the odds? Time to get out of it.

He suddenly realized that he was still carrying James Mulholland's ID around with him. He had to bury Mulholland. How long would it take for the cops to trace James Mulholland through his license or his credit card? Would have been great if he'd been stopped at any time over the past couple of days! "Slipping.

I'm fucking well slipping," Leonard said to himself. Yeah, it's time to get out. He wasn't focused like he used to be. Ever since Mickey started talking about the kid. What a time to be talking about a kid! Give her what she wanted because over the years she'd never asked for anything for herself, never pushed him. Well, except for her family. She'd ask for things for them. Money. And he'd grumble to himself, and she knew how he hated doing anything for them. Because of their rejection of her. Her sadness never spoken, never intruding between them.

"What are we going to do, Mickey? About the baby? About us? About maybe they'll get to me. Soon. What will you do? We don't need the baby." But he wouldn't say it to her. He wouldn't come right out and say she couldn't have it. Even though he had no idea how they were going to come up with a baby on such short notice and leave. Get away. Like it wasn't that they could get one at the supermarket or walk into the hospital and say I want a baby that looks like Mickey and has her disposition. The sweetness—and the toughness. He just couldn't order up something like that.

"Why did you have to start crying Mickey? Why did you have to show me all of your pent-up want in that one moment? Why didn't you just say, we ought to think about it? Give me time to let the idea jell—or fade away?"

Those god-damned tears. The ones she shed in her loneliness for her family which he never saw except for the redness of her eyes and her nose where she had blown into her handkerchief and which the use of her compact couldn't quite hide. And when he'd returned from 'Nam and her tears that he was safe, tears of joy. And when the smoke had cut him, undoing all the work that they'd done on him in the Army hospitals and when he opened his eyes and she sat there, shedding tears noiselessly because he had beaten the odds again. But the tears when she heard about the kid were different from all of the others.

These tears hammered into him, spilling noiselessly out of her eyes but thudding into him like hailstones. Baseball-sized hail-

stones that left him short-winded with their force and wondering
what he'd done? To them—to Mickey and him? But he meant
it—the promise he'd made to her. At least, right then, he meant
it. Now he'd had too much time to think about it, and for the first
time in his life, except for that one time in the cave with the spiders, he was afraid. Not for himself. For them. What were they
going to do?

And what about the kid? Was it too late?

But first he had to dispose of James Mulholland. He locked
his office door and retrieved his ID from the safe and James
Mulholland's passport. He sat at the desk and meticulously cut up
the credit card, the driver's license, and the passport into small
pieces onto a newspaper. Satisfied, he made several smaller piles
and flushed the pieces down the toilet. He then figured up his
credit card recipts and wrote a check for the amount to be drawn
against his account. That should wipe out Mulholland's checking
account. He wouldn't bother to check the Post Office box in nearby
Lundale, a twenty minute drive, just in case his box was already
under surveillance. He sat at his desk, searching for an escape.

The tapes. How much time did he have?

"You're home early," Mickey said drying her hands at the
kitchen sink. "I have some good news." He thought her smile was
brighter and her eyes threw sparks as though her good news was
ready to burst from her. Leonard held himself in check, took her in
his arms and held her for a moment.

"What was that for?"

Leonard shrugged unable to destroy her moment. "What's the
good news?" He held the newspaper in one hand.

"We don't have to look any further."

"For?"

"For my baby."

Leonard seated himself at the kitchen table. What could he
say? Things were moving too fast. Out of control. He placed the
newspaper, folded, picture concealed, on the table.

"Coffee? You don't seem overjoyed," some of the elation gone out of her voice.

Leonard didn't respond, and she filled a mug with the inscription printed on the side. 'Home is where the heart is.' In place of the word there was a large red heart. She made a mug of tea for herself and sat across from him. He couldn't look at her happiness. Couldn't destroy it. He forced a smile. His hand lying on top of the newspaper. Unable to open it.

"When did this all happen?"

"Over the past month or so. That's why when we were at the Belhurst having dinner that night, it came as the answer to my prayers when you suggested that we adopt a child. I'd never expected it. You did mean it didn't you, Leonard?"

"Yes." He stirred his coffee and took a sip not looking at her. Unable to bring up the article in the paper. "So what happened?"

"A new family moved in with the Thanhs. You don't know them. They're cousins to the Thanhs. They've been living with them for some time until they can find a place of their own. One of the daughters was raped by a high school football player. Her family took it to the police, but the boy's family, they're very well to do, got into the picture and wanted it hushed up. They kept it out of the newspapers. They offered to pay for an abortion. They threatened the girl with exposure, and the police leaned on the girl's father. The family agreed to a settlement. The daughter was beyond her trimester but hardly showed. It was too late for an abortion. They took her out of school. Made her quit. She's very bright. Already spoke good English and was doing very well in school."

"So how do you fit into all of this?"

Mickey stood and added hot water to her teabag. Sat back down and stirred a spoonful of sugar into her tea; took a deep breath and said, "I took her, with her parents' permission, to a private hospital and registered her in my name. I posed as her mother and told the registrar that I would take care of all the bills; that I didn't have medical insurance. A doctor checked her, and she and the baby are healthy. He doesn't see any complications. I'll take her when she goes into labor. Would you mind if I brought her here? She's very close? Like any day now. She is so frightened. Leonard, the baby will be born a Grissom. I am so happy." She stood and came around the table and kissed him, holding his head against her stomach.

Leonard put his arm around her slim waist and listened to the life in her stomach wondering what the difference would have been if she was having the baby?

"How soon will she ... the girl ... be coming here?"

"I'm going to bring her here this evening. The neighbors won't see her."

Leonard released her. Pushed his cup aside and opened the paper to the front page. The words HIT MAN leaped out at him again. Even more strongly it seemed because he knew the words were there. Made him feel evil, dirty, less ... human. Maybe it was because of her talking about the kid. Her hand dug into his shoulder as she leaned forward and looked at the picture. Several strands of her hair dragged across his cheek. He breathed deeply trying to smell her perfume that subtly remained just out of reach. All he could think of was the minefield and the events, which would shatter the fragile syndesis of their life. He pressed his face against her hip. Her hand stroked the back of his neck.

"What does it mean?" She returned to her side of the table, sat, the newspaper spread out in front of her as though she might be sick on it. Her face strained. He could see the hope of her having the baby fading, leaving her face stark while indicting him for his error, for unnecessarily exposing himself and by that exposure, her dream. She didn't say anything. Didn't condemn him verbally. But her eyes drove spikes of reproach into him.

"It means I think they may be closing in."

"How many people do you know who would connect you to this ... this person?"

"It would take only one. I haven't heard from Sal yet."

"You think he saw the article?"

"He read the one that gave only the physical description so I imagine he saw this. He gets all the newspapers from the Albany area. I also think that the police may be on to something now. I've already taken steps to eliminate Mulholland."

"You think that people would mistake you for this picture?"

"I can't chance it."

"I want the baby."

"We won't have time." He began thinking about how much time he could buy. He could easily shift to another identity, as could Mickey. He had prepared for this eventuality years ago when he was unsure of what the next day might bring. They could pick up and move out in a minute. Just walk away like they'd never existed. He was prepared for the two of them. Hauling a kid along would be another matter.

"Then I'll stay behind with my child." She had already assumed the role of motherhood. "I'll take care of it. I've been reading about how to care for a newborn baby. You didn't know that, did you? Even when I was knitting, you didn't suspect?"

"No. I didn't know." He didn't know that she had this hidden part of her. That she was doing this thing for herself.

"This is very important to me."

"More important than us?" He wanted to say me, but he was afraid of the answer, wasn't sure how she would take it. He didn't feel betrayed, but felt he had lost something. Something that could never be replaced even if she went with him, without the kid. It would never be the same between them. He knew that, and she probably did too, but it didn't matter to her. He wasn't sure if he wanted to share her. If he could!

"It goes beyond us, you know. It's not about us. It's about a baby who is going to be born and will be without a mother or a father. It's about us taking responsibility for someone other than ourselves, like putting our strong love into a child. You must take care of us. You must make this happen in our lives. You must do this or leave. I will stay here." Her eyes intent, boring into his.

"I don't know if I can. If I want to. Everything I've done has been for you. You never told me what you were doing. That you had been preparing for this. I'm not ready for this all at once. I need time." Leonard lifted his cup and drained the last few drops. They were cold and bitter.

"From what you say, there is no time." She sat back in her chair and folded her hands on the table in front of her.

"No."

"You must take care of us. Will you?"

He didn't have to think about that. Who was he kidding?

"Yes. You know I never would have had a life if you hadn't been there. You've always been my life. I guess, I'll have to learn to share you. Maybe, I can do that. I'll try."

The phone began ringing, jarring the space between them. Mickey tensed; went rigid in her chair. "I'll get it," Leonard said scraping his chair back.

"It looks a lot like you, kid. The sketch in the papers."

Sal rarely called him at home.

"If you're looking for me, I guess it does."

"The accent was the clincher. It'll make a lot of people start thinking ... if they know you."

"I guess it would, but it could also be a hundred other people too, Sal. Look around you. The description doesn't just fit me. How many people really look at a sketch? And remember it."

"Maybe you should have waited for instructions before you snuffed him, Leonard. Al couldn't talk."

"But we didn't know if he'd be able one of these days. It would have been tougher then."

Silence.

"You think the sketch ... that someone will recognize me?"

"I don't know."

"How many people look at those things? They got the weight wrong also. People will be looking for a fat guy, ya know. You ever remember a sketch? The cops do this all the time. Besides, I don't socialize that much."

"Yeah, you're probably right." He dropped the subject and didn't mention the accent again, which surprised Leonard. "Everything is getting fucked up. We got more problems down here. With this guy owns a carting company ..."

"Garbage?"

"The guy is competing for 'stops.' Is going against the Trade Association, ya know? Has become an outlaw. Cut the cost of the contracts to do business. Sending the wrong message to our clients. Thought you could handle this one. Take some a the heat off us and send a message to anyone else getting ideas."

"How soon?"

"Need it done within a week" He gave a date, the name and location of the company, a physical description of the mark, his daily time schedule to and from work and where he lived. "Only thing is Leonard, I gotta know where and when the hit is going to take place so that none of my people are around. We're keeping a close eye on this guy to see who he meets with and talks to. He doesn't squat but we know about it, ya understand?"

"I understand. Price?"

Sal gave him a higher than usual figure and included a bonus.

"Sounds good," Leonard said. Too good. Came up too quickly.

"We'll have a meet. After. You said something about wanting to retire. We might be able to work something out. Especially with you becoming a family man. Ya see, I been thinkin' about that. Didn't I tell you that I thought we could work somethin' out?"

"Yeah, Sal, you did. You said you'd try to work something out. I'm glad to hear that. It takes the pressure off. It'll make Mickey very happy."

"Okay, Leonard, keep in touch. When you call, just leave the date and time. No one's gonna make anything outta that."

Mickey had been standing by the door leading into the hallway.

"Sal?"

"Yeah. He's got a situation he wants me to take care of. In the City."

"Then everything's okay?"

"He even said we could meet and talk about retiring."

"That's wonderful."

"Let's go back in the kitchen. I think we should talk." Leonard put his arm around Mickey and guided her back to the kitchen. She had to understand that it wasn't as wonderful as it sounded.

XX

Miko brought the girl home that evening. Three days. That's all he was going to allow himself. Was it enough time? Had to put it all together in three days. He had tried to convince Miko that the baby would be an impediment, baggage that would slow them down, would mark them if Sal or the Feds or anyone found out about it. But she was adamant, fierce in her determination that she would have the baby. Had told him that everything they had together, built for themselves, couldn't compare with the joy of having this child.

Jeezuz, it was like she was having it, that it was her ... their kid— growing inside of her, burgeoning, pushing her swelling stomach out in front of her, making her face puffy and slowing her walk—binding herself to the mother. He couldn't just leave, no matter if he had to share her with this ... kid. This child that neither the biological mother, nor the guy who had planted the seed, nor the girl's parents, nor anyone in the fucking world wanted, including him. He wondered if the yet-to-be-born kid, curled up inside that young girl's body—already formed in a sea of fluids, unseeing, but perhaps feeling, sensing life outside the womb connected by a tube that gave it nourishment—would ever know how tenuous its life was about to become? Only Miko stood between the kid and extinction. And Leonard 'asshole' Grissom, the great benefactor, the moral equivalent of John Wayne Gacy, giving succour to the offspring of a poor, taken-advantge-of-dink. While the fucker who initiated this violation stood free, shielded by his fucking parents who traded on their civic reputations to protect their all-american boy from the wiles of a predatory, grasping, six-teen-year-old Oriental. And of course, a charge of statutory rape.

"Leonard, this is Li," Mickey said.

Leonard had heard the car come up the drive, the overhead garage door grate back, car doors slam, footsteps and knew when she was in the house and was standing in the doorway. He rose from his recliner and clicked off the TV, turned and stared into the dark, frightened eyes of a young Vietnamese girl. He'd seen dozens like her in the villages, the same frightened look, shuffling with their duck-walk, along dirt roads to or from villages—resignation etched in their faces and their movements, carrying their swollen bellies into an uncertain future.

The image was stark, not clouded by the dullness of time. He took her flaccid but delicate hand in his. The face looked up at him and the small mouth stretched like a rubber band into a tentative smile. Leonard sent her back a smile. Miko would tell him later that it was more a scowl. But he'd tried.

"I'll take her up to her room," Miko said, interrupting his non-talk.

They made a short stop in the kitchen. The refrigerator door slammed. The voices chattered, the sound, foreign, floating back to him across dusty years as they mounted the stairs. Leonard sat for a long time in the recliner.

"Leonard!"

Miko's voice stabbed into his head, jolting him awake. He sat up and looked at his watch. He ran up the stairs. The light was on in the spare bedroom across the hall from theirs. The sheet was thrown back. The girl was in labor. Mickey had laid a pad and some towels under her.

"We got time to get her to the hospital?" Leonard asked, reflexively checking his watch.

"Her contractions are very close together; I think I see the baby's head." Mickey watched Li's face, her own face reflecting the efforts of the young girl.

"Want me to call the Emergency Medical Team?"

"There's no time. I need some warm towels, water, a bowl and a pair of scissors to cut the cord. See if you can find some string. Make sure everything's clean. Hurry!" She went into the bathroom. She was running water into the sink.

Sweat bathed Li's face; small white teeth clenched her lower lip, her upper lip curled back and she began pushing, forcing, grunting; her strong, young body helping the baby emerge.

"Leonard, please hurry," Miko said as Leonard watched the struggle of the young girl.

Leonard took one look at the head and fluids emerging with it and left the room as Mickey tore away the membrane covering the baby's face. He was cheered that he didn't have to watch any more. He'd felt queasy. Death had never bothered him. It had always been impersonal, a name on a contract, remote. This was the first time he had witnessed a life beginning. He hurried downstairs with an armful of towels from a hall closet, fumbled with the dryer as he read the directions and was relieved when it went on and he could hear the towels spinning in the dry warmth. He found a pair of scissors and a plastic mixing bowl in the kitchen and put them under the hot water faucet while soaping them down. He cut a piece from a ball of string, washed it and put it in the bowl.

"Leonard!"

"Coming!" He took the warm towels out of the dryer without folding them and ran up the stairs, two at a time. He placed a chair next to the bed and placed the towels and scissors on the chair.

He turned away; went into the bathroom unable to look at the head of the infant. He took the mixing bowl into the bathroom and filled it with warm water. Slowly. In the mirror he saw Mickey support the baby as the shoulders slid out but looked away when she put two ties in the membranous appendage connecting mother and child and picked up the scissors and leaned toward the baby resting on the towels. He took the bowl of water back into the bedroom just as a squall burst from the wizened form that Mickey held up as he set the bowl of water on the night table. He watched her clean the baby, holding it gently but firmly as she wiped it dry, wrapped it in still-warm towels and placed it beside the mother. The girl smiled as the small mouth fluttered toward her breast and greedily sucked the life-giving nipple.

The girl's face suddenly contorted with pain as a strong contraction gripped her, lifting her knees off the bed as she planted her feet and arched her body.

"Get the plastic bucket out of the bathroom," Mickey said as she helped the girl, still clutching the baby, out of the bed.

Leonard placed the bucket beside the bed, as Mickey took the swaddled bundle from the mother and handed it to Leonard. At first, he held the baby away from his body, unsure how to hold this ... red-faced infant. In a moment of clarity, he brought the child against his shoulder, awed by the diminuitive size of the infant. He moved away from the bed as the mother squatted over the bucket. Leonard found himself sweating, his stomach churning again as he heard the sounds of the maternal, held-back afterbirth, discharge into the bucket behind him. He put his face against the infant's and breathed in the sweetness of this new life.

"Okay, we'll take the baby," Mickey said as she retrieved it from Leonard and nestled it back into its mother's arms. "Call the hospital and let them know we're bringing Miko Grissom in with her newborn baby, just to make sure we don't have any complications. The number's inside the cover of the phone book. I'll clean up here and then change."

Leonard, relieved of his burden, freed of the smells and sounds of the new birth, made the call and then went into the guest bathroom where he rinsed his face and brushed his teeth. He grabbed a jacket from a closet and waited for them in the hallway.

They paused at the kitchen door while Leonard brought their coats from the hall closet.

"We're ready. I'll help Li. You take the baby."

For a moment, Leonard again held the small bundle in his arms. He couldn't define his feelings, didn't dare. But they weren't the same as before.

"Oh, by the way, is the baby a boy or girl?"

"A girl."

"Got a name?"

"Lenore. Lenore Trung Grissom."

"Trung?"

"Vietnamese. They were two sisters who were heroines in our history."

"Oh. What if it had been a boy?"

"Leonard."

"No."

"We would have talked about that."

Miko opened the car door for Li, waited for her to settle back, took the baby from Leonard, handed her to the new mother, and slid in beside her.

"You were very good with ... you know ... handling the mother and baby." Leonard said over his shoulder as he backed the Range Rover out of the driveway. He used the remote to close the garage door. He expected Mickey to say that it was a woman thing. But she didn't.

"I had brothers and sisters. Our village had no hospital. We had no doctor. My mother had one stillborn. When I was old enough I helped my mother and the midwife bring my younger sisters and brothers into the world. It wasn't always easy. I guess you don't forget things like that." She turned her attention to the baby.

Li sat with her eyes closed, her head against the back of the seat. She looked exhausted, Leonard thought, when he glanced at the young girl in the mirror. Mickey patted her forehead with a towel.

They left Li at the hospital with the baby for observation. The physician told them that the hospital would release them within a day or two, if there were no complications.

"We don't have much time, Mickey. But having the baby to-night helps. I think we can handle it. With the baby included.

Lenore, eh? Nice sound to it. I like it." He reached across the gear box and the gulf between them and took her hand. On the way home, Leonard stopped at a supermarket and lifted a shopping cart into the Range Rover.

The call came at 9a.m. the next morning as he expected. He had to cut it pretty close because of the heavy traffic, a funeral, a detour, and the rain. The rain slanting against the windows with a steady beat; windshield wipers frenetically trying to catch up or stay ahead, tires sending out thick sprays of water in front of him to splash against his windshield. He parked as close as he could to the phone. He'd have to get out of the car.

He picked up the receiver on the first ring. He huddled against the phone, feeling the rain on his back. He was glad that he'd grabbed a raincoat and a hat before leaving home.

"Yeah."

"You were supposed to give me a date and time for the hit and where you intend pulling it off," Sal said. The voice came through, cutting, the words snapping out.

"I've been planning. How close I can get to him without tipping him off. You know, I had to look all over for a map of the Bronx? I checked his route from the map. I see a couple of possibilities, but I think my best bet is to catch him when he arrives at the yard where he keeps his fleet. His guard will be down. Thinks he's got it made. You said the trucks are out by the time he gets there; the garage and fuel pumps are at the back, and his company trailer is almost backed up to the main gate. That seems like the ideal place. Hit him before he gets in the gate."

"You got a time?"

"I'll be waiting for him when he arrives. 0700. The day after tomorrow. In and out …fast."

"Sounds good to me. Can't have any screwups on this one."

"You're sure he won't have any security."

"No, but he'll be packing. He flashed it when a couple of our guys tried to muscle him. He's a tough son of a bitch. Our snitch

tells us he's wired, so this is even more reason he's got to go. Everything we say goes right to the cops."

"He paying before?"

"Yeah, like everyone else. Someone got to him. Probably the
Feds, and now he wants to be a hero."

"Can't have that."

"Fuck no."

"I'll get the job done, but I been thinking about the payoff."

"You already agreed."

"I didn't take into account the risk involved in this one."

"C'mon, Leonard."

"The job's worth more than that or you'd be doing it yourself."

"You're squeezing me, kid."

"How much are you getting for the job, Sal?"

"Believe it or not, nothin'. The man says this affects all of us
one way or another. That's why he wanted me to handle it 'cause
there wouldn't be no loose ends. This guy gets away with this an'
we're all gonna feel the heat, ya know what I mean? Others will
start breaking away, making their own deals. Ya understand the
problem?"

"Yeah, I understand. But this is short notice. I got no slack.
I'll do it plus ten percent." Leonard purposely drove the price up.
To get a reaction; to see where it would lead. To see how much Sal
wanted him there. He knew the price was too high.

"Five percent and you're killing me, kid."

"Split the difference and I do the job. Clean, like always."

"Just don't leave no tracks."

"In advance, Sal? I got a bad feeling about this one."

"What? I don't do business that way, kid. You know that. Half
now and the rest when the job is done. That's the best I can do."

"Understood. Make an exception."

"No way!"

Leonard knew that Sal was getting angry. How bad did he
want him on this job? In the City on that particular day?

"Okay, this is the way it is. I just want to make sure Mickey has something, you follow me? We've been spending a little above our heads lately. I swear, I don't know where the fucking money goes. This one sounds risky. I go down and she's left sucking hind tit."

"Okay. I don't like it. You know I don't like it. But I'm willing to make an exception ... this time. You fuck up an' I'm out a bundle. You're sure I can pass the word that the job is done by 0700 the day after tomorrow?"

"You can take it to the bank."

"More like I get taken to the cleaners. Okay, it may take a day or two. Why not pick up the money here?"

"I got time. I'll wait."

"This is going to change things, Leonard. I can't do business like this."

"Yeah, I know. Remember who my trainer was!"

"Aw shit, you're right. I trained you good," Sal laughed. "You're a piece of work, kid. One of a kind, ya know? I'll get back to you."

"Miko, I've got to make a trip out to the self-storage unit and pick up a few things. Anything you want me to take out there?" Leonard said when he returned home.

"No, will you be gone long?"

"Out and back. I'd like you drive me into the City as soon as I return."

Leonard gave her the location for the drop and the pickup as he made his preparations.. She was to pick him up in two days. If he wasn't there, she was to return home and gather the girl and the baby and leave the house, and under no circumstances, return.

"Just remember, you're Mrs. Harry Walker. The registration in the truck is set. Pay cash at the hospital when you pick up the girl and the kid, then you won't have to show any ID. Book yourselves into a motel in Harriman. It's going to be tight, babe."

"What happens to Li?"

"She stays with you. She can nurse the kid until you're ready to send her home. You paid off her parents?"

"They're taken care of. Well taken care of. I mentioned the IRS would like to know about the tax-free money they had, and the INS might want to review their status. They'll be all right. I also told them that Li would call them every day. Li has no problem with the arrangements. Leonard, I'm worried."

"Don't. The only thing I can tell you is that if this works out, we'll be on our way to retirement. With the baby."

"Sal?"

"He doesn't know yet. Don't call him no matter what. You're on your own after this one if it doesn't work out. Just remember, keep moving. I changed the plates on the truck before I came in. The registration is in the glove compartment."

XXI

That evening, the rain stopped, and a Range Rover dropped a grimy derelict off in the industrial section of the Bronx, in Pelham. They had passed several police cars, but none in the area. Leonard moved quickly to the rear of the truck and lifted out the shopping cart followed by two black trash bags. The Range Rover drove away. He rearranged the contents of the bags and re-positioned them in the cart. He made adjustments to his clothes and pushed his cart into a nearby alley to the limit of the reach of the streetlight at the far end. He prepared his laager for the night, pushing between several trash cans deep inside the darkness. He paused to see if the scraping of the cans had drawn any attention. Several rats scurried from around him. He fastened the lids on the cans.

He scrounged in the trash for a piece of dry cardboard; found a box that was soiled on the inside. He broke it open and put the soiled side on the ground. He pulled a worn and tattered-edged army poncho from one of his trash bags to cover himself. He wedged the cart against the wall so that it couldn't be moved without waking him. He settled onto the asphalt and leaned against the wall. He was two blocks from the truck park and office of the Inter-Borough Waste Company. He nestled into place, patted the Randall inside his sleeve and moved his butt so that he could feel his taped dogtags in his back pocket. So much for good luck pieces. He listened to the ticking of the raindrops from the fire escape and the eves onto the cardboard and trash along the alley.

He heard two screams, a car backfiring or was it a pistol shot? an unintelligible argument that lasted twenty minutes between two drunks, male and female, footsteps running past the entrance to his alley, sirens of police cars, the raucous ugly sound of fire

engines approaching and receding in the distance. A spotlight made
a hasty probe of the alley. A steady breeze off the bay carried the
noxious odor of a distant landfill. Leonard didn't check his watch
before he dozed off. Around 2 a.m. he heard the trucks rumbling
out through the gates of the waste company, along the street on
their way to collect the detritus of the City. The movement of the
trucks obliterated the other sounds. He must have been asleep
when the garbage collection crews arrived at the gate earlier because he didn't hear their cars nor the gate scraping back nor their
voices as the night watchman admitted them. At 5 a.m., Leonard
opened the thermos which held the remains of his coffee from
home and finished off the luke-warm drink. He folded the poncho
and put it in the cart. He made his way through the tenebrous
dawn and the layered putrescence of air that hung over the cobbled
streets and alleys, along the still wet, adjacent streets, avoiding the
potholes filled with water, up one alley and down another, tensing
up as a clatter disturbed the tentative silence, close enough to his
objective area to check the activity in and around the fleet park.

Many of the buildings fronting the carting company were
boarded up and abandoned. Graffiti was the current art form with
gang names and symbols sprayed in red and black and blue and
yellow and green along with slogans and curses and hate—love
had no place in the urban etchings. By 7 a.m. the owner's Jeep
4X4 had not appeared. By 8 a.m. the night watchman opened the
gate for the day and admitted several employees. At 8:30, the Jeep
Waggoner appeared, and Leonard pushed his way up the street
several blocks to a McDonald's. He parked his cart inside the door.
He bought two large coffees and two egg sandwiches. Outside, he
stowed one of the egg sandwiches in an ammunition box in the
trash bag. He refilled his thermos when he was out of sight in an
alley. He propped what was left of the coffee balanced in the
styrofoam cup on top of the trash bags and poured in the creamers, stirring it slowly as his eyes roamed the neighborhood. He ate
one of the egg sandwiches and drank the coffee holding the sandwich and cup in his hand as he walked, pushing the cart with his

forearms and body. People avoided getting close to him. He heard their curses.

He pushed his cart past the carting company, peering into the yard at several trucks jacked up like beached whales in various stages of repair near a large garage at the back of the lot. Sounds: metal against metal; a radio disk jockey inveighing his twisted logic across the airwaves, voices cursing, laughing, someone drilling, and then, there were blue sparks arcing into the air from within the shop, engines running, sputtering, coughing, roaring and black exhaust curling up before disappearing into gray, cloudy tatters. Rubber burning. Trash burning. All constants after 0800. Along with the smell of the distant landfill. All day he surveyed the lot, as much a part of the scene as the rotting melon rinds and potato peelings, and the brackish saliva dripping from the gaping mouths of the returning garbage trucks. Watched the shifts return and the cars scatter out from the gate at the end of the shift. The Jeep Wagoneer had left earlier. He compared it with what he saw that morning.

Before 0700, that day, an empty, garbage-strewn street, potholed with severe urban acne. But no cars. No activity. No one waiting or watching or sightseeing or absorbing the atmosphere, sniffing the air or listening. Just him and his cart bumping and teetering along the broken network of sidewalks and shattered curbs. He was convinced the owner followed the same routine every day except that the owner's day started at 08:30 in the morning. The night watchman had been standing there waiting, had been controlling movement through the gate even before the owner appeared. The routine was locked in. Sal wanted Leonard there at seven. Leonard didn't even consider that this might not have been an ordinary day for the owner.

Leonard wandered the streets near the carting company. Nothing would happen before tomorrow. However, he watched each car, van, truck for a sign of interest and stayed close to the entrance of the alleys, crossed the streets quickly after assuring himself that he could make it across safely. Had cover once across the streets.

Two blocks from the Inter-borough Waste Company a car came flying around the corner, hugging the curb, weaving out from the parked cars and bore down on him; he stepped back between two cars and hunkered down, his hand between the wire sides of the cart he'd spread, widened, so that he could reach inside the trash bag. The barrage of bullets never came. Teenagers laughing, pointing at him. A beer bottle came flying back from the car. It bounced off the car beside him. He flattened himself out on the pavement and watched the bottle land two feet from his head. He braced himself, expecting an explosion. Nothing. The bottle bounced and shattered, spreading silvery shards of glass near his head. Leonard rose, knees shaking, heart pounding. Time to get off the street. He was too uptight.

He returned to the alley near the carting company. He went deeper into its carvernous mouth and found a pile of boxes and garbage cans. He burrowed into the boxes. Less than twenty-four hours to go. He ate his other egg sandwich and sipped his coffee. He thought of Mickey. He thought of the baby. They seemed far away. They seemed like they were out of reach; that he would never get to them. That even if he did, they would still be far away, on a distant planet, or in another time zone, and he didn't know the codeword or the password or the secret sign that would open the door to their lives. He didn't have to stay here. He didn't have to go back to them. But he did! He had to! He was sure about the first, to stay and do the job, which was—to stay alive. Whether he could go back to them depended on the outcome of the first. He slept like he had slept many times in 'Nam or on a job. Sitting up, patient, half awake. Half asleep His mind giving the illusion of being awake because he was thinking so hard, and if he wasn't awake he should have been dreaming—the thoughts running through his head were fragged dreams, remnants of the things that he had yet to do; that still hung out in front of him like poultry in the open market or shorn pig's heads, sightless, mouths open in lugubrious smiles. He knew he wasn't dreaming But was partially awake. Partially asleep in the deep shadows left behind as the sun shifted toward the west beyond the smells, sounds and the boarded up and rundown buildings that made up that part of the war zone in the Bronx.

The crackling of footsteps on broken glass and the scraping of a can as it was catapulted along the alley by a misstep woke him, brought him out of the partial world of sleep into full wakefulness. Through squinted eyes he watched a form bend over him. A whispered, septic curse pushed out through the black hole of a mouth. A hand pulled the poncho down from Leonard's neck and blindly fumbled through the layers of clothes. The man was leaning against the wall as he searched, the hand against the wall held a length of pipe. Leonard thrust up, throwing the poncho aside, and grabbed the hand holding the pipe and brought the other hand up with the Randall to a point under the man's chin.

The man's face, creased with dirt, fuscous, stretched like dried leather when he felt the point of the blade. He tried to back away but Leonard held him in place and pushed one foot against the man's ankle. His tongue hung loosely like a dog panting. He swallowed, his adam's apple bobbing up and down like a cork on water, moving the dirt filled creases in his neck like so many fishing lines as his mouth closed and opened and he tried to speak.

"I ... I ... was checkin' ta see if you was alive.... Jus' checkin'. Ya wasn't movin'. I thought ya was dead. Ya looked dead, ya know? I was gonna git a doctor for yas."

Leonard positioned his feet under himself and stood. He had not let go of the man's wrist. It was skeletal. The man was a sack of bones. Bony face, under a Met's hat, pulled low on his fretted forehead, sunken, stubbled cheeks, runny nose, and a slack mouth. He kept licking his lips and wiping his nose with his free hand. The man's eyes rolled back and forth like a frightened animal. Leonard put pressure on the man's wrist and the pipe fell to the ground, clanging as it bounced several times and rolled to a stop.

"You got a name?" Leonard asked in a raspy voice.

"Two-step."

"Your real name."

"Roy ... That's it, Roy."

Leonard's eyes drilled into Roy's, staring at him until Roy's only escape was to close his eyes. Leonard knew that Roy was frightened. He began to form a plan.

"Roy, we're going to hang out together for the next couple of days. What d'ya think about that?"

"Means I can't keep my appointments although I sure would like to do that, ya know, hang out with ya." His eyes shifted past Leonard and back again, not looking directly at him.

"Ya know, Roy, I think you're tryin' to fuck with my head."

"You a Narc?"

"No."

"Well if it's all the same to you, I think I'll head on out."

"You ain't listenin'. You and me's hangin' out together for the next couple of days or so. You got that?" He waited until Roy nodded. "See anyone you know, tell 'im I'm Mac. To you, I'm Mac the Knife. Can you remember that?" Leonard waited for an answer. He watched Roy twitch himself into a response, his hands nervously reacting to an attack of itching across and around his body. Leonard stepped back.

"Okay. What's in it for me?" his eyes narrowing slyly. He scratched at the side of his face shifting from one foot to the other.

"For starters, what say we get a bite to eat and pick up a fifth. Any liquor stores nearby?"

"Yeah, not far from here. You buyin'?"

"Start of a partnership."

Roy grinned, his tongue pushing through the gaps in his teeth to lick his white crusted lips.

They moved the cart along the street; Leonard pushing and Roy walking ahead of and to the side of the cart, his hand on the basket. Leonard stopped at the same McDonald's as he had that morning. Again he parked his cart inside the door. Another shift was on, but the suspicion was identical and the revulsion, obvious. Customers stepped away from them. Leonard ordered a bag of burgers, and fries, a couple of cartons of milk and a large coffee for himself. He dug into his pockets pulling out a wrinkled bill here, another there, completing the transaction with change from a shabby coin purse. The girl recoiled at taking the money directly from his hand, and Leonard, muttering, laid it on the counter. He expected that she would scrub the counter and wash her hands when they left. He took a handful of napkins and asked for extra sugar and cream. They walked out of the restaurant, pushing the cart, trailed by a putid cloud.

Roy shivered, hugging his body with both hands. They avoided any other derelicts.

"I gotta have somethin', man," he said, teeth chattering like a pair of castanets. He led them to a liquor store. Leonard had Roy follow him in and stand by the counter and keep an eye on their basket. He selected a fifth of Old Crow off the shelf and went through the same routine with the clerk as he had earlier at McDonald's. Leonard carried the bottle wrapped in a paper bag; tucked it alongside the trash bags. They returned to the alley where he'd spent the night. They sat side by side, their backs against the wall. Leonard poured part of the contents from the bottle into the styrofoam cup that he'd saved from breakfast. Roy drank with both hands wrapped around the cup, careful not to spill any. He wiped his mouth and held the cup out for a refill.

"First, ya eat something." He handed Roy a cheeseburger and watched the emaciated derelict force it down. He held out the cup again, and Leonard cut the portion and watched Roy drain it. The shivering stopped, but he wouldn't eat anymore food.

"Tired," he mumbled.

Leonard found another box and laid it out for Roy who curled up and went to sleep. Night dropped on them. There was no dusk in the alley, only the sharp edges of the remaining daylight at one end of their narrow passageway and straight up, overhead, between the buildings that seemed to lean over them. Leonard sat in the dark, listening to the City night sounds while he drank his coffee and ate the burgers. He threw the remains of the fries down the alley. Heard rats skittering on the pavement towards the food. He put the remaining burgers in the metal ammo box buried in the cart so as not to draw the rats. When he finished the coffee he turned the cup over and shook what drops were left onto the pavement. He pulled out his taped dogtags and ran them back and forth through his fingers. How long would his luck hold? He tied Roy's shoelaces together and sat back against the wall.

The rumble of the trucks awakened him. He pulled out the thermos and drank the luke warm coffee from the bottle. He ate one of the remaining hamburgers and went over the plan in his mind. He ran his hands over Roy's clothes and finally came up with a flat, worn, wallet. He took out the ID and the social security card. Roy groaned but didn't wake up. He took in the information on Roy's ID with his penlight, careful to keep the beam low. Still carried his union card and a picture of a woman. Maybe that's what kept him drinking. Looking at that picture every day. He wondered if he collected social security payments. Roy Benish. So Roy did have a last name. He put Roy's papers in his own pocket and returned his wallet.

He woke Roy at 05:30 after untying his shoe laces when the derelict struggled to get up complaining that something was wrong with his legs.

"I'm not feelin' so good," Roy said, flopping back down on his side.

"C'mon, Roy, there's nothing wrong with you. Git cher ass up."

"Fuck you. I'm sick, man," he groaned.

"Here, maybe this'll help," Leonard said, pouring an ounce of liquor into the cup. He capped the bottle and put it in the cart. He watched Roy gulp it down and sigh.

"Feel better," he said, wiping his mouth with a begrimed hand.

Leonard handed him a cold hamburger and a carton of milk. He took one of the burgers for himself and drank the remainder of the coffee from the thermos.

"Be a good idea if you got something in your gut, Roy."

"How 'bout 'nother drink. Small one."

"After we talk a bit. You got family?"

"Not so's anyone would notice. Nah, I walked out on 'em when I started hittin' the bottle." He pronounced it in two disticnt syllables bot-ul. "Couldn't hold a job. Wife an' me argued alla time 'bout the booze. Had a good job. Machinist, ya know. Paid good. Schenectady. GE. Couldn't hack it. Couldn't take the arguin' all'a time."

"Kids?"

"She wanted to wait. I show you a picture a my wife?" Roy started to reach inside the folds of his clothes for his wallet.

Leonard put a hand on his arm.

"Some other time, I gotta deal for ya. Ya wanna deal?"

"She's a good looking woman. Didn't want kids right away, ya know. Said she wanted a career first. Shit, she was a friggin' bank teller. Wanted to wait."

Leonard thought he was going to start crying. He sniffled, rubbed his arm across his face and turned weepy eyes on Leonard.

"Ya says ya wasn't a Narc, right?"

"Right."

"I be breakin' the law?" He opened the carton of milk and took a sip, pushed the hamburger aside.

"Nah. You'd be doing me a favor." He dug into his clothes and came out with a fifty dollar bill and ran it in front of Roy. He watched his eyes skate across the Grant. "Ya know what this is?"

"Yeah, half a C. So whadda I gotta do for it?"

Leonard tore the bill in half. "Put this in your pocket so ya get the feel of having it close to ya. Rub it. It'll buy a lot of booze when it gets its mate." He waited while Roy put the half a bill away in his shirt pocket. He patted the pocket.

"Ya know that garbage company down the block?" He waited while Roy tried to jump-start his memory. Finally, he nodded. "All I want ya ta do is take this bundle and when the night watch-man shows, see if he'll take it. Tell him Mac sent it."

"Wha's this guy's name?"

"Sal. His name is Sal."

"Why the fuck don' cha do it ya'self"

"Cause he said he'd whip my ass whether I returned this shit or not. I heisted it from him, ya know?"

"You're fuckin' wi' me."

"Okay, so I'm fucking with ya. Give me the half a bill back an' I'll do it myself."

"How do I know you're not settin' me up?"

"How do I know you can even walk that far?"

"This stinks. Where'd ja get that kind of money?" He asked, his words slurred.

Leonard could see the furtiveness creep into Roy's eyes, wondered if he'd hold up long enough to do the job, if he'd try to nail him for more than the half a C.

"You read about the pusher that got whacked over in Morris Heights? In the projects? It was in the *News* the other day…. I did it. I had to cut outta there." Leonard took a small roll of bills stuffed into the top of his sock. Roy's eyes widened.

"Yeah, I think I read that. You did it? "

Leonard flicked the Randall from his sleeve. Roy backed away.

"Man, you a bad ass. Where ya get a blade like that?"

"You gonna do the job?"

"We still be partners?"

"We'll see how this works out. See if ya can handle somethin' simple like this."

Leonard rolled his sleeve back and looked at his watch while Roy took a piss against the opposite wall of the alley. It was 0650.

"Okay, lets do it. Here take a short snort to success." Leonard handed him the bottle.

"I like that. To success!" He raised the bottle in salute, drank and let out a contented sigh followed by a hacking laugh. "Here's to success." He still clutched the neck of the bottle

Leonard pulled the bottle away before he drained it. Roy straightened, threw his shoulders back. The short snort generated a lot of courage. Leonard paused in the alley. Concealed from the street. A van was parked along the chain link fence about thirty feet from the entrance, its rear doors facing the main gate. A black four-door sedan was parked on the opposite side but further down the street, beyond the entrance; its dark tinted windows concealed anyone inside.

"Now all you gotta do is take this bundle over to the fence and holler for Sal. Have him check the bundle." He placed the bundle on Roy's shoulder. "See it's not heavy, but don't drop it. It's got some fragile shit inside. Tell Sal that this squares us, an' ask him if he would stop hasselin' me. Got that? Tell 'im Mac sent it. You're acting like my go-between, ya know. Like between labor and management."

The last drink had done the trick. Roy took the bundle, staggering slightly, but hugged it to his shoulder with one arm.

"For Christ's sake don't drop it or I'll be up shit creek."

He watched Roy step out onto the street, out of the shadows of the alley, look up and down the street and cross the open space, stumble once on the edge of a pothole, regain his balance and continue to walk. Leonard reached into the shopping cart and drew out an M-79 grenade launcher already loaded with a 40mm HE—high explosive—round. He put a bandolier with three more rounds on top of the trash bags. He extracted another round, WP—white phosphorous—and laid it beside the bandolier. He sited on the van as the rear doors opened and one of the Hmongs stepped out and called to Roy. Leonard flicked off the safety. Roy stopped as the Hmong fired. Leonard took aim. Roy hit a wall, straightened and sagged as the rounds tore into his body. The Buick pulled up to where Roy lay. The driver jumped out and began firing into what had been Roy. Leonard squeezed the trigger and the round floated across the open, noisome space and hit the van. The gunman in the van threw up his arms with the explosion. The driver of the sedan staggered back. Leonard loaded the WP round into the M-79. Took aim and squeezed the trigger again, and the round tore through the shattered windshield of the black sedan, filling the car with a white explosion as the car burst into flames. At that moment the timer on the bundle Roy carried went off lifting Roy as well as the gunmen in several directions off the ground. The watchman peered around the corner of the trailer and ducked back out of sight. Leonard elevated the barrel of his weapon and arched an HE round into the yard. He checked again to see if anyone moved. He pushed the shopping cart against the wall, stripped off his outer garments and piled them on top of the trash bags in the cart; scrubbed his hands and face as best he could with his handkerchief. He set the timer in one of the trashbags and pushed the cart out into the street. He ran back up the alley as the cart rolled a few feet, wobbled as it got hung up on the rutted pavement, paused for a moment and exploded as it fell on its side. He broke the M-79 down as he ran and carried it and the bandolier with the remaining round until he found a sewer grate near several abandoned buildings. He shoved the weapon down into the sewer. He walked out onto the street several blocks away as police cars from all directions converged on the waste company.

Leonard stopped at a small cafe that advertised two pieces of toast, an egg and coffee for ninety-nine cents. He ordered the 'special' as he walked to the back to the rest room where he scrubbed his hands and face with cold water and a thin dried-out bar of soap. He wiped his hands and face with several sheets of coarse paper towel. He flushed Roy Bemish's expired driver's license and social security card down the toilet. He put his cap back on and sat at the counter and began to eat the ninety-nine cent breakfast and ordered a second cup of coffee.

"What's all the noise? I heard some explosions and what sounded like Chinese New Years," he said to the counterman, a tall, thin hollow-eyed man who wore a white paper hat, T-shirt and dirty apron which he used as a towel to wipe his hands.

"Ahh ... who knows. 'Round here somethin's always happenin'. Fuckin' city," he muttered under his breath. He stood wiping the counter where he could stare out the window.

"Sounds like the cops are coming from all over the place."

"Prob'ly's over at the garbage company. They been havin' a lotta pro'lems. Mob shit."

Leonard finished the eggs and drank the coffee. The counter-man hadn't touched them with his bare hands. He left the toast.

As customers began to arrive, Leonard paid his bill and left.

He took the subway to the north end of the Bronx where Mickey met him. Leonard turned on a New York City station and heard about the shooting at the Inter-borough Waste Company. There was no explanation for the shooting of a homeless man, the newscaster said...

"Police would only say that several high explosive rounds had hit a van and a late model Buick. None of the occupants of the van or the car survived. The victim was tentatively identified as Leonard Grissom from a set of Army dog tags found on the body. The police concluded that it was a gangland rivalry and Leonard Grissom was an unintended victim. No mention was made of the owner of the carting company except to say he was being questioned. More news will follow as we get more information. Positive identification of the other victims will be delayed because of the condition of the bodies.... We'll pause now...."

XXII

They heard the phone ringing as soon as they ran the car into the garage. Leonard had expected the call. Had planned on it. He didn't know how many times it had rung before they got home. Leonard went into the study. Mickey sat down and picked up the phone.

"Leonard?" she asked, her voice tremulous, fearful, like she was expecting bad news, but hoped for good.

"Mickey, this is Sal."

"Sal, is Leonard there with you?" Her voice, with the right amount of hope in it.

"Leonard's not home yet?"

"No, he left last night, said he had business. That you had something you wanted him to do. That it had to be done this morning." Now, her voice questioning, puzzled.

"Ahh, shit. It must be true."

"What? What's true? Did something happen to Leonard? Tell me! What's going on?"

"Calm down, Mickey. I called earlier. I tried his office. Where were you?"

"I had to get out and shop early before Leonard got home. You know how ... oh, you wouldn't know how he likes everything just right when he comes off a ... business trip. Where is he, Sal? Why isn't he here?" Her voice edging into hysteria, tears choked back.

"Easy, Mickey. 'Fraid I got some bad news. Hate to have to tell you by phone like this. Ahh ... the job went belly up. I don't know what happened. He was supposed to complete the transaction by 0700 this morning, but he must have run into cops or another gang there for the same purpose. I don't know. The cops aren't saying anything. The Feds are looking into it now."

"But why?"

"Uhh ... it was pretty important that this guy reconsider what he was doing. He was undercutting us. Leonard was there to uhh ... straighten out the whole deal."

"But what happened?"

"Leonard's dead, Mickey. I'm sorry. All they found on him was his old Army dogtags. I don't know if they'll track him back to you or not. I don't know how that works."

"He always carried them with him." She choked, held back a sob. "He carried them for luck. Oh, Leonard."

"Easy Mickey. Ya know he was like a son to me? Did you know that? I thought of him like a son. We were going to work out something so the two of you could retire."

"What's going to happen? What's going to happen to his body? I can't leave him there!" Mickey started sniffling, and groaning under her grief. She sobbed. It burst out of her.

"Leave it, Mickey. He was carrying explosives, and what's there ain't worth looking at."

"But I have to bury him. I owe him that," she sniffled.

"He's dead, ya understand? Drop it. Let the dead bury themselves." His voice had turned ugly, but then, became solicitous. "Are you okay? I mean you gonna be okay, financially?"

"Leonard was afraid this was going to happen. He was counting on the money from this ... uh transaction."

"Well, that won't get you very far."

"I can't collect on his insurance, can I?"

"How much was it for?"

"$100,000."

The line went silent. Leonard thought that Sal had hung up until he picked up the sound of his breathing at the other end.

"This is going to hurt me, but suppose I make up this shortfall? I was going to send him the payment for this job, but I got hung up with some other business and didn't get it off. It'll take a day or two to come up with all the cash, but Leonard was a good man, and I hate to see you left hanging out there. Did he, uhh … by any chance leave any papers with you or anything about our uhh … arrangement."

"He never kept anything at home," she sniffled. "I don't know what he kept at his office. I could look for you. I have a key. When he's away I …."

"Why don't I bring the money up myself, maybe we could run over there and take a look."

"That's nice of you, Sal. You've done so much for us. Thank you. Is Ginger coming with you?"

"Nah, she's up to her ears in a street festival the church is putting on."

"Oh."

"We'll all get together sometime. I'm sorry about Leonard, Mickey. I'll see you the day after tomorrow."

Leonard unhooked the tape recorder from the phone in the study. She looked up as he came into the hallway. Worry lines had creased her smooth, tight skin. He put his arm around her and pressed his lips against the top of her head.

"How 'bout that. He says I was like a son to him. He's all heart isn't he?"

"Did I sound convincing?"

"You did fine, babe. I think he's given me up. He set me up, Mickey, to save his own butt. I think you're next. I guess he's going to do it himself. But I've got to make sure he comes here."

"What about the baby and Li if he comes here to the house?"

"And what if he asks for the key to the office, takes it, and waxes you and the baby right here? Hmm, I don't know, babe. Maybe we'd better get Mrs Harry Walker on her way."

"No. The baby is important, but you're part of my life too." She rose from the chair and lifted her face to him and he kissed her, their lips barely touching. There was none of the tightening in his scrotum, none of the enflaming arousal. That was over. He had to figure this out. He had to protect her and the kid. He held her in his arms, her face against his; his mind churning through options, scrolling through the alternatives.

"Let me work on this. Try to figure. First, though, I want to add something to this tape." He took her by the hand and led her into the study. He showed her the tape and wrote out what he wanted her to say. They rehearsed it several times. When she finished making the tape, he tore up the note and flushed it down the toilet.

"I've got to clean up, and then I want to get a couple of hours sleep. We've got a lot to do before Sal arrives."

When Leonard awoke, Mickey was gone. He pulled the drapes in the living room. Lighted the fire in the fireplace and sat in his recliner, a cup of coffee beside him. She had picked up Li and the baby after she had brought him home, after she made the tape. Before she left to become Mrs. Harry Walker, Mickey brought the baby in and stretched out on the bed, the baby between them. Their arms intertwined over the infant, and they watched the small hands grasping at the air, her blue eyes open, her brown hair like rust on the top of her head.

"She's beautiful, Mickey." He touched the fine hair on Lenore's head and ran his hand along Mickey's cheek. "Like her mother."

Mickey took his hand and pressed her lips into his palm and closed her eyes.

"I don't want to leave you," she said.

"I don't want you to go." He looked at his watch. "It's about time, babe. Better get on the road. Remember everything is in both our names. Harry Walker. You have the money?"

"Yes. You don't think Sal will wait until the day after tomorrow."

"I wouldn't."

He had kissed the baby, on the forehead and on her small tiny hands. He hadn't expected the emptiness to start so soon, that they wouldn't even be out of the house, and he'd feel the gut-wrenching loneliness. She had helped to keep it back, the dark shades of desolation. He had never been away that he didn't feel he'd see her again. Here, he was at home and was certain that this would be the end. He had reached the end of the tunnel, propelled there by Sal's betrayal. To wait until they came for him. He finally went to sleep.

The fire played its rhythms across the logs, smokeless, but sending out heat. As a boy he was told to expect that if he went to Hell it would look like that except there would be towering flames and intense heat that reddened the skin, but didn't burn, only caused severe discomfort. There would be no water. Only unquenchable thirst. He felt that thirst now. To live. His Hell had become a place of dense, thick darkness, that he could taste. It left his tongue dry and his throat constricted. The absence of love. He had that now, understood it. Love, and he wanted to live. But not at the expense of Mickey and the kid. He hadn't told her, hadn't come right out and said that she would be on her own. Forever.

Time. He extinguised the fire, and doused the lights. Put on a light leather jacket, tucked the .22 with the silencer into his belt and went out to the garage to the BMW. He patted the dashboard like a friend.

At the mall he found a vacant phone booth. He dialed the number and listened to it ring. After four rings, the answering machine broke in with its message. Leonard waited for the beep and held the taperecorder to the phone:

"You were supposed to give me a time for the hit and where you intend pulling it off."

"I've been planning. How close can I get to him? You know, I had to look all over for a map of the Bronx? I checked his route from the map. I see a couple of possibilities but I think my best bet is to catch him when he arrives at the yard where he keeps his fleet. You said the trucks are out by the time he gets there; the garage and fuel pumps are at the back, and his company trailer is almost backed up to the main gate. That seems like the ideal place. Hit him before he gets in the gate."

"You got a time?"

"I'll be waiting for him when he arrives. 0700. In and out fast."

"Sounds good to me...."

Mickey's voice broke in..

"Sal, I'm awfully upset about all this, this house, feeling him around me, I've got to get away. I can't handle it, you know? I found this loose tape in his dresser drawer. Hearing his voice..." Her voice caught in a sob. "He must have forgotten it. I'll meet you at his office the day after tomorrow. I'm going to get away for a day or so." She gave the address of Leonard's office and directions on how to get there.

Leonard put the tape recorder in his inner pocket and returned home. He showered again and went back downstairs to wait. Tonight? Tomorrow? Definitely some time tomorrow. They wouldn't wait until Mickey returned. They'd leave someone here. Wouldn't they? Or would they? He waited. He closed out the clock in his head, closed out the second hand going round and fusing into the minute hand which in turn made its revolution to become another hour. He'd waited before. Shut his mind down like turning off the lights. He pushed his thoughts off to the edge and would bring them out selectively, look at them, dissect them. The only thought that held him now was seeing the van and the black car waiting by the gate of the carting company. Waiting for him. Waiting for him on Sal's orders. Waiting to fire five, ten, twenty, thirty rounds into his sagging, falling, twitching, jerking, dead body. The clothes containing the torn, bullet-ridden flesh; the layers of rags he wore sopping up the blood, but the blood still seeping out or spurting out from the numerous rounds that had found a place in his skull, or face, or in his hands covered by dirty woolen gloves with the fingers cut out, or in his scabrous legs where the pant legs had crept up past the bony ankles and sticklike shins. When one or two would have done it. But wanting to be sure that he never moved again. Perhaps having heard from Sal how he had cheated death so many times when he should have died. So after the first rounds, when the body lay still, they gave life to it by firing their hatred into the lifeless form, causing it to jerk from the impact, appearing to still be alive, giving them all the more reason to keep firing until the first 40mm round to hit the van had brought the firing to a halt. He was sure they didn't move again after the second round. The guy in the car must have thought that he could save himself. Must have seen the white phosphorous round angling toward him, growing larger, not knowing that it would explode with a flash and blossom into a white burning chrysanthemum of hell. Did he see his death? Did either of them? The explosion settled everything. Roy hadn't heard it. Roy was very dead. Poor, sad, stupid, greedy, pickled jerk, clinging to life with half a Grant buried in his pocket. I did him a favor, Leonard thought. I did them all a favor.

Could he convince Sal to make the trade—tapes for her life and his? No way would that happen. She would begin calling tomorrow to find out what the deal was. He set that aside. He owed Sal. Owed him for giving him and Mickey a life together, making it happen. But also owed him for setting the van and the black car outside the gate of the carting company. Owed him for the death of Leonard Grissom and the chance to begin again. He wouldn't thank him for all this because it had become too difficult to overcome the sense of betrayal. Sal wanted him dead. Wanted Mickey dead. Sal had to die. And Leonard wasn't sure if he could do it. Towards evening he made himself a sandwich and drank a glass of milk. He wondered if his stomach had begun to ache because of what he had been eating or because of the tension. Lodged in the center of his belly, dull, throbbing. The milk helped.

The window in the kitchen door shattered. Crude, he thought. How would Mickey's killer spend his time while he waited? Would he look around the house first? Check the refrigerator? Turn on the TV and sit in Leonard's recliner and speculate about when he could live like this? Would he go upstairs and look through her clothes, put her pants to his face to pick up her scent through the detergent, handle her cosmetics, sniff her perfume bottles, run her comb through his hair, handle her shoes, smell them. Would he be aroused by the closeness of her and would he wait for her, touching himself from time to time to remember, bringing himself close to relief, but holding back, thinking about the woman. He, the violater of their home, cleared his throat, coughed. How long had he waited outside to be sure that no one was at home? The beam of his penlight cast a narrow beam around the room. He followed the beam into the living room, flashed right and left, stopped when it came to the soles of Leonard's feet. He had no time to lift the flashlight. He was dead before the flashlight had come to a stop after rolling along the floor, sending its beam where it stopped at the wall.

"Had you all the way, rookie," Leonard said to the body on the floor. He put the safety on the .22 calibre pistol with the silencer attached. He shined the dead man's light on his body. The black hair had begun to gray. He turned one of the hands over. The once work-hardened hands had become soft. No callouses. He hadn't even taken out his weapon. "Sal, you let them go soft on you. Get lazy." One dead Hmong.

They were in there. What had they expected to find without knowing where to look? A muted glow shone through the blinds. No other lights, except the night lights, were on in the building. He could see it from where he parked his car, a block away. They had parked behind the building. He walked towards his office, approaching the back near the rear entrance. Their car was parked in the rear parking lot. He hung back in the shadows, beyond the mercury vapor glow cast by the lot light. He heard water splashing on the ground and a sigh. He saw the shadowy form of a man step back from the dumpster, bend forward slightly as he zipped up his fly. Leonard started towards him when the lights flashed on in his head.

"Hey Sal, found this guy snoopin' roun' out back."
A hand yanked his head back. Leonard opened his eyes. Sal

turned. He hadn't changed except for the eyes. Fear? Sal was afraid. He stole a look around his office. The room was a shambles.

"The radio said you were dead, kid."

"You set me up, Sal. They were waiting for me. Why?"

"You were getting expensive. Costing me too much. That sketch in the paper was pretty good." Sal stepped back and took hold of Leonard's chin and moved his head from side to side. "To make peace, I had to deliver up the guy who waxed Big Tony Buconti and Greasy Genovese. Remember those two? We made a pretty good piece of change on those two. Mugs. But their family has a long memory. Besides Leonard, you've been whining about retiring. You and your whore."

Leonard tried to pull away, but his arms were pulled back until his elbows were almnost touching. He grunted with pain and relaxed, let his body hang loose. There were five of them.

"He carrying, Pauli?" Sal asked. Pauli mumbled something and handed Sal the .22 and his Randall. "Still running around with the shiv, Leonard? I thought you outgrew that after the ADA thing. Maybe before we go, I'll let Pauli work on you with this. How 'bout it Pauli?"

Pauli snickered. "Maybe I'll start with his pecker first." The other two laughed. One, another Hmong, stood at the blinds looking out onto the parking lot. Another Hmong stood at the door to the office. And the fifth man stood in the doorway to the bathroom.

"So is the whore coming back? Hey, do you know how many times I fucked your little Miko while you were laid up in the hospital? She let me. She lay there and let me. Like a stick. What d'ya think of that, sucker? Oh, by the way, both me and Dao tried her out a few times before we put her in the bar. I guess I didn't tell you that, did I."

Leonard again strained to get at the big man, only to have Pauli yank his arms back again, raising him on his toes. Tears ran down his face. He snuffled, feeling the mucous making a trip from his nose to his upper lip. He tried to wipe his mouth against his shoulder.

"Tell me about the tapes. Seems you haven't been completely honest with me, kid. That's against the law unless you've notified the other person. You were breaking the law." He shook a finger in Leonard's face. Laughed. Drew back his arm and smashed Leonard in the mouth. He lost consciousness and didn't feel the floor.

A glass of water in his face brought him back. He was sitting in one of the straight back chairs in the office. Water dripped from his face. He licked his swollen lip, ran his tongue around his teeth, tasted the blood from his nose. Pauli gripped his shoulders.

"Why the tapes?" Sal asked. "Were you going to turn me over? Work a deal? With the Feds or the State?"

Leonard shook his head.

"C'mon, answer me." He backhanded Leonard, almost closing his left eye completely.

"Insurance. To stay alive. Just to stay alive."

"To retire?"

"That too."

"What good are they to you now? How many do you have?"

"From the beginning. After Dao."

"I want them."

"Deal?"

"What do you want? You know I can't let you go. By the way, where's Mickey?"

"The deal is you let Mickey and the baby go. I told her not to tell me where she is. She's going to call to see if the deal goes."

"Baby? Whatsa matter with you two? Shit. Tai, go pick up your buddy and bring him back. Pauli give him the keys." The door slammed.

He had fifteen maybe twenty minutes at the most before Tai came back.

"Okay, so I tell you she's off the hook. What then?"

"How do I know you won't go after her?"

"I give you my word."

"Sal, your word doesn't last as long as piss in the wind."

"You're the one I wanted, kid. You're not going nowhere."

"In the safe. The tapes are in the safe."

"What safe? We tore this place apart."

"Tell fatso to let me go and I'll show you." Pauli's hands drifted from the back of the chair. Leonard stood and flexed his arms, checked out the side of his face and fingered his swollen lip. He wiped his nose on his sleeve. "In the bathroom." He glanced in the mirror as he entered the room, stepping on towels and his spare clothes that lay spread out on the floor. He swept them out the door with his foot. He opened the cabinet door under the sink, removed the bottom of the cabinet, and eased out the tiles. Sal and Pauli bent down to look.

"Need some light. I can't read the numbers on the dial."

"Gotta hand it to you Leonard. Pretty clever." They moved to let the light hit the dial.

He could feel the sweat running down his back and from under his arms. He wiped his hands on his pants after spinning the dial to the first digit. Pauli started to react when Leonard wiped his hands. Second digit. Third digit. And back to 0. A hand grabbed his collar and sent him sprawling on his back as Sal said, "Lemme me at that. I'll open it. This fucker might have a piece in there."

As the handle clicked, Leonard squirmed toward the bathroom door and reached for his belt buckle as an explosion filled the room with heat and smoke. He heard Pauli and Sal scream. He jammed the short belt buckle blade into the groin of the man standing outside the bathroom door. His gun dropped to the floor as he groaned and reached for his groin. Leonard grabbed the gun, flicked off the safety, shot the wounded Hmong as he bent forward and whipped it toward the gunman at the entrance to the office who staggered forward off balance as the door behind him swung against his back. Leonard fired. Mickey stood in the doorway, the front of her blouse blossoned with a red stain. As she fell, she reached out for support, pulling on the gunman as he lifted his weapon. Leonard fired into him. Smoke filled the office. A figure staggered screaming out of the room, clothes aflame, hair burning. His eyeballs streamed like mucous down his face. He fired his weapon, and unseeing turned it on Pauli as the fat gunman, his clothes smoldering, tried to shove his way past Sal. Pauli dropped. Sal stood screaming, sightless, firing blindly, even after the gun clicked on empty.

Leonard shouted, "Mickey, Mickey," over and over as he crawled to her. "Aw, Mickey, don't die on me. Please don't die on me." He buried his face on her chest. Her sightless eyes stared up at the flames creeping along the ceiling. He found her purse and pulled out the Beretta and turned it on Sal who had fallen to his knees, writhing in agony, unable to do anything except burn. Leonard shot him in the groin shouting, "Burn, mother fucker, bleed and burn." Sal screamed over and over until the embers of white phosphorous reached his brain. Leonard placed Mickey's gun in her hand. He grabbed her purse and staggered down the rear staircase. He paused outside to look up at the flames inside his office. He heard the sirens already in the distance and remembered the documents in the Range Rover. He ran over to the utility vehicle, and grabbed everything in the glove compartment. A few minutes later he climbed into the BMW. Harry Walker drove away from the burning building.

The sirens passed him. He could smell the smoke on his clothes and through it, Mickey's perfume when he had laid his head on her breast. He looked in the mirror and wiped the blood from his face. He could see the whole building going up in flames in his rear-view mirror. Leonard parked in a mall and dug into Mickey's purse. Found the receipt for the motel she was staying in. Why did she come back? Was it for him? Was it really for him?

He tapped lightly on the door. Li peered over the chain across the narrow gap, gasped and opened the door to let him in. She stepped back, her eyes wide.

"The baby, how's the baby?" He asked, unable to control the tears that spilled down his cheeks.

"The baby's fine. What happened? Where's Miko? She said she had to get something from the office." Leonard watched understanding spread from her eyes to her whole body as she began to shake. "She's not coming back is she? She's dead."

Leonard put his arm around her and held her until the shuddering stopped.

"I want to clean up. I need to figure what we're going to do. What I'm going to do? What you're going to do? What we do with Lenore?" He left her sitting on the edge of the bed, the baby asleep in the middle of the bed.

He lay for a long time in the hot tub of water. She wasn't here. She'd never be here again. What had he really expected? You get what you pay for, he thought. He used Mickey's tooth brush to clean his teeth. Li and the baby were in the other bed.

He wasn't sure when it was that the small, thin girl climbed into bed and welded her body next to his. He stroked her long hair until he fell asleep.

EPILOGUE

Marvin, the rural letter carrier, tooted his horn until Sue came out to the porch.

"Got a package here for a Master Sergeant Cory Masterson. Just says Crescent Hills, New York. Kinda looks like it had a tough time getting here. Sorry 'bout that."

Sue smiled at him and took it into the house. Cory sat at the kitchen table eating a late breakfast. Dog, his pitbull, sat at his feet, its intelligent eyes watching every morsel of food that went into his mouth.

"Whatcha got, honey?"

"Package. Been banged around a little. No return address."

"Hmm." Cory looked at it, turning it over to examine all sides." He took his jackknife out of his pocket and slit the paper open, unwrapped it, and ran his knife along the center fold of the cardboard box, lifted the flaps and took out an inner package wrapped in newspaper. He cleared a space and laid it on the kitchen table.

"What the heck? Tapes. Dated 1973, right up to this year."

"Is there a note?" Sue asked leaning on his shoulder.

"Yeah." He took out an envelope from the bottom of the box and opened it. He held up the note for Sue to read.

> Sarge,
> I did all three of them. Whelan, Sawyer and Schultz. Listen to the tapes and you'll understand.
> The watch in the bottom should come as no surprise. Have a life.
> Your friend,
>
> Leonard Grissom

"Who's Leonard Grissom?" Sue asked.

"Just a guy I knew In 'Nam. Thought he was dead."

The package was postmarked the day before the police found dog tags with the name, Leonard Grissom, in the pocket of a homeless man in the Bronx.

"Let's try one and see what's on it." Sue said.

"How about the first one?" He inserted the oldest casette in the radio/cassette player. The voices were garbled. They waited but couldn't understand who was talking or what was being said.

"Leonard always was a fuck-up," Cory said. He picked up the watch.

GLOSSARY OF TERMS USED IN
KILLER'S GIFT

Ao dai- Traditional Vietnamese woman's dress with a high neck and long sleeves with long panels that fall front and back from the waist. Worn with trousers.

Artillery- equipment for injecting drugs.

Aunt Mary, Aunt Hazel, Aunt Nora- Marijuana, heroin, cocaine; also bouncing power-cocaine; bozo- heroin.

Baby sit- Guide someone through their first drug experience.

Bac si- Doctor.

Claymore- An American anti-personnel mine, aimed above ground, blasted hundreds of steel balls in a wide swath. Used in defensive positions if available.

Cherry- a virgin or soldier new to combat. Usually a FNG- fucking new guy.

Di di or di di mau- Vietnamese: go or get out!

Dust off- An emergency medical evacuation by helicopter.

Geeze- To inhale cocaine.

Grunt- Combat soldier; usually an infantryman.

Gook- Derogatory term used for any oriental person. Also dink, slope, or slant.

HE- High explosive.

Kit Carson Scout- Former VC/NVA soldier. Served as scouts for US Forces.

Lipton Tea- Inferior quality drugs.

Laugh and scratch- To inject a drug.

LZ- Landing zone.

MPC- Military Payment Certificate. Currency used by US Forces in Vietnam.

Puff the Magic Dragon- A C-47 equipped with Vulcan machine guns, set up in the cargo doors to provide intensive fire support to ground troops.

Rockers- One of the curved stripes under the chevron that indicate the grade of a sergeant.

REMF- Rear Echelon Mother Fucker. A pejorative term used by combat troops to refer to those assigned duties in the rear.

Skag- Low quality heroin.

Stops- Reference to customers in the garbage hauling business in New York City.

Tunnel rats- US troops who fought the VC in the underground tunnels linking villages as well as military complexes.

USAID- US Agency for International Development.

VC- Viet Cong. Victor Charley. Vietnamese Communist members of the National Liberation Front. The enemy.

White mice- The Vietnamese military police.

Wax- To kill. Also ace, grease, off, waste.

IATS]